Penguin Books
Community Architecture

Nick Wates was born in England in 1951 and educated at Bedales and University College London. In 1970 he taught woodwork in Botswana before entering university, where he received a First in Architecture, Planning, Building and Environmental Studies (1973) and a Diploma in Development Planning (1975). Since then he has worked as a freelance journalist and consultant, specializing in community architecture, as well as being an active environmental campaigner in the London neighbourhoods of Euston and Limehouse where he has lived. He is married to an architect, Caroline Lwin, and has two children. Full-time posts have included coordinator of the Tolmers Village Association, a community group in central London, and news editor of the *Architects' Journal*. He is the author of *The Battle for Tolmers Square* (1976), co-editor of *Squatting: the Real Story* (1980) and editor of *The Limehouse Petition: for a Future Inner City* (1986). He has been a regular columnist for *Building Design*, was consultant for the BBC 1 'Omnibus' programme 'The Hackney Way' (1987), and is a member of the international editorial board of *Open House International*.

Charles Knevitt was born in America in 1952, of British parents, and educated at Stonyhurst and the University of Manchester, where he received an honours degree in architecture (1975). He began writing as a freelance journalist in 1974 and one of his first articles was a profile of Rod Hackney, 'Community Architect Mark I'. He was appointed editor of *What's New in Building* in 1978 and from 1980 until 1984 was architecture correspondent of the *Sunday Telegraph*. Since then he has been architecture correspondent of *The Times*. He was also, for three years, a consultant on Thames Television's 'Thames News' and on 'Space on Earth', a six-part Anglia Television series for Channel Four, for which he wrote the accompanying book. He is married with a daughter and lives in Teddington. In 1985 he devised *The Times*/RIBA Community Enterprise Award Scheme under the patronage of the Prince of Wales and is its secretary. The following year he was appointed Director of the Inner City Trust.

Nick Wates and Charles Knevitt – who have both received the International Building Press Architectural Journalist of the Year Award – first teamed up in 1984 to research and write this book. In 1986 they founded Community Architecture Information Services (CAIS) Ltd with Jim Sneddon and Caroline Theobald, and organized 'Building Communities: the First International Conference on Community Architecture, Planning and Design', which was held at the Astoria Theatre, London, in November 1986.

Community Architecture

How People are Creating Their Own Environment

Nick Wates and Charles Knevitt

Foreword by the Rt Hon The Lord Scarman, OBE

Penguin Books

To the pioneers

Penguin Books Ltd, 27 Wrights Lane, London W8 5TZ (Publishing and Editorial)
and Harmondsworth, Middlesex, England (Distribution and Warehouse)
Viking Penguin Inc., 40 West 23rd Street, New York, New York 10010, USA
Penguin Books Australia Ltd, Ringwood, Victoria, Australia
Penguin Books Canada Ltd, 2801 John Street, Markham, Ontario, Canada L3R 1B4
Penguin Books (NZ) Ltd, 182–190 Wairau Road, Auckland 10, New Zealand

First published 1987

Copyright © Nick Wates and Charles Knevitt, 1987
All rights reserved

Made and printed in Great Britain by
Richard Clay Ltd, Bungay, Suffolk
Filmset in 9/11 Monophoto Photina

Except in the United States of America, this book is sold subject
to the condition that it shall not, by way of trade or otherwise, be lent,
re-sold, hired out, or otherwise circulated without the
publisher's prior consent in any form of binding or cover other than
that in which it is published and without a similar condition
including this condition being imposed on the subsequent purchaser

Contents

List of Plates

Acknowledgements

The authors would like to acknowledge editorial advice and contributions from those listed below; but they take full responsibility for the views and opinions expressed.

Christine Bailey
Debra Bartlett
George Clark
Ben Derbyshire
Marc Dorfman
Nicholas Falk
Paul Finch
Ian Finlay

Tony Gibson
David Goodman
Chris Gossop
Rod Hackney
John Lane
David Lewis
Paul Lusk

Caroline Lwin
Gordon Michell
Jonathan Miller
Robin Nicholson
David Rock
Jim Sneddon
Caroline Theobald

John Thompson
John F. C. Turner
Diane Warburton
Colin Ward
Barbara Wheeler
  Early
David Wilcox
Tom Woolley

Various other people helped the authors in numerous ways during the research and writing. Many thanks to:

Leighton Andrews, Phil Bixby, Virginia Bond, Laurie Chiarella, Kelly Code, Alice Coleman, Anne Cowlin, Paul Curno, Robert Davies, Stephen Davies, Louisa Denman, Sir Andrew Derbyshire, Sara Drake, Helen Drummond, David Hall, Ben Hayden, Bill Hillier, Michael Hook, Lyne Hulton, Lucy Knevitt, Jules Lubbock, Cindy Marshall, Edward Mills, Sir John Moreton, Douglas Mulhall, Elissia Noble, Ian Potts, Martin Purdy, Jon Riley, Henry Sanoff, Esther Sidwell, Rebecca Smithers, Kate Theobald, Kim Ward, Jon Watson, David Wilkinson, Sue Wolk, Stella Yarrow, plus Mae, Max and Polly.

Financial Assistance
This book was made possible with the financial assistance of the following:

Ahrends Burton & Koralek
Calouste Gulbenkian Foundation
Community Architecture Information
  Services (CAIS) Ltd
Franklin Stafford Partnership

Rod Hackney Foundation
Hunt Thompson Associates
Lane Bremner & Garnett
Stanhope Securities Ltd
Wates Foundation

Foreword by Lord Scarman

For the last few years, our cities have been in the headlines, and most of these have been grim. Newspaper sub-editors, composing front pages by night, have had no shortage of violent images with which to shock their readers on the way to work next morning. The television screen has brought a terrifying image of the inner city into millions of quiet living-rooms around the country.

It is no wonder that residents of inner city areas despair of persuading the rest of us to act effectively to help them improve their living conditions. Some, who are optimistically inclined, have said that recent disorders have at last focused public attention on the plight of the inner cities; but I suspect that most of those who live in these troubled areas believe that the violent symbols of decay will stamp their area for life. New stereotypes are being created, which threaten to become self-perpetuating, frightening off those who can invest time, energy and funds in recreating communities.

These images of the city are not new. T. S. Eliot's view of the city as waste land, devoid of life and community spirit, echoes the voice of literature of earlier centuries:

> Unreal city
> Under the brown fog of a winter dawn
> A crowd flowed over London Bridge, so many,
> I had not thought death had undone so many.

It is high time to destroy these impressions of city life. Let us abandon our despair and pessimism and think constructively for the future.

In this book Nick Wates and Charles Knevitt dare to conceive of a future for the city. Their book unveils the new spirit which is shining through many communities – a spirit which could take the city off the front page as something to be gawped at, and return it to the community as a place in which to live, work and play.

The 'community architecture' movement which they describe is certainly about architecture. But it is more than that. They are describing a new lifestyle: a quiet revolution. In their book, they argue that the prob-

9

lems of the city will never be resolved unless people in communities are entrusted with the power of decision. Local people must assume responsibility, while the role of the experts is one of giving advice but not making the decisions.

The authors demonstrate living examples of groups who are fighting their way through red tape to get the homes, workspaces, parks, play schemes and community centres they want, not the schemes others think they should have.

The theme of the book is that people must be given more control and more effective choices over their lives. It is a crucial change, if we are to avoid further social disorders. In Brixton six years ago I found that a key factor in local community tensions was the degree of alienation felt by people locally. Brixton in 1981 expressed a problem that has spawned an entire industry to solve it: the problem of urban decay, which hits most drastically and disproportionately at the poorest and the most disadvantaged groups in society. These are the people who cannot afford to move out of the inner city to the leafy suburbs: notably, the old, who tend to live in the oldest housing, which is consequently often in most need of repair, and the members of the ethnic minority communities. Our inner cities have suffered because there has been a lack of regard in inner city planning for human needs – a failure to keep developments within a human scale. The impersonal nature of major cities has stoked up tensions and the physical design of many of our giant housing complexes has created new problems of policing and law enforcement. The police can deal only with the legacy that the planners hand down to them.

I recall one particular development in Brixton. On paper, it looked marvellous: a great area of flats, beautiful walkways, garages underneath. In theory, this was fine; in practice, it was dreadful: most became areas where vandalism, glue-sniffing and drug-taking were rife. The cars of those residents who could afford them were vandalized. The police had an impossible job because the buildings had infinite hiding-places and escape routes.

There are problems of scale that many who planned housing estates overlooked. In the 1930s peripheral estates, on the edges of cities such as Glasgow, often far removed from useful employment, from reasonable shopping facilities, with few communal or social facilities, and inadequate public transport, became a new form of ghetto. Families were uprooted and settled in these estates, but in no way were homes and communities being created: houses were provided, but a house is a lifeless object whereas a home is part of a community.

Yet there is in Brixton and similar areas energy, commitment, imagination, and enthusiasm for voluntary enterprise. What local communities need are the resources to enable them to put their energies into action – financial resources certainly, but also the resource of professionals who are willing to work alongside communities rather than on their behalf.

The professional as enabler is increasingly a feature of community development in Third World countries. In the Third World, the professional is often the people's guide to the boundaries of legality and illegality, finding ways of creating solutions and by-passing obstacles. Over recent decades in this country we have seen dedicated community activists undertaking a similar role in the UK. As President of the UK Council for 1987's UN International Year of Shelter for the Homeless, I am encouraged by the obvious recognition of the fact that community participation and self-help – two strong themes of the International Year – are dimensions where the Third World has much to teach us.

Community enterprise is a continuing process. As the authors recognize, there are no instant solutions: communities change in their needs and aspirations, cities grow and shrink, and there is a continuous process of renewal which can be helped – or hindered – by experts. The real task for today is to create a partnership between those different sectors that have different resources to offer: the public sector, which can often assist with supply of land, the private sector, which has the finance, the professionals, who have the skills, and the voluntary movements – housing associations, cooperatives, self-build associations, etc., which know the immediate needs and have the commitment to resolve them. It is a task which must be addressed urgently.

The international dimension of this issue is important. The true builders of the cities of the Third World are the people themselves. Governments which for years had sought to supply housing for people, bulldozing the illegal settlements which sprang up around and in their cities, were eventually forced to concede. Instead, there is a strong move towards supporting the efforts of people to house themselves, rather than supplying housing which is often inappropriate and almost always too expensive for the poorest families. That trend was one of the factors which led to the first world Habitat Conference in 1976, and gave rise to the United Nations decision (at the suggestion of the Sri Lankan government, which itself was changing from a policy of housing supply to one of housing support) to designate 1987 as the International Year of Shelter for the Homeless.

The potential of the community spirit which underlies Third World housing has been well-defined by two of the principal researchers in the field, Jorge Hardoy and David Satterthwaite of the Human Settlements programme at the International Institute for Environment and Development set up by the late Barbara Ward. Writing of the Latin American *barrio*, or neighbourhood, they record

> Politically, it is at a scale within which the inhabitants became interested in participating. Administratively, it could represent the basic unit for decentralizing decision-making and project formulation, implementation and evaluation. Economically, it could become a suitable scale for the location of small- and medium-sized workshops and non-polluting enterprises . . . Environmentally it is the ideal size for step-by-step actions which are inevitably the best hope for low and lower middle income groups for a rapid improvement in their habitat. Socially, despite its changes in size and dispersion within a metropolitan area, it is at the scale where throughout history most valid community organizations and activities have taken place.
>
> (Hardoy and Satterthwaite, *Shelter in the Third World: People's Needs and Governments' Response*)

The community architecture movement represents an important element in the drive by people for more say in the decisions that shape their lives. It offers the opportunity for democratic action and should help to renew the strength of our democratic processes. It is giving people more say in the decisions which are of initial importance to them. In the Third World context or in our own, that is welcome and important.

When people are involved in decisions they feel confident and secure. A community that gives people confidence and security is a powerful community. That is the challenge that community architecture is engaged to meet – building powerful communities that can handle change and adapt to it.

It is a challenge which has to be met if civilized life is to survive.

SCARMAN
House of Lords
February 1987

Authors' Preface

Community architecture has emerged as a powerful force for change in the creation and management of human settlements. Like many of the other new currents which are presently transforming societies all over the globe, its strength lies in being both an *activity* rooted in re-discovered natural laws and a broad political *movement* cutting across traditional boundaries. The activity of community architecture is based on the simple principle that the environment works better if the people who live, work and play in it are actively involved in its creation and management instead of being treated as passive consumers. The movement is providing the political and organizational impetus for transforming the development industry and putting these principles into practice.

At the time of writing, community architecture is developing at an unprecedented rate on many fronts. This book is intended to assist that development by sketching out the movement's evolution and the current state of the art. It is written for the general reader, but also contains information essential for those professionally involved.

Chapter 1 provides an overview of the main arguments which are elaborated in the rest of the book. Chapter 2 traces the movement's history and describes the recent breakthroughs which have catapulted it to national and international prominence. Chapter 3 describes the paralysis and bankruptcy of conventional approaches, which have made a new approach so necessary. Chapter 4 looks at some of the pioneering community architecture schemes and shows how the approach is successfully creating prototypes for all kinds of development. Chapter 5 explains why community architecture works by identifying the natural laws on which it is based. Chapter 6 examines the new organizational forms, techniques, roles and attitudes necessary for making community architecture work. Chapter 7 looks at the main changes needed for the full potential of community architecture to be realized, and concludes with the authors' personal view of the prospects for the future. In order to assist those who wish to take their interest further, a detailed bibliography, glossary and directory of organizations is provided in the appendices. For handy reference, a chart comparing community architecture with conventional architecture appears on pp. 24–5 and a concise history of the movement is given in Appendix 3.

The emergence of community architecture is a worldwide phenomenon and the book has been written in such a way as to be useful to readers everywhere. The examples used, however, are mainly from Britain, because the movement has developed a unique momentum here in recent years due to a remarkable combination of factors, including the keen interest of the heir to the throne – His Royal Highness The Prince of Wales. Since the principles and issues involved are broadly similar worldwide, the recent British experience is of relevance to people living in other parts of the developed or developing world.

Although the community architecture movement has taken off in recent years, it is still in its early days. New prototypes, methods and techniques continue to be developed and the theory continues to be refined. Like any new art or science – and community architecture is both – its evolution proceeds by continual feedback from many small steps being taken, and in many parts of the globe. It would be impossible to provide all the answers at this stage. But we hope that this book – the first on the subject – will speed up the learning process. To assist us with future editions information on new developments will be gratefully received.

Nick Wates/Charles Knevitt
5 Dryden Street
Covent Garden
London WC2E 9NW
England

August 1987

Chapter 1

Rebuilding Communities
Introducing Community Architecture

I know of no safe depository of the ultimate powers of society, but the people themselves; and if we think them not enlightened enough to exercise their control with a wholesome discretion, the remedy is not to take it from them, but to inform their discretion.

Thomas Jefferson (1743–1826) US President (1801–9) and architect.

The crucial issue today is how to give people more pride in their environment, involvement in their housing and more control over their lives, all this leading to increased confidence and hope, a development of new organizational skills and a consequent flourishing of new enterprise. We are talking about the regeneration of thousands of local communities, and this is the really essential point about the whole thing. How can we achieve such an aim while ensuring that it isn't pie in the sky? The fundamental point to stress is the urgent need for partnership between the public and private sector, between local politicians, community groups and non-public sources of finance. To restore hope we must have a vision and source of inspiration. We must sink our differences and cut great swathes through the cat's cradle of red tape which chokes this country from end to end.

HRH The Prince of Wales, 13 June 1986

I am convinced that, after the fundamental question of preserving peace, it is the form and organization of urban areas that is now looming up as the greatest social challenge for the world for the rest of this century.

Colin Buchanan, Professor of Transport, Imperial College, London, 1968

On the night of 6 October 1985, violence erupted on the Broadwater Farm estate in north London. As families and the elderly cowered in their homes, gangs of youths – armed with bricks, knives, bottles and petrol bombs – confronted hundreds of police armed with riot shields and batons. What had been thought of as a model housing estate on its completion only twelve years previously became, for several hours, a battleground. By the end of the disturbances, 223 police and twenty

15

civilians had been injured. One policeman had been hacked to death. The senior police officer for the area described them as 'the most ferocious, the most vicious riots ever seen' in Britain.

Over the next few days, an agonized debate began. Was there something wrong with young people that they could behave in such a way? Were Britain's cities doomed to become 'no-go' areas in which decent people feared to walk the streets? Was there a fundamental design fault with housing estates like Broadwater Farm, whose deck-access walkways were used as launching pads for missiles against the enforcers of law and order? Were the riots really a law-and-order issue – or the manifestation of environmental, economic and social grievances which had not been heard? Had the billions of pounds poured into housing, unemployment benefit and social welfare nationally since the war been of no avail? What, precisely, was going wrong?

For the eruption at Broadwater Farm could not be dismissed as an isolated incident. Alarm bells had been ringing since 1981, when for days on end the nation's television screens showed scenes of looting, violence and arson by uncontrolled mobs in deprived inner-city areas in various parts of the country: Brixton, south London; St Pauls, Bristol; Toxteth, Liverpool; Handsworth, Birmingham; Moss Side, Manchester. Destruction of property alone ran into tens of millions of pounds. The social cost was less easy to quantify.

Most of the public debate in the aftermath of these urban riots had initially focused on the need to improve and strengthen the police force and to devote more government money to housing and welfare services. Steps – albeit limited – were taken on both fronts.

But the Broadwater Farm incident was a forceful indication that these traditional remedies for urban unrest were not getting to the root of the problem, and increasing attention was paid to another aspect of the problem, one which had previously been little noticed by those in authority. This was the possible link between social unrest and *the degree of control that people have over their environment*.

In his public-inquiry report for the Home Secretary on the Brixton 'disorders' in 1981, Lord Scarman, a former High Court judge and Chairman of the Law Commission, had included the following recommendations:

Local communities should be more fully involved in the decisions which affect them. A 'top-down' approach to regeneration does not seem to have worked. Local communities must be fully and effectively involved in planning, in the

provision of local services, and in the managing and financing of specific projects
. . . Inner-city areas are not human deserts. They possess a wealth of voluntary
effort and goodwill. It would be wise to put this human capital to good use . . . It is
essential that people are encouraged to secure a stake in, feel a pride in, and have
a sense of responsibility for their own area.[1]

This aspect of Scarman's findings went unreported and unremarked at
the time. But after the Broadwater Farm incident it was rediscovered and
given prominence by a movement which, in the intervening period, had
emerged as a powerful new force in environmental politics – an extraordinary coalition of community organizations, academics, environmental
professionals, politicians of all parties, church leaders and the Prince of
Wales.

The Community Architecture Movement

The movement is called 'community architecture'. It is an umbrella term
which also embraces 'community planning', 'community design',
'community development' and other forms of 'community technical aid'.
It emerged from a growing realization that mismanagement of the built
environment is a major contributor to the nation's social and economic
ills, and that there are better ways of going about planning and design.

The modern urban environment in Britain, as in many other parts of
the world, has become widely recognized as a disaster story characterized
by ugliness, squalor, congestion, pollution, wasteland, vandalism, stress
and the destruction of communities. 'Development' has come to be
regarded as 'a bad thing', and the demolition by controlled explosives of
housing estates built at vast expense only a few years before is almost
commonplace. Conventional architecture and planning, rooted in the
paternalistic and centralized creation and management of the environment by experts, have clearly failed; the ideals behind them have
been lost, the visions have faded, the policies lie in tatters.

In contrast, a handful of pioneering development projects all over the
country have demonstrated that it is possible to escape from this disaster;
to build housing that people want to live in; to give people a sense of
pride and reinforce their identity with their local community; to build
social facilities that are needed and properly looked after; to develop
neighbourhoods and cities in ways that enrich people's lives by being
genuinely responsive to their needs and aspirations.

Contrary to popular belief, the magic solution is not simply vast quantities of public money. Although more investment in the built environment is desperately needed, the crucial task is to improve the way resources are used. The key is to get the *process* of development right; to ensure that the right decisions are made by the right people at the right time. And the main lesson to emerge from the pioneering projects (and backed up by an increasing volume of theoretical research) is that *the environment works better if the people who live, work and play in it are actively involved in its creation and management.* This simple truth – the core principle of community architecture – applies to housing, workplaces, parks, social facilities, neighbourhoods and even entire cities. And it applies to both capitalist and socialist economies, whether rich or poor.

Discovering how to make it possible for people to be involved in shaping and managing their environment is what the community architecture movement has been exploring over the past few years. Starting with architects and planners working with, instead of against, community groups, it has grown rapidly to include a new breed of professional organizations providing technical aid to the community; new enabling schemes started by professional institutes and voluntary organizations; decentralization programmes by local authorities; and a variety of partnership programmes involving the public sector, with developers and financial institutions, working closely with the voluntary sector. New prototypes for development of housing, social facilities and neighbourhoods have emerged in which the people are no longer the consumers of what others provide, but are in control.

It has been a hard – and often heroic – struggle, marked by bitter campaigns and frustration. Those in the vanguard of change are rarely welcomed or appreciated initially, and the traditional development industry and planning system have, over the past fifty years, come to be based on an entirely contrary principle; that managing the built environment is far too complicated to be entrusted to ordinary people and should be left to the experts. Despite its becoming increasingly obvious that this does not work very well, those promoting community architecture have had to fight every inch of the way: against bureaucracy, professional institutions, the property industry and political dogma of all shades. For every successful community architecture project there have been dozens of attempts which have fallen by the wayside.

The breakthrough for the public perception of community architecture in Britain came on 30 May 1984 when the Prince of Wales spoke out on the subject. In a speech at Hampton Court Palace at the 150th anniversary celebrations of the Royal Institute of British Architects, he started with a bitter attack on the architectural and planning professions. Reducing some of the audience to tears – some of joy, some of sorrow – he declared that: 'Some planners and architects have consistently ignored the feelings and wishes of the mass of ordinary people in this country.' He went on to praise community architecture as one of the few new ideas giving optimism and hope for the future.

To the consternation of much of the architectural profession, the government and many of his own palace aides, he followed up his remarks by visiting more than a dozen community architecture projects throughout the country, inviting community architects to private dinners at Kensington Palace, becoming patron of the first award scheme for community architecture, commissioning community architects for projects on his Duchy of Cornwall estate and making several more outspoken speeches over the next three years.

Through his royal endorsement, Prince Charles gave the community architecture movement the respectability and credibility it so badly needed to overcome the obstacles confronting it. It marked its breakthrough as a popular movement. As architect Rod Hackney, the movement's most able politician and propagandist, commented at the time:

It was dynamite. Suddenly, the future king has come along and said that the way to work isn't the way most architects are working but *is* the way community architects work. That means that the image of community architecture has suddenly leapfrogged over a lot of establishment figures who have been opposing it. He didn't just close the door on architecture, he opened the door for the way out. He has shown the direction. The Cinderella of the profession has at last found its prince, and the RIBA and the Government will now ignore it at their peril.[2]

The effect was soon felt. Projects in the field suddenly found it easier to get funding and approval from authorities. The media started running stories on it. Senior politicians in all the main political parties began to take a serious interest in it. So did the professional institutes, which performed double somersaults in their attempts to convince the Prince that they were doing what he wanted. Such is the influence of royalty.

A second breakthrough came on 1 December 1986, when it was announced that Hackney had won a ballot of the whole membership of the Royal Institute of British Architects to become its next president. Civil war over the direction which the architectural profession should take appeared to have come to an end, with a decisive victory for community architecture.

19

Lessons of the 'Quiet' Revolution

The growth and recognition of community architecture in Britain has been paralleled – perhaps less sensationally – by similar activity throughout the world. In the United States, for instance, where the movement is better known as 'social' architecture, it was sparked off by urban riots in the 1960s; since then its development has followed a very similar pattern to that in Britain, including overcoming institutional objections from both within and outside the professions. In developing countries, based on the success of architects and planners working closely with the inhabitants of shanty towns from the late fifties, it is now widely accepted that it makes more sense to improve and upgrade than to tear down and rebuild as was the general policy only a decade ago. The importance of people participating in the planning of their own homes and neighbourhoods was a central theme which arose out of the United Nations Habitat Conference on Human Settlements in Vancouver in 1976. It united delegates from both First and Third World countries, and has increasingly shaped the development of international policy and cooperation on human settlements ever since.

From this worldwide environmental revolution, often referred to as the 'quiet' revolution, some conclusions are beginning to emerge;

1. That when the people who inhabit any environment are effectively involved in its creation and management, it 'works' better. It is likely to be of higher quality physically, will be better suited to its purpose, will be better maintained and will make better use of resources – finance, land, materials, and people's initiative and enterprise. Also, the process of involvement, combined with the better end product, can create employment, can help reduce crime, vandalism, mental stress, ill health and the potential for urban unrest, and can lead to more stable and self-sufficient communities, and to more contented and confident citizens and professionals.

2. That for such a process to work effectively, there has to be a fundamental change in the roles of all the people involved in the development process. For professionals – whether architects, planners or others – it means using their knowledge and skills to help people solve their own problems rather than dispensing wisdom and solutions from a distance; becoming *enablers* and educators rather than preachers and providers; assisting people in their own homes and neighbourhoods to understand their problems and devising solutions to help

them solve them. For politicians and bureaucrats, it means helping to make things happen rather than stopping them – becoming *facilitators* or supporters instead of gatekeepers or suppliers. For citizens, it means the *willing acceptance of responsibility* for the environment, and being prepared to devote time, energy and resources to learning how it works and how to improve it. For everyone it means developing a 'creative partnership' with all the others involved.

3. That community architecture is not in any sense anti-design, even though it is not a style such as Post-Modern or Classical Revival. It may well herald an alternative to much of the monumental, style-conscious, eye-catching architecture that dominates the pages of the architectural magazines. This is because the judges of success are no longer the panels of professionals who give awards to their peers or magazine editors in search of titillating images, but the users of the buildings and environments themselves. There is an emphasis on the *process* of design, rather than the end *product*, but not at the expense of the latter. Several of the best 'designer' architects in Britain are also, occasionally, part of the community architecture movement, for instance. 'Good design' therefore becomes that which works well, is of human scale, is recognizable and understandable, and which 'looks good' to its users. But this is not at the expense of the traditional architectural virtues of 'commodity, firmness and delight'. On the contrary, many professionals argue that the more they involve the users, the richer their architecture becomes, and that what is created is a new vernacular, harnessing new technology and making it appropriate to the needs of modern society.

4. That while community architecture demands a radical change in the relationships between those involved in development, it transcends traditional Left/Right politics. It is not rigidly pro nor anti public or private ownership of land, public or private development agencies, high rise or low rise buildings, for instance, believing that dogmatic attitudes to such issues have prevented any resolution of the central problem of people's alienation from their environment in recent years. What it does require is an understanding of the complementary nature of power at different levels and of the need for design solutions and tenure and organizational patterns tailored to the needs of each and every specific location and circumstance. It also requires a massive change in establishment thinking so that resources are channelled more effectively and put at the disposal of residents and local communities. In this respect, community archi-

21

tecture is part of a much broader pattern of change – often referred to as the Third Wave – that is emerging in post-industrial societies, in which traditional cycles of dependence are being replaced by new frameworks of self-reliance.

Coming of Age

In many respects the *activity* of community architecture is not new but merely the rediscovery of ancient wisdom made relevant to a different age. That wisdom was lost during the rapid industrialization and urbanization of the past two hundred years, when the increasing complexities of life led to the intervention of third parties to design, regulate and control building and development. But the current revival of interest and its emergence as a *movement* has its root in the community action, conservation and amenity movements of the 1960s, when communities began to protest about the destruction of their environment by forces outside their control and demanded more say. In the seventies these groups began to link up with professionals, who were beginning to give them the technical advice and vision they needed to convert their ideas into positive proposals. By the early eighties the movement had had many notable successes in the form of built projects and it was gaining in confidence all the time. By the mid-eighties the message was finally beginning to get through to those with power and influence: politicians, financial institutions and, through the media, to public opinion.

Community architecture is now poised on the brink of a new era with immense possibilities. Its time has come. Blueprints are available for most development situations, the theoretical framework is established, the professions are starting to change and there is increasing public understanding and support.

Yet there are still many difficulties to be overcome. The emergence of such a potentially powerful force for change has inevitably been marked by suspicion, confusion and hostility in many quarters. Entrenched attitudes and jealousies persist and there are still many sceptics and cynics who cannot see the wood for the trees. Resources are still desperately lacking where they are most needed and there is a desperate shortage of people with the relevant expertise at all levels. And a great deal more needs to be understood about precisely how and why particular methods succeed or fail. Community architecture is in a continuous process of learning and development. It is an adventure story shared by people all

over the developed – and developing – world. While it is already transforming the way the environment is designed, built and managed, its full
economic and social implications have yet to be discovered.

Like most other popular labels, the term 'community architecture' has
acquired a meaning beyond its dictionary definition. But taken literally,
community architecture is 'architecture' (the 'art or science of building')
which creates or reinforces 'community' ('identity of character; fel-
lowship').[3] And herein lies its greatest promise. The architect, David
Lewis, has said: 'No one knows the community better than the people
who live there. Equity – a sense of personal investment in one's community – is the critical basis for the working of democracy and citizen-
ship.'[4] By combining design, organizational and entrepreneurial talent
with local knowledge and commitment, community architecture provides
a new way of addressing one of the timeless – yet currently most pressing
– problems facing mankind; the creation of harmonious communities
and human settlements.

What Makes Community Architecture Different

	Conventional architecture	Community architecture
Status of user	Users are passive recipients of an environment conceived, executed, managed and evaluated by others: corporate, public or private sector landowners and developers with professional 'experts'.	Users are – or are treated as – the clients. They are offered (or take) control of commissioning, designing, developing, managing and evaluating their environment, and may sometimes be physically involved in construction.
User/expert relationship	Remote, arm's length. Little if any direct contact. Experts – commissioned by landowners and developers – occasionally make superficial attempts to define and consult end-users, but their attitudes are mostly paternalistic and patronizing.	Creative alliance and working partnership. Experts are commissioned by, and are accountable to, users, or behave as if they are.
Expert's role	Provider, neutral bureaucrat, élitist, 'one of them', manipulator of people to fit the system, a professional in the institutional sense. Remote and inaccessible.	Enabler, facilitator and 'social entrepreneur', educator, 'one of us', manipulator of the system to fit the people and challenger of the status quo; a professional as a competent and efficient adviser. Locally based and accessible.
Scale of project	Generally large and often cumbersome. Determined by pattern of land ownership and the need for efficient mass production and simple management.	Generally small, responsive and determined by the nature of the project, the local building industry and the participants. Large sites generally broken down into manageable packages.
Location of project	Fashionable and wealthy existing residential, commercial and industrial areas preferred. Otherwise a green-field site with infrastructure (roads, power, water supply and drainage, etc.); i.e. no constraints.	Anywhere, but most likely to be urban, or periphery of urban areas; area of single or multiple deprivation; derelict or decaying environment.

Use of project	Likely to be a single function or two or three complementary activities (e.g. commercial, or housing, or industrial).	Likely to be multi-functional.
Design style	Self-conscious about style: most likely 'international' or 'modern movement'. Increasingly one of the other fashionable and identifiable styles: Post-Modern, Hi-tech, Neo-vernacular or Classical Revival. Restrained and sometimes frigid; utilitarian.	Unselfconscious about style. Any 'style' may be adopted as appropriate. Most likely to be 'contextual', 'regional' ('place-specific') with concern for identity. Loose and sometimes exuberant; often highly decorative, using local artists.
Technology/ resources	Tendency towards: mass production, prefabrication, repetition, global supply of materials, machine-friendly technology, 'clean sweep' and new build, machine intensive, capital intensive.	Tendency towards: small-scale production, on-site construction, individuality, local supply of materials, user-friendly (convivial) technology, re-use, recycling and conservation, labour and time intensive.
End product	Static, slowly deteriorates, hard to manage and maintain, high-energy consumption.	Flexible, slowly improving, easy to manage and maintain, low-energy consumption.
Primary motivation	*Private sector*: return on investment (usually short-term) and narrow self-interest. *Public sector*: social welfare and party political opportunism. *Experts*: esteem from professional peers. Response to general national or regional gap in market, or social needs and opportunities.	Improvement of quality of life for individuals and communities. Better use of local resources. Social investment. Response to specific localized needs and opportunities.
Method of operation	Top-down, emphasis on product rather than process, bureaucratic, centralized with specialisms compartmentalized, stop-go. impersonal, anonymous, paper management, avoid setting a precedent, secretive.	Bottom-up, emphasis on process rather than product, flexible, localized, holistic and multi-disciplinary, evolutionary, continuous, personal, familiar, people management, setting precedents, open.
Ideology	Totalitarian, technocratic and doctrinaire (Left or Right) big is beautiful, competition, survival of the fittest.	Pragmatic, humanitarian, responsive and flexible, small is beautiful, collaboration, mutual aid.

Chapter 2

The Breakthrough
A History of Community Architecture

When we want your opinion, we will give it to you.
  Motto suggested for Liverpool City Council by the Eldonian Community
  Association, Liverpool, 1986

The greatest problem with embarking on a new approach is breaking through
established dogma and stigma and set ways, particularly with professionals and
town-hall bureaucrats. The best way to do this is to show by practical example
and hope that the example, if successful, can act as a precedent.
  Rod Hackney, 1985

I have a message for the two professions most involved in the destruction of
our environment. To the politicians – trust your communities. To the
architects – we'll rehabilitate the buildings, you'd better rehabilitate your
profession.
  Patrick Doherty, Project Director, Derry Inner City Project, 13 June 1986

Many many thanks to you both, from us the tenants of Newquay House. You
have opened up a new life to us with your kindness and consideration, knitted
together a community that was straying apart, shown us there was hope in a
decaying area and worked and fought very hard, long hours – for which we
are all very grateful . . . We are stimulated now and we will not let the work
you have done go to waste. We are determined to reach the goal you have
shown us can be reached . . . Without fail we all very much hope you will
remain with us throughout the changes. Not only are you our architects, you
have become our friends.
  Letter signed by twenty-six tenants of Newquay House, London, to architects
  Ben Derbyshire and Caroline Dove of Hunt Thompson Associates

The gathering momentum of community architecture here and elsewhere in the
developed world is wholly welcome as an antithesis to alienating Modernism
and as an antidote to professional arrogance.
  Editorial, *Architectural Review*, April 1985

Just ten years elapsed between the emergence of community architecture in Britain as a conscious and identifiable movement on the fringes of the architectural profession, in 1976, to the election of the movement's most able politician and propagandist, Rod Hackney, as president of the Royal Institute of British Architects.

It was a turbulent decade. But by its conclusion the architectural profession had been transformed and a new national multi-disciplinary association of environmental professionals had been created and had blazed a trail of rapid expansion. From being a radical alternative, community architecture had become part of mainstream conventional wisdom in the professions and had been endorsed by all sections of society – from the grassroots activist to the heir to the throne – as well as politicians from all four main parties. It had become a political movement of substance with long-term economic and social as well as environmental implications.

The movement is the product of a fusion of experience from many different parts of the broader environmental field; from many disciplines and from many isolated local projects. A new theoretical framework has crystallized, enabling people to make better sense of their experiences and to build on common links between issues and events previously seen as being separate. At the same time, a progressive style of campaigning tactics has evolved, based on challenging the status quo with positive alternatives, rather than simply abstract protest. This chapter describes how these developments have lead to a breakthrough in the prospects for a better built environment.

Roots

The movement's roots can be traced back to the widespread community action of the 1960s and early 1970s, much of which was a response to prevailing techniques of urban planning and architecture. Well-intentioned but misguided policies implemented by central and local government at that time led to the wholesale destruction of existing communities in comprehensive redevelopment and rehousing programmes, often accompanied by rampant property speculation. Throughout the country, but particularly in the major conurbations, citizens took to the streets in protest, forming themselves into tenants' associations, residents' groups, traders' associations and other forms of voluntary organization, to defend their homes, their livelihood and their environment. Often they were assisted – and sometimes led – by idealistic

27

young professionals and students disillusioned with the direction in which their training and professional institutions were taking them.

Occasionally, by a skilful combination of direct action and media manipulation, these groups were successful in halting the bulldozers. More often they failed, and became embittered and dispirited. But even when they were successful, they rarely managed to go beyond preventing antisocial development from going ahead. The planning and development industry was unresponsive to what it saw as negative reaction, rather than as a potentially positive force. Few alternative schemes which were proposed were ever implemented, even though they were usually more rational, humane and almost invariably a cheaper option. Compromise was the order of the day, and this partly contributed to the community action movement petering out by the mid-1970s. But it had given birth to a new style of political action, an alternative to orthodox party politics, being based on participatory rather than representative democracy. Many valuable key lessons had been learnt and were subsequently built on. Among those of relevance to community architecture were:

1. That community groups were unlikely to succeed unless they were able to match the technical capability and organizational skills of the opposition – in planning, architecture and the legal framework of development, for example.
2. That genuine community participation in environmental decision-making – the central demand of community action – is an extremely difficult, hazardous and complex affair, requiring both the citizens and their professional advisers to develop new attitudes, techniques and skills.
3. That community control over developments at local level would remain impossible – or only be possible with sustained struggle – until there was a change in attitude at national level about the way in which the development industry and local government should be structured.
4. That participation by people in their own environment is inherently a political issue and yet does not fit into a conventional party political pigeonhole. As Colin Ward, one of the earliest and most influential writers on the subject, wrote in 1974 about tenant control of public-sector housing estates: 'It would be foolish to suggest that [it] is not a political matter. It is political in the most profound sense: it is about the distribution of power in society. But fortunately it is one of those issues which cuts across normal party divisions. It finds sup-

porters amongst adherents of all political parties, and none.' He went on to recommend: 'Its advocates ought to exploit this spectrum of support' – which, as we shall see, they were to do later with dramatic effect.[5]

Setting the Stage

Largely based on the experience of community action, a series of parallel but related developments took place from the beginning of the 1970s which were eventually to make the community architecture movement possible.

Pioneering projects
Pilot projects involving the participation of users were started at local level in many parts of the country. For instance, in Liverpool in 1969 Shelter set up the Neighbourhood Action Project (SNAP) where for the first time architects were situated in a neighbourhood office and worked with local residents. In the same year the architect Ralph Erskine, when given a commission by the local authority in Newcastle, established an office in a former undertaker's shop in the Byker district and involved residents of slum property in designing new council homes (see p. 77). Two years later, the North Kensington Amenity Trust was formed in west London as a partnership between voluntary associations and the local authority, and embarked on a multimillion-pound, mixed-use re-development on land under the elevated Westway motorway. In Glasgow, architects and students from the university formed an organization called ASSIST and pioneered the rehabilitation of tenements with the involvement of the residents. And at Dryden Street in London in 1972, the architectural firm Rock Townsend established the first user-controlled managed workspace (see p. 92). These, and many other projects, established precedents for others to follow, and a growing body of knowledge and practical experience evolved.

New types of organizations
New forms of organization specifically geared to involving people in their environment were set up by professionals and voluntary groups. The Free Form Arts Trust and Interaction, two of the first independent environmental agencies committed to working with community organizations, were formed in London in 1969. Interaction later spawned NUBS (Neighbourhood Use of Building and Space), providing the first free arch-

29

itectural services to community groups. In 1972 in London, the Town and Country Planning Association set up a Planning Aid unit, providing free planning assistance to community groups. In Liverpool, Neighbourhood Housing Services was established in 1973 as a 'secondary cooperative', providing technical assistance to the growing housing cooperative movement. In Birmingham in 1974 the local authority set up locally based project offices to tackle housing rehabilitation. And, in the same year, groups in Covent Garden established the Covent Garden Forum, effectively the first non-statutory neighbourhood council in the country.

Intellectual foundations

The intellectual foundations of community architecture were built using the experience of what was happening in projects on the ground in the developed and developing countries, and putting them within a context of global trends of post-industrial society. Critiques of post-war planning and architecture had first begun to appear in the 1960s, with such seminal books as Jane Jacobs's *The Death and Life of Great American Cities* (1961) and John Habraken's *Supports* (1961). The most influential writers during the early 1970s were Robert Goodman, in *After the Planners* (1972); John Turner and Robert Fichter in *Freedom to Build* (1972), and Turner in *Housing by People* (1976); Colin Ward in *Tenants Take Over* (1974) and *Housing: An Anarchist Approach* (1976). Few of these books achieved mass circulation or had much impact on the general public. But they were extremely influential in schools of architecture and planning, and provided a new generation of campaigners with an intellectual armoury which backed up the experience being gained on the ground. On the broader theoretical front, there were a number of books on similar themes which did achieve mass circulation and began to create a shift of thinking in the same direction: for example there was the futurist Alvin Toffler's *Future Shock* (1970); E. F. Schumacher's *Small is Beautiful* (1973); Ivan Illich's *Tools for Conviviality* (1973) and *Disabling Professions* (1977); and Charles Reich's *The Greening of America* (1971).

Government response

Throughout this period the government introduced legislation and guidelines which made community involvement in the environment easier. In 1968 the Town and Country Planning Act required that the public must be adequately 'informed' and 'consulted' before the approval of plans. The following year the Skeffington Report, *People and Planning*, the world's first government report on public participation, was published, advocating greater public participation in the whole planning process. As a result, public participation – albeit of a limited nature – became part and parcel of the work of planning authorities both in developing structure plans and in development control. The 1969 Housing Act encouraged the retention and improvement of houses and neighbourhoods rather than their wholesale demolition and replacement, making it easier for people to be involved. This was reinforced in the 1974 Housing Act, which introduced General Improvement and Housing Action Areas, making available a range of grants both to individual owners and for environmental improvements.

Developing international links
The early 1970s also saw the development of networks allowing the exchange of information and experience internationally. The first International Design Participation Conference was held in Manchester in 1971, drawing participants from many parts of the world. Four years later a symposium was organized in Sweden by the International Youth Federation for Environmental Studies and Conservation at which a valuable, but short-lived Community Action in Europe network was launched. The importance of people participating in their environment emerged as one of the central themes of the historic United Nations' Habitat International Conference in Vancouver in 1976, which finally brought the subject of human settlements into the centre of political debate, particularly at a spectacular 'counter' conference which was run simultaneously by non-governmental organizations. The Habitat International Council, which was launched in Vancouver as a federation of non-governmental organizations, has played an important role ever since as a policy-making pressure group and advisory body in the field of human settlements. These networks enabled people to draw inspiration from a number of innovative projects worldwide. Particularly influential in the mid-seventies were the self-governing Free Town of Christiania on a large area of squatted land in Copenhagen, the revitalization of the Nieuwmarkt neighbourhood in Amsterdam through imaginative community pressure and direct action, the building of the medical student centre at the University of Louvain designed by students with architect Lucien Kroll, and the development of a network of seventy design centres providing assistance to community groups in the United States.

For the most part, these developments – pilot projects, new organizations, theory, legislation and international connections – took place independently of one another. There was little publicity linking the significance of what was happening. The lessons drawn from international experience tended to be localized and specific, and there was little communication between those actively involved. While the increasing involvement of people in their environment was clearly being seen as an important social movement by many of those involved, it lacked the common identity necessary to give it public profile and political clout.

That changed in 1976 when a handful of British architects formed what they called the Community Architecture Group of the Royal Institute of British Architects (RIBA). It was the first time the term 'community architecture' had been used formally.* Although there were few tangible results for some years, the label and the group's shrewd political tactics were to prove a winning combination.

The group's leader was Rod Hackney, then known only as architect for the award-winning Black Road self-help general improvement area in Macclesfield (see p. 70). Within a decade of the group's formation, Hackney's role extended to include being an unofficial adviser to the Prince of Wales and President-elect of the RIBA.

The Battle for the Professions

From the early seventies it was clear to all those campaigning for people to have more control over their environment that the professional institutes – which controlled professional education and codes of conduct – were one of the main obstacles. They tended to be ruled by older members of the profession – firmly wedded to the so-called Modern Movement in architecture and planning – who Rod Hackney had once dismissed as 'a whole generation of people producing the wrong product'. They were seemingly incapable of taking the initiative necessary to adapt to a new age. Until the advent of the Community Architecture Group (CAG), most of the professionals pioneering community architecture were largely operating outside the professional institutes, which were seen as impenetrable bastions of reaction. The New Architecture Movement, for instance,

---

* The term 'community architecture' appears to have been first used by Fred Pooley in his inaugural address as President of the RIBA in 1973 (see Bibliography – *Royal Institute of British Architects Journal*). He used it to refer to public-sector provision of architecture for the community by local authorities. The first use of the term with roughly its present meaning was by Charles Knevitt in a profile of Rod Hackney in 1975, called 'Community Architect Mark I' (see Bibliography, articles).

formed by over one hundred radical architects in 1975, focused its attention on unionizing architects and reforming the Architects' Registration
Council of the United Kingdom (the body established by Parliament to
control standards in the profession, which in practice is strongly influ-
enced by the RIBA). The Community Architecture Working Group, by
contrast, derived its strength from campaigning from within.

Although it had little real power within the RIBA, the group persuaded
the institute to put its name to a number of important initiatives over the
next few years, and this helped to build up a national organizational
framework for the movement. An Architectural Aid scheme was started
in 1978 in Norfolk, with architects holding 'surgeries' for the general
public at Citizens' Advice Bureaux. The first of several 'architecture
workshops' was opened the same year in Newcastle to develop environmental education programmes. A pilot community project was funded at
Highfield Hall near Bolton. In 1982 a Community Projects Fund was
established which provided community groups with funds to pay architects and stimulated hundreds of community projects all over the
country. The Community Urban Design Assistance Team (CUDAT) programme was introduced from the United States with a pilot project in
Southampton in 1985. Several conferences were organized and pamphlets published. And eventually, in 1986, a community architecture resource centre was established in the RIBA headquarters at Portland
Place, London.

Despite these successes, however, a constant state of guerrilla warfare
existed. With virtually no representation on the ruling council, the
Community Architecture Group's relationship with its parent organization was always tense, and confrontation rather than cooperation
persisted. The group had to operate by stealth and occasional appeals to
the profession's conscience. It used the media as an effective weapon in
its campaign and occasionally resorted to threats of pulling out of the
RIBA altogether and establishing an alternative, rival institute. (A precedent for such a move had been established in the early nineteenth
century when the famous engineer Thomas Telford set up the Institution
of Civil Engineers after being forced to resign from the Royal Academy –
the professional forerunner of the RIBA – because the warehouses,
bridges and canals he was building were not considered to be 'architecture'.)

As it happened, an alternative institute was launched anyway in the
form of the Association of Community Technical Aid Centres (ACTAC).
As well as coming under fire from its own institute, the RIBA's Community Architecture Group was heavily criticized by professionals,

mainly from other disciplines, who believed that the activity that had become known as community architecture was not solely 'architecture', but involved all the environmental professions equally. They accused CAG of 'hijacking' the movement for user-control over the environment by promoting the term 'community *architecture*' and concentrating on the role of the *architect* in the process. The term they preferred was 'community technical aid'.

ACTAC was formally launched in London in October 1983 with backing from across the political spectrum. Key speakers at the launch included Sir George Young, Conservative Under-Secretary of State for the Environment, and George Nicholson, Labour Chairman of Planning at the Greater London Council. The aim of the association was to provide support facilities for organizations providing technical assistance to community groups, and to help communities set up such facilities where none existed; in short, to champion the cause of community technical aid and campaign for multi-disciplinary technical aid to be available to communities throughout the country.

Starting with only fifteen member organizations in the autumn of 1983, the association grew rapidly. Within two years it had over fifty members, employing between them over 310 full-time and 562 part-time staff, and a combined annual turnover of more than £5m. Thirty-five of the member organizations had themselves been formed since 1980. Although the association itself had funds to employ only three members of staff, the balance of power between the professions had changed decisively; for the first time there was a national multi-disciplinary association dedicated to user involvement, with the users playing a significant role.

By 1984, the community architecture movement was firmly established, at least within the construction and development industry. Hardly a week went by without references to it in the trade press; the two leading weekly magazines for architects – the *Architects' Journal* and *Building Design* – had both started running regular features on the subject. An increasing number of completed pioneering projects on the ground had demonstrated that it worked for almost all development situations and the lessons were being applied on a larger scale. In Glasgow, for instance, community-based housing associations had successfully renovated over 10,000 flats, and the principles of tenant involvement and control pioneered by ASSIST architects in the early seventies were transforming the city's housing policy.

Interest had spread outside the architectural and planning professions.

The Royal Institution of Chartered Surveyors had also launched a voluntary aid scheme providing free surveying advice. An increasing number of local authorities were taking positive initiatives by supporting technical aid schemes, setting up special projects with professionals working directly for tenants, and restructuring and decentralizing their technical departments. A national network of Groundwork Trusts – independent, non-profit making, charitable companies which link the private, public and voluntary sectors at regional level to improve the environment – was being planned following a successful pilot scheme in Macclesfield. And the Department of the Environment – encouraged by the success of its Priority Estates Programme, which introduced estate-based management on public housing estates – was steadily increasing a new special grants programme for funding organizations supporting community technical aid nationally.

The full international extent of the movement was demonstrated with the publication in 1984 of twenty-six case studies from all over the world in *The Scope of Social Architecture* by Richard Hatch, Professor of Architecture at the New Jersey Institute of Technology in the United States. Citizen participation had emerged as a major theme in the 1981 European Urban Renaissance Year, and the Commonwealth Association of Architects focused on community architecture at its Nairobi conference that year. In 1984, the International Union of Architects (UIA) awarded its first annual gold medal for 'outstanding achievement in the field of architecture' to the Egyptian architect, Hassan Fathy, who is best known for bringing architects, craftsmen and the community together in the creation of shelter for the poor. And in the same year the Union organized an international student competition, 'The Architect as Enabler', which received 186 entries from forty-four countries, demonstrating growing interest from architecture schools throughout the world.

But there were still immense difficulties. Despite proven success, projects on the ground often faced immense obstacles, largely rooted in obsolete political dogma and resistance to change. In Liverpool, for instance, the Labour-controlled council put a halt to the highly successful new-build cooperatives (p. 77), declaring them to be 'part of a deliberate and calculated attack on municipal housing by the Tory party nationally, aided and abetted by the local Liberal/Tory alliance'. A conference on community architecture in the city organized by the city-funded polytechnic was stopped at the last moment on the grounds that the Labour party had not been offered a prominent-enough speaking slot. In Macclesfield the Conservative-controlled council made persistent attempts to evict Rod Hackney from his street-corner offices (see p. 70), on the extraordinary grounds that 'office' use was inappropriate in a residential area. (The irony of the fact that there would no longer have been a residential area had it not been for Rod Hackney's offices seemed to escape them.) In St Ives in Cornwall, the Conservative county council went so far as to ban an architect hired by local residents from entering a redundant school to assess its suitability for conversion into a community centre. Its own proposals for demolishing the building and building a new fire-station on the site had been opposed by a petition signed by one third of the town's population.

Even where there was no outright political opposition, all community architecture projects had to overcome immense bureaucratic hurdles. Simple applications for funding and approvals could take up to a year, creating frustration and despondency. Many positive initiatives were strangled at inception or were wrecked by compromise. The architect Caroline Lwin summed up the mood of those on the ground after helping a group of parents construct a play centre in the East End of London (p. 86): 'It could have been such a joyful experience. Instead it's been blood, sweat and tears all the way.'

On top of all this the movement was desperately short of finance and skills. Most projects still depended on professionals working at least in part on a voluntary basis or on spec. The schools of architecture, with one or two exceptions, had still not started teaching the new skills necessary, and even where finance was available it was hard to find high-calibre staff. Most depressing of all, the movement was faced with a barrage of cynicism, particularly from some prominent architectural critics who rarely left their offices in central London and, perhaps, saw it as a threat to their livelihood. References to community architecture included such descriptions as 'vacuous', 'pissing in the wind' and even 'dangerous'. The national media could not even be persuaded to see it as an issue.

Something was needed to lift the movement on to another plateau and give it renewed impetus. Dumbfounding everyone, most of all those involved, that something turned out to be the intervention of the heir to the throne – His Royal Highness The Prince of Wales.

The Prince of Wales Factor

In May 1984 Prince Charles was invited to speak at the 150th anniversary celebrations of the Royal Institute of British Architects at

Hampton Court Palace, and present the Royal Gold Medal for Architecture to Charles Correa, from India. He told the most distinguished members of the profession and their guests (which included the Environment Secretary, Patrick Jenkin) that architects had failed to listen and respond to the needs of ordinary people; for the first time he publicly supported community architecture, naming architects Rod Hackney and Edward Cullinan as the real heroes. These remarks were barely reported until much later, as the media focused on his attack on the design of two London projects, the National Gallery extension in Trafalgar Square and the Mansion House Square scheme by the late Mies van der Rohe. He described these as looking like a 'monstrous carbuncle' and a 'giant glass stump' respectively.

The RIBA had made frantic attempts to stop – or at least drastically modify – the speech in the hours leading up to its delivery, but to no avail. Public opposition by the heir to the throne to two of the most prominent and controversial post-war architectural projects in London was bad enough, but to praise community architecture and name two of its most able practitioners was to lead to the most bitter rivalry and the most extraordinary example of institutional paranoia yet seen.

The Hampton Court speech can now be seen as the watershed in helping to achieve the political breakthrough in community architecture two years later. Although the immediate impact of what the Prince said was lost in the tabloid headlines about 'carbuncles' and 'stumps' it led to a series of events which gave the movement a considerably enhanced status among the general public, the profession and media editors.

The original source of his comments about community architecture remains unclear. Jules Lubbock, architecture critic of the *New Statesman*, says he introduced the Prince to the subject over dinner at the Royal Academy some while before the speech, and followed it up by sending him some cuttings. A profile of Hackney also appeared in a special report in *The Times* two weeks before the speech and it is likely that the Prince had read it.

There is another possible explanation, however, or at least another possible contributory factor: the Duke of Gloucester, Prince Richard, is a former partner of Bernard Hunt and John Thompson of Hunt Thompson Associates, architects of the Lea View community architecture project (p. 73). The three read architecture at the same time at Cambridge and had set up in practice together before the premature death of Prince Richard's elder brother forced him to give up his profession and perform royal duties instead. As the only architect member of the immediate royal family, and living a stone's throw from Prince Charles's private apartments at Kensington Palace, it would have been natural for Prince Charles to consult his cousin about current trends in architecture, and Prince Richard might well have taken the opportunity to promote a cause close to his own heart.

Whatever the spark that ignited the interest of Prince Charles, it is worth recalling what he had to say on the subject on this first of many occasions:

> For far too long, it seems to me, some planners and architects have consistently ignored the feelings and wishes of the mass of ordinary people in this country . . . To be concerned about the way people live, about the environment they inhabit and the kind of community that is created by that environment should surely be one of the prime requirements of a really good architect.
>
> It has been most encouraging to see the development of community architecture as a natural reaction to the policy of decanting people to new towns and overspill estates where the extended family patterns of support were destroyed and the community life was lost. Now, moreover, we are seeing the gradual expansion of housing cooperatives, particularly in the inner-city areas of Liverpool, where the tenants are able to work with an architect of their own who listens to their comments and their ideas, and tries to design the kind of environment they want, rather than the kind which tends to be imposed upon them without any degree of choice.
>
> This sort of development, spearheaded as it is by such individuals as a Vice-President of the R I B A, Rod Hackney, and Ted Cullinan – a man after my own heart, as he believes very strongly that the architect must produce something which is visually beautiful as well as socially useful – offers something very promising in terms of inner-city renewal and urban housing, not to mention community garden design. Enabling the client community to be involved in the detailed process of design, rather than exclusively the local authority, is, I am sure, the kind of development we should be examining more closely. Apart from anything else, there is an assumption that if people have played a part in creating something they might conceivably treat it as their own possession and look after it, thus making an attempt at reducing the problem of vandalism. What I believe is important about community architecture is that it has shown 'ordinary' people that their views are worth having; that architects and planners do not necessarily have the monopoly of knowing best about taste, style and planning; that they need not be made to feel guilty or ignorant if their natural preference is for the more 'traditional' designs – for a small garden, for courtyards, arches and porches – and that there is a growing number of architects prepared to listen and to offer imaginative ideas.[6]

The reaction – both positive and negative – that the speech provoked (hundreds of letters were received by Buckingham Palace, virtually all of them supporting the speech, while many architects were, and still are, critical of it) may have convinced the Prince that he had touched a raw nerve and that it was something worth pursuing. Lobbied by Michael Manser, president of the RIBA, he agreed to host a private dinner at Kensington Palace to discuss architecture generally. Hackney attended the dinner and, it is understood, he was then invited to organize a series of others also at the palace, on various aspects of promoting community architecture, such as education and development finance.

Over the following months the Prince paid a series of private visits to community architecture projects – Black Road in Macclesfield and some of the Liverpool co-ops; Limehouse Basin and the Lea View Estate in east London; the Zenzele self-build housing co-op in Bristol; riot-torn Lozells Road next to Handsworth in Birmingham; the Community Design Service in Cardiff; Edward Cullinan's Lambeth Community Care Centre; Hackney's Weavers Triangle scheme in Burnley and his Colquhoun Street scheme in Stirling, for example. He became patron of *The Times*/RIBA Community Enterprise Award Scheme (the first national award scheme for community architecture projects), handing out its prizes in June 1986. Support also came in the form of commissions for community architects: Joe Poynton, a member of the RIBA's Community Architecture Group, for a Duchy of Cornwall estate at Curry Mallet, Somerset; Ben Derbyshire, another CAG member and a partner of Hunt Thompson Associates, for the refurbishment of a Duchy block of flats, Newquay House, in Kennington, south London; and Edward Cullinan, who was commissioned to design new entrance gates for Kensington Palace. He returned to the subject in several speeches. Most notable among these were his addresses to the Institute of Directors' annual convention at the Royal Albert Hall in London, in February 1985; at the Community Enterprise Awards presentation ceremonies in June 1986 and July 1987; and at the Building Communities Conference in November 1986.

The main purpose of the Albert Hall speech was to interest businessmen and women in his social concerns, and to try to persuade the financial institutions – in particular, the banks, insurance companies and pension funds – to invest part of their massive resources in the inner cities. (The fact that his message fell largely on deaf ears on this occasion meant that he had to return to the subject again later.) He spoke about 'a trail of devastation throughout the country – particularly in the north of England'; 'the desperate plight of the inner-city areas'; 'the cycle of economic decline leading to physical deterioration and countless social problems'; and the 'inhuman conditions' in which people were being forced to live.

He referred to 'shattered communities . . . day-to-day survival in a hostile environment . . . money by itself is not necessarily the answer, as demonstrated by most post-war redevelopment schemes'. He went on: 'The real answer, I would contend, lies in the enormous human potential and resource waiting to be given the incentive and encouragement to play a fuller part in contributing to the common good; waiting to be released from the over-numerous shackles of bureaucracy and the all-pervading atmosphere of "the professionals" knowing what is best for you.' Reporting on his visits to community architecture projects, he said he had been 'electrified' by what he had encountered, and described how it had 'filled me with enthusiasm'. He talked about architects as 'enablers' and 'catalysts' and about using the community architecture approach to commercial and industrial ventures, as well as to refurb and self-build new housing schemes. He warned against the mental barrier that existed between the private and public sectors involved in inner-city renewal – 'the "them" and "us" syndrome which leads to mutual distrust taking the place of mutual understanding'. He also predicted that this attitude could eventually lead to Britain becoming a 'fourth-rate nation'. But ending on a high note, as he always does, he concluded: 'The possibilities in the field of regeneration are immense, the challenge is awesome, but the rewards, I feel sure, will be nothing less than a *Great* Britain once again.'[6]

All this, needless to say, was music to community architects and those people living and working in the schemes which he had visited. Others put it down to the fact that he was rapidly coming under the influence of the 'nut-cutlet' brigade (many were putting it around that the heir to the throne had gone quite loopy), while there was genuine concern in political quarters that the Prince was starting to stray into the no-go areas of constitutional monarchy – getting involved in national (even party) politics.

Many would argue, however, as the Duke of Edinburgh did in a speech in February 1987, that issues such as housing (and the inner cities) were *above* politics. It was only politicians who were keen to destroy any national consensus, preferring to maintain their adversarial thrust and edge over the opposition parties.

Apart from occasional articles in the national press and the rare television programme (for example, Ramsay Short's BBC Television documentary in 1974), community architecture had never enjoyed such a high profile. But it was shortly to face a crisis which might have led to Hackney's banishment from Court and media interest being confined to the professional journals once more. That crisis came to be known as the 'Divided Britain Affair'.

The Divided Britain Affair

The 'Divided Britain' controversy arose out of a telephone conversation between Hackney and Peter Sharples, a young reporter on the *Manchester Evening News*, in October 1985. The contents of that conversation were – and still are – hotly disputed. What can be stated is that two days earlier Hackney had had a private meeting with the Prince on board the royal train in a Somerset railway siding, where various matters relating to community architecture and Britain's inner cities were discussed.

As a result of the telephone interview, the *News* splashed across its front page: 'Exclusive – Prince Charles: My Fear for the Future'. Next to it was a picture of the Prince and Hackney touring riot-torn Toxteth. The story claimed that 'The biggest fear of Prince Charles is that he will inherit the throne of a divided Britain.' It continued: 'The Prince is prepared to force his way through parliamentary red tape to ensure that his country is not split into factions of "haves" and "have nots" . . .' Hackney was quoted: 'He is very worried that when he becomes king there will be "no-go" areas in the inner cities, and that the [racial] minorities will be alienated from the rest of the country. He does not want to become king in an atmosphere like that.' [7]

Buckingham Palace issued a statement: 'We can confirm that Mr Hackney was on board the royal train and did take dinner with the Prince of Wales. We have no idea what was discussed, but obviously the Prince is extremely concerned about the plight of the inner cities and is doing everything he can to find a solution to the problem.'

Through an arrangement with the *Manchester Evening News* for sharing stories, the report was simultaneously splashed across the front page of the London *Standard*. Hackney, at the RIBA in London for a meeting, was besieged by reporters from every national newspaper and from radio and television current-affairs programmes. He denied the major content of what he had been reported as saying – but then went further to express his own views, very similar to those of the Prince quoted above. It was to prove to be the start of a traumatic ten days for Hackney and, one suspects, for the Prince. Reporters and photographers camped outside Hackney's Black Road office and eventually tracked down his farmhouse in the Peak District too. The Prince, on a tour of Australia, was reported to have told journalists in an 'off-the-record' briefing that he had been 'betrayed' by his friend from Macclesfield. Some pundits suggested that it was a deliberate leak, and said it put Prince Charles on a par with his great-uncle, King Edward VIII, who, as Prince of Wales fifty years earlier, had said 'something must be done' about unemployed Welsh miners. 'If the Prince wishes to say something, he is quite capable of doing it for himself,' said a Buckingham Palace spokesman tersely. Reports that the Queen was displeased with her son drew the response from the same source: 'The provenance of that story was very dubious indeed.'

The political fall-out was, not surprisingly, immense; the full repercussions are still being felt. The evening the reports appeared, the Labour Opposition seized on the remarks attributed to the Prince to attack the Government in a heated House of Commons debate. Gerald Kaufman, the shadow Home Secretary, held up a copy of the *Standard* and demanded of the Government; 'Is this Government determined to preside over the deterioration of the Queen's realm?' He went on, directing his comments to Douglas Hurd, Home Secretary: 'Does this Government lack the will or compassion or patriotism to insist on including the whole of our society and all people in a national commonwealth? Is it resigned to presiding over a Britain in which, as Lord Scarman warned, disorder will become a disease endemic in our society?' Neil Kinnock, the Labour leader, and the Tory backbencher Anthony Beaumont-Dark and Enoch Powell entered the fray as abusive exchanges flew across the Despatch Box.

Whatever the truth of the newspaper reports of the affair, the Prime Minister, Margaret Thatcher, in America at the time, was also said to be fuming. She is understood to have called Prince Charles from Washington and demanded to know exactly what he thought he was up to. His reply went unrecorded.

There was a further disclosure that the 'caring' Prince had paid secret visits to dossers at Charing Cross Station in London, and the Palace let it be known that all manner of people were consulted by the Prince for their advice. All sorts of strange remarks were reported as the media continued to look for new 'angles' on the inner-city story. Harold Brooks-Baker, for example, editor of *Burke's Peerage*, recommended the creation of black peers and the employment of black butlers to cure society's ills! Cartoonists had a field-day. But the overall response from commentators – from Brian Walden in the London *Standard* to Frank Chapple in the *Daily Mail* and Woodrow Wyatt, 'the Voice of Reason', in the *News Of the World*, and leading articles in *The Times* and *The Star* – was all supportive of the Prince's concern, whether or not it was true that he had expressed himself through Rod Hackney.

What the whole saga ensured, however, was that from now on the spotlight would be focused on Hackney, the Prince's adviser, and his ideas; and although it took six months to achieve a *public* reconciliation between the two (privately it is understood to have taken a couple of days) the net result was not only to further the cause of the community architecture movement, but to guarantee its debate throughout Britain as one possible solution to the inner-city malaise.

Going Public

If the Prince's intervention in 1984 marked the public breakthrough for community architecture, then events in 1986 marked its political breakthrough. After the Hampton Court speech it was no longer primarily an internal professional debate but had become an issue on the public agenda. All sections of society were starting to express an interest in its potential as well as in its leading personalities. It began to show the signs of a popular campaign rather than being just an obsession of a relatively small number of community activists and their professional advisers. And in addition to the impetus provided by the championing of the cause by the Prince of Wales, other factors reinforced the growing belief that perhaps community architecture held a solution to many of the problems faced by people living and working in a decaying built environment.

A renewed spate of inner-city riots in the autumn of 1985 gave added impetus to the search for new solutions, being the most tangible expression of the frustration which still existed in pockets of urban deprivation in various parts of the country. In the autumn of 1986 Lord Scarman paid a return visit to Brixton to mark the fifth anniversary of the publication of his report into the disturbances there. Little had changed and few lessons had been learned in those five years, he said. As if to emphasize his point a brand-new £½m community centre in the St Pauls district of Bristol – built with government-allocated funds following riots there in 1981 – was rejected by the community it was intended for and stood empty for many months. It had been designed by the local authority without involving the community association, which claimed it was unusable.

Hackney was invited to speak at fringe meetings at the four major party political conferences and to the Tory Reform Group. Dr David Owen, leader of the SDP, aligned himself with his local community association, the Limehouse Development Group, by launching 'The Limehouse Petition', opposing developers' plans for the area and putting forward a community architecture alternative. Jeff Rooker, Labour's housing spokesman, visited the pioneering new-build housing cooperatives in Liverpool and made a speech emphasizing the party's commitment to end paternalistic provision of public housing: 'It is élitist to think experts, officers, councillors and, yes, MPs know best. It is the people who know best. Our task is to provide the resources, the legal framework, and above all the political will to upset the existing order so that people can decide.'[8] The leaders of the other three parties, including Mrs Thatcher, and the Prince of Wales, had already trodden the same path in Liverpool and been equally impressed. Mrs Thatcher had described the Grafton Street Cooperative as 'superb. The houses are excellent value for money and there is a good environment and atmosphere. The residents took part in the designing and layout as they should each be entitled to do.'[8] The Secretary of State for the Environment, Kenneth Baker, gave his support too in an interview in January 1986: 'Community architecture has always been considered to be a bywater of the architecture and development world. I hope it is going to become the mainstream of it.'[9]

In the private sector the construction and development lobby announced its Phoenix Initiative, to act as marriage-broker between central and local government and the development world to regenerate large areas of the inner cities; and Business in the Community launched its demonstration partnership environmental projects with an emphasis on community initiative. An increasing number of conferences emphasizing the bottom-up approach were held and endless reports were published on the plight of the inner cities, emphasizing the contribution which communities could make, from such diverse quarters as the Archbishop of Canterbury's Commission and the Office of the Chief Rabbi, to the House Builders' Federation and the Building Employers' Confederation. Some local authorities started showpiece community architecture projects, such as Westminster Council's Martlett Court. And the appointment of Tom Woolley, one of the most energetic campaigners for community architecture since the early seventies, as head of Hull School of Architecture appeared to mark a watershed for architectural education.

On the ground, community groups found new confidence. In Liverpool, for example, the Eldonian Community Association adopted the slogan 'We do it better ourselves' and started work on a £6·5m community planned and managed mixed development with central government funds. In Belfast the residents of Divis Flats won their fight to have the hated blocks demolished and new homes built. And in London, the Whitechapel Development Group launched a £45m community scheme for a mixed town-centre development in competition with private developers. The first year of the Community Enterprise Award Scheme, sponsored jointly by *The Times* and the RIBA, attracted 184 entries from throughout the United Kingdom. The winner of the special award was the Derry Inner City Trust in Northern Ireland, which created employment for 500 people in an ambitious self-help regeneration project, making it the second biggest local employer after Du Pont Chemicals.

Although the battles within the architectural profession continued, they began to seem more and more incestuous and irrelevant to what was happening outside. Attempts were made by the RIBA to bring its Community Architecture Group (CAG) into line by imposing a new Community and Urban Affairs Committee above it, controlling its membership, removing its separate identity and preventing it from developing its own initiatives; but the horse had already bolted. The group (now under the chairmanship of Manchester architect Ian Finlay) had instigated the setting up of a National Community Partnership of nearly twenty national voluntary organizations, which had far more clout to pursue its main objective of securing proper funding for community projects. Attempts by the RIBA to wrest control of the Community Enterprise Award Scheme out of the hands of *The Times* were also successfully defeated.

The upsurge of activity and public interest was crystallized in November 1986 by Building Communities, the First International Conference on Community Architecture, Planning and Design, which was held over two days at London's Astoria Theatre and was supported by over forty national and international organizations. The title caught people's imagination and everyone wanted to be in on the act. To accommodate all those who wanted to address the two-day conference, speakers had to be limited to ten minutes each. Extra space had to be taken at the last moment to accommodate over seventy exhibitions. The conference chairmen were Lord Scarman; Ted Watkins, the community leader from Watts in Los Angeles; the leading academic and consultant, Dr Thomas Blair; and the journalist Simon Jenkins. Hackney was conference president.

The Prince of Wales gave the keynote address. Seemingly unembarrassed as Hackney introduced him as 'the champion of the community architecture movement, our patron and friend', the Prince said he thought the subject the conference was addressing was 'one of extraordinary importance'. 'I'm here frankly because what is known as the community architecture approach makes a great deal of sense to me and I would like to see more people become aware of what it actually means.'

It was more of a celebration of community architecture and community enterprise than the term 'conference' would imply. It was attended by more than a thousand delegates from all sections of the development industry, government and the voluntary sector. Speaking at the end of the event, Paul Ekins, Director of the Other Economic Summit, caught the mood when he said: 'The whole seems to be more than the sum of the parts . . . we've been witnessing the Greening of Architecture.' Over a hundred media correspondents attended, ensuring unprecedented reportage in the national press, on radio and on prime-time television news and current-affairs programmes. The community architecture movement had become national news.

The conference was used to launch two important new initiatives: the National Community Aid Fund and the Inner City Trust. Both are aimed at removing the single most important obstacle to the further development of community architecture: the lack of resources available to community organizations to execute their own environmental projects. The fund, organized by the National Community Partnership (see above), raises money to enable community groups to employ professional advisers. The Inner City Trust, with the Prince as its patron, provides grant aid, in cash and in kind, for capital projects generated through self-help community initiatives.

The final triumph of 1986 came just two days after the close of the Building Communities Conference when Hackney won an election for the Presidency of the RIBA. Normally the two-year post for the profession's most influential figurehead goes to a senior elder statesman nominated by the Institute's ruling council. Hackney challenged the council's choice, Raymond Andrews, forcing a ballot of the 27,000 member architects in Britain and abroad. In the most controversial and widely publicized election since the Institute was founded in 1834, he won by a sizeable majority of 1,700 votes on a record poll.

Hackney had never disguised his willingness to make a bid for the RIBA presidency one day, but no one expected it so soon. Increasing membership disillusionment with the inept leadership of the profession over recent years, combined with the growing success of the community architecture movement and Hackney's own status as a formidable politician, gave him the opportunity he needed. The profession had become sharply divided. As Brian James reported in *The Times*: 'On the one hand, the establishment; senior architects in stately competition for commissions for ever higher, ever more hitech monuments to Mammon and the municipalities; on the other, Hackney and his upstarts, convinced that the architect's place in 1987 was in a street-corner surgery advising the tenants of derelict streets how to acquire the skills, raise the money and get the permission to rebuild the inner cities.'[9a] The upstarts won – and the effects were soon apparent. Even before Hackney formally took up office in July 1987, the Institute was acting as host for the British launch of United Nations' International Year of Shelter for the Homeless; and the way was paved for sweeping organizational reforms and staff changes. The architectural profession had turned a corner.

Hackney's election as President of the RIBA marked the political breakthrough for the community architecture movement. From being a rootless guerrilla movement it now had the prestige and resources of the profession's most powerful organization behind it. Within weeks of Mrs Thatcher's Conservative Government winning a third term of office in June 1987, Hackney was called in to advise on the inner-city crisis, newly placed by the Prime Minister at the top of the political agenda.

Hackney's position was strengthened a few weeks later when he was elected President of the International Union of Architects as well. Also on the international front, the movement was reinforced with the formation, in June 1987, of the Habitat International Coalition as a high-profile pressure group to campaign for community architecture worldwide and liaise with governments and international agencies. The coalition (which grew out of the former Habitat International Council) comprises representatives of non-governmental organizations concerned with human settlements from all continents. 'Community architecture has come of age,' Hackney told *Building Design*. 'We're no longer fighting the corner, we've got the corner. Governments, having tried their approach and found that it failed miserably, are saying we need help.'[9b]

By 1987, community architecture had proved itself in thousands of projects at street-, neighbourhood- and city-scale. The question remained whether the approach was capable of tackling the enormity of the crisis facing human settlements globally. Hackney was optimistic: 'Lots of little sand grains make big beaches. Participation and self-help work at the micro-level. The big challenge of our times is how we can make them work at the macro-level.'[9c]

Chapter 3

Cities That Destroy Themselves
The Bankruptcy of Conventional Architecture

Our inner-city areas have been devastated by the actions of previous
generations of architects, planners, housing officers and politicians working in
isolation from the people they serve, effectively condemning thousands of people
to a life of urban squalor and hopelessness. Participation is the key to the way
forward, but there can be no half measures if it is to be successful.

    John Thompson, *Community Architecture: The Story of Lea View House,
    Hackney,* 1984

Present systems of production are organized in such a way that most decisions
are made very much 'at arms' length'. Decisions are made by people remote
from the consequences of the decisions. Architects make decisions about people
whose faces they have never seen. Developers make decisions about land where
they have never smelled the grass. Engineers make decisions about columns
which they will never touch, nor paint, nor lean against. Government
authorities make decisions about roads and sewers without having any human
connection at all to the place about which they are making those decisions.
The construction workers who nail the boards and lay the bricks have no
power of decision at all over the details which they build. Children who are
going to play between the houses have no power of decision at all, over even
the sandpits where they are going to play. Families move into houses which
have been laid out 'for' them and have no control whatever over the most
fundamental and most intimate aspects of the plan in which they are going to
live their lives. In short, the production systems which we have at present
define a pattern of control which makes it almost impossible for things to be
done carefully, or appropriately, because *almost without exception* decisions are
in the wrong hands.

    Christopher Alexander, *The Production of Houses,* 1982

Apathy is frozen violence.

    Patrick Doherty, Project Director, Derry Inner City Project, 13 June 1986

There is growing realization worldwide that the physical environment in
which people live their lives is crucial, both to their social and mental

well-being. People's ability to work, bring up children, think, learn, socialize and remain healthy is immeasurably improved by a conducive and responsive environment – and seriously impeded without one.

Yet, in contrast to man's extraordinary advances in science and technology – whether in outer space or conquering disease – the ability to create and maintain humane and efficient settlements has advanced little if at all. Indeed the clock has been put back in many respects rather than forward.

The spectacle of immensely costly public housing estates being dynamited or abandoned within a few years of construction – despite chronic and persistent homelessness – hardly makes news any longer. Neither does the fact that the design and management of much of what remains in service make it equally detested by its occupants and are increasingly blamed for family break-ups, illness, crime and other social disorders. Yet paternalistically provided public housing is only the most visible symptom of the disastrous way in which so much of our built environment is created and managed. Few people are fortunate enough to be able to say that they live in a home which is beautiful and suits their needs, in a street in which they feel they belong and in a neighbourhood which they feel proud of. Instead they are likely to talk about crude new developments which are alien and inappropriate; about public property vandalized and badly maintained; about the lack of amenities and facilities; about insensitive road planning, traffic congestion and deteriorating public transport; about how beautiful, well-made buildings have been unnecessarily destroyed and replaced with ugly, badly made ones. They will speak about the destruction of communities; a stream of award-winning buildings which leak and are socially and operationally unusable; the impossibility of finding competent builders and craftsmen; and about local businesses driven to the wall because of senseless restrictions and zoning policies. They will talk in the pub about absence of street life; lack of community spirit; and how there does not appear to be anything that can be done about it all.

This general malaise has been recognized for some time but solutions have remained elusive. For the sake of expediency, governments, professional institutions and academics have prescribed a series of universal top-down remedies which have almost invariably created as many problems as they have solved. Lack of government investment is often blamed, but even when money has been thrown at the problem the solutions have often failed. The community architecture movement on the other hand has approached the problem from the bottom up, by dealing with *specific* problems in *specific* communities and devising *specific* solutions. A better insight into the nature of the problem can therefore be gained by looking at a specific community and the problems it has faced over a period of years.

The Problems: Limehouse

The example we have chosen is Limehouse, in London's East End. Limehouse is typical of the run-down inner-city areas of Britain that are increasingly the main focus of concern. It is a predominantly poor, multi-racial neighbourhood with some 3,000 residents and 100 businesses. The difficulties facing such areas are, however, particularly sharply focused in Limehouse because its location next to Canary Wharf, where a massive new office complex is under construction, is causing land values to rise. An examination of the way the area has developed – or rather not developed – over the last decade illustrates clearly the ways in which the built environment is being mismanaged. This in turn helps to explain why community architecture has emerged as a popular alternative approach and is so desperately needed.

Symptoms 1. The Homeless

'London 1984: LIVING HELL' screamed the banner headline in the *Daily Mirror* on 13 March 1984. The rest of the front page was taken up with a photograph of six children, aged from three to eleven, who shared a bedroom which was so small that they had to sleep in shifts. Their parents slept in the family's only other room, which measured 6 × 12 ft. On the inside pages of the paper was a horrendous description of how tens of thousands of young homeless people were tramping the streets of Britain and how tens of thousands more had no option but to live in cramped and sordid hostels. 'This is Britain, the civilized society, in 1984,' campaigned the *Mirror*. The main target of the article was Princes Lodge, a hostel for 169 homeless families in Limehouse where the six children sharing a bedroom had been photographed. A report by Environmental Health Inspectors claimed, rightly, that it was 'unfit for human habitation'. Sparked into action by the *Mirror*'s story, national housing pressure groups quickly joined local community organizations and the local authority in noisy demands for its closure.

But as so often in environmental politics over recent years, the anger was directed at the wrong target: at the symptom instead of the cause. Had those who campaigned so vigorously for the closure of Princes Lodge directed their attention to what was happening to the environment in the immediate vicinity, they would have discovered far more disturbing evidence of the malaise which is afflicting our cities, a malaise which affects everyone and of which the homeless are only the most visible casualties.

Symptoms 2. Demolition-mad Paternalism

Within a few minutes walk of Princes Lodge with its 169 homeless families there were, in 1981, 368 flats owned by public authorities standing empty. Most were in five-storey blocks built between the First and Second World Wars, similar to those in which over half of the population of Limehouse live. One such block was Brunton Wharf; a handsome, well-planned and well-made building with eighty-six flats and eight shops, owned by Tower Hamlets Council. Until six years previously, it had been very popular with residents, some of whom had lived there since 1924, when it was built. The communal courtyard was beautifully maintained and the ground-floor-flat gardens were well kept.

But the council wanted to modernize the block and decided to move people out; 'decanting' is the official phrase. Many people did not want to go, but were given no option. Delays then occurred in the programme. Some vacancies were filled temporarily with people from the council's waiting list. Others were occupied by squatters. The new community, however, had no roots and no sense of permanence. The complex informal patterns of self-policing and maintenance which the previous community had evolved over the years could not instantly be replaced. The estate began to deteriorate physically and started to look untidy. The local paper described it as a 'cesspit'. Neighbouring residents blamed the newcomers – many of whom were black – for the deteriorating state of affairs. Vandalism, violence and racial tension increased steadily.

Unable to understand or cope with these problems, the council decided to demolish the estate, even though it had no other use for the site.

Then Circle 33, an experienced housing association, entered on the scene, offering to buy the block, and refurbish and manage it for people in need at no cost to the council. Circle 33's area manager, Simon Kaplinsky, described the decline of Brunton Wharf as 'a classic example of an anonymous bungling bureaucracy destroying a living community'.

But worse was to come. Not only did the council reject the association's offer, but it also rejected an offer from a property consortium formed by local designer and developer, Thomas Brent, to buy the block for £70,000 or whatever the district valuer said it was worth. Because the block was in such good condition structurally, with many attractive design features, Brent claimed he would be able to sell converted flats in the block for between £11,000 and £14,000 each – making them some of the cheapest in London and well within the means of many people on the council's waiting list, who would be given first option to buy.

Brent's offer was turned down by a special committee of the council's Development Committee on 3 August 1981. Admitting that the Committee had not seen details of how Brent intended to convert the property, vice-chairman Dennis Twomey told the *Observer*: 'We wouldn't want to push people into a position where they were forced to buy flats which we thought were unacceptable to live in.'[10]

In 1982 the council paid demolition contractors over £200,000 to demolish Brunton Wharf. Five years later the site was still a waste land surrounded by corrugated iron.

A similar fate befell Brightlingsea Buildings, owned by the Greater London Council. Despite an offer from the same housing association to buy these fifty flats, they were left empty for three years until the £200,000 could be found to demolish them. Former resident Joe Royle told the local paper that the destruction was 'diabolical': 'The flats are ideal. If they had let me rent one, I'd have done it up myself.' This site too was still vacant in 1987. Other blocks of flats senselessly demolished in the early 1980s include Kotoko House (75 flats), Shipwright House (64 flats), and Providence House (78 flats). All but one of these sites were still vacant in 1987.

Other publicly owned housing in Limehouse has simply been left to rot. Six picturesque canalside cottages, owned by the British Waterways Board, have lain empty for almost twenty years, despite frequent offers by individuals and housing associations to buy them. Homeless families squatting in them at no cost to anyone have been forcibly evicted and the corrugated iron replaced at considerable expense to the public purse.

In 1986, 1,230 people were accepted into homeless accommodation by Tower Hamlets Council, and the cost to the ratepayers of housing homeless families in bed-and-breakfast hotels exceeded £13m. Nine thousand people were on the council's waiting lists and the situation at Princes Lodge hostel for the homeless remained unchanged, despite the *Mirror's* campaigning journalism.

Symptoms 3. Rehabilitation for Nobody

The local authority's reluctance to refurbish blocks of flats is more understandable when you see what a mess they can make of it when they do. Padstow House escaped demolition, but suffered an only slightly less depressing fate. In October 1982 the three hundred tenants in this five-storey block built around a tarmac courtyard received a letter from the Director of Community Services headed 'Tenants Consultation: Padstow House – Improvement Scheme'. The letter informed tenants that the council proposed to carry out 'major improvements' to the block, which was built in 1938. After briefly setting out details – 'Central heating and hot water, full internal and external repairs and decoration, lifts and improved balcony access, controlled entry system, direct mains water supply, a new look to the courtyard' – the letter concluded: 'I feel sure you will agree that these works will improve the quality of life in the area.'

But this improved 'quality of life' was not intended for the current tenants of Padstow House. Although many of them had lived there for over twenty years and grown attached to the neighbourhood, they were simply 'decanted' and dispersed throughout the borough. They were given no option.

And yet this was only the beginning of the catastrophe. Padstow House itself was then 'improved' to designs by the council's architects department without any consultation with either past or future inhabitants and, after partial completion in 1986, tenancies were offered to people with high priority on the council's waiting list.

On being shown round the refurbished block, Dr Alice Coleman, Director of Land Use Research Unit at Kings College, London (who had directed a study of 100,000 flats throughout the UK) commented that it was a 'complete waste of money'. An architect who had recently completed the renovation of a similar block, working *with* the tenants, described it as an 'appalling disaster' and was visibly upset. 'It will be a slum again within six months,' he predicted. Although providing the flats with new basic amenities, the council's refurbishment had completely failed to deal with the basic arrangement and organization of the block, which was the main cause of tenant dissatisfaction in the first place.

For instance, one of the keys to refurbishing such blocks successfully has proved to be redefining common and private space so that as much of the common space as possible becomes the responsibility of individual

53

tenants. This can be done by amalgamating ground- and first-floor flats and providing them with private gardens and direct access on to the street. Entry to flats at upper levels should be directly from the street and balcony deck access should be avoided, since it means people are constantly walking past other people's windows – a frequent cause of tension. The council's renovation of Padstow House made no attempt to tackle the problem of common space and instead created new balcony access where none had previously existed. Almost in recognition of failure, a complex central entrance locking system was provided with permanently mounted security video cameras. This system prevents people from having personal post-boxes and – because it is possible to stand on a rail on the ground floor and swing, with ease, on to the first-floor balcony – does not work for security purposes anyway.

The refurbished flats have not proved popular. Prospective occupants invariably comment on the prison-like atmosphere. The first ten turned down the offer. Tenants in residence complain of social tension caused by poor sound insulation both within and between flats, lack of maintenance of common areas, the impossibility of getting furniture in because of poky front halls and the difficulty faced by visitors in getting in. 'I can't think of anything I like about the flat. It's ridiculous. I just want to get out,' one says. The construction costs alone of the 'improvements' to Padstow House were £2m, or almost £30,000 per flat; as the tenant quoted above observed, 'money down the drain'.

When council tenants on the neighbouring St Vincent Estate realized they were in danger of suffering a similar fate, the tenants' association commissioned its own consultant architects to show how the estate could be improved without people being 'decanted'. The consultants' first recommendation was that the tenants be allowed to appoint an architect of their own choice to work with them on the estate. The proposal was turned down by the council on the grounds that it would take work away from its own in-house team of architects.

Symptoms 4. Utopian Housing Nightmares

As in most cities, the most popular homes in the Limehouse area are three- and four-storey brick terraced houses built over a hundred years ago. With front doors opening directly on to the street, secluded back gardens and a simple construction system which allows for flexibility and personal choice, they provide people with a combination of privacy, sociability, independence and freedom which has rarely been matched by the construction industry since. Unfortunately, there are not many left in Limehouse. Most of those that survived the Blitz in the Second World War were systematically demolished by the council to make way for the brave new Utopia of the post-war planners and architects.

The least popular housing in Limehouse is the product of that Utopian vision; that most recently built by the local authorities. Residents of Kiln Court, built in 1977, find it hard to understand why the council should have demolished the terraced houses they were brought up in which used to stand on the site, and, at vast expense, moved them into a seven-storey block of sixty-two flats made of purple-brown bricks, which looks like a misshapen factory and is surrounded by unusable pockets of land, thorny shrubs and tarmac play areas enclosed by sixteen-foot brick walls and chain-link fencing. Certainly they were not involved in any of the decision-making or in choosing the design.

Ironically, the Kiln Court housing scheme was built well after architects and planners were thought to have learnt from the mistakes of the tower-block era, three fourteen-storey products of which stand close by and are classified as 'hard to let'. Yet only the shape is different. Neither have much to do with creating homes and neighbourhoods. To get to one's flat in Kiln Court in 1987 involves negotiating a maze-like network of alleyways, flights of steps, dark graffiti-covered stairways with broken windows and urine-soaked lifts, and dreary rubbish-strewn internal corridors with broken light fittings. The basement car-parks are frequented mainly by vandals, glue sniffers and alcoholics. Cars left there are rapidly wrecked and burnt out, so cars are mostly left on pavements instead, where only the radios get stolen.

One tenant, who used to live in a terraced house on the same site, comments: 'I wish I was back in my house, I put up with it now because I have lived in the area all my life. But my children can't wait to marry and move right out. They don't want *their* children to put up with this.'

Symptoms 5. Planned Wasteland

The skill of successfully planning and managing open space has also eluded the local authorities. One of the main reasons advocated for building high-rise housing in the sixties and seventies was to provide large public open spaces for people to enjoy for recreation. But it is hard for residents of the two estates just mentioned to enjoy the acres of tarmac and grass surrounding them. Even were they not normally covered with litter, broken glass and dog excrement, what is one supposed to do there?

The laying out of the first phase of Limehouse's new park – known as Ropemakers Fields – in 1982 by Tower Hamlets Council initially seemed more hopeful. At the suggestion of local tenants, two tennis-courts and some children's play equipment were incorporated and surrounded by shrubbery. A plain new brick building was erected containing an office of a park-keeper and, somewhat surprisingly, two public toilets. (Limehouse's two existing public toilets, built at the end of the last century, had just been closed due to lack of staff.)

Sadly the park deteriorated rapidly. The tennis-courts remained largely unused, initially because the park-keeper who held the only key to the gates did not work in the evenings and at weekends when most people wanted to play tennis; later, because the keeper's post was axed altogether. No attempt was made to establish a tennis club which might have enabled local tennis enthusiasts to take over the running of the courts. The type of play equipment – metal structures on tarmac – was chosen without consulting parents or children and was located close to flats. After several accidents and the predictable complaints about noise, the play equipment was removed. Virtually all the shrubs died; because there was a dispute over who should maintain them – between the contractor who planted them and the Parks Department – no one did any maintenance at all during the crucial early period of their growth. At no time have any of the residents of the flats which directly overlook the park been invited to play a part in its management.

The final phase of the park development was shelved because the council claimed it had run out of money. In the previous two years alone, nearly £$\frac{1}{2}$m had been spent demolishing flats in the area that people wanted to live in and were prepared to pay for.

Symptoms 6. Killing Community Culture

Apart from a one-room old people's club and a youth club, social facilities in the area are virtually non-existent. To get to any shops involves crossing a busy main road, as the area's shopping street was demolished to make way for the Utopian housing projects. There is no focus to the neighbourhood and few opportunities for social interaction apart from the pubs. The development of voluntary organizations and cultural activity is hampered by lack of premises. There is no community centre, cinema, theatre or adequate venue for live music, exhibitions or dancing. A survey carried out in 1980 identified widespread demand for social, shopping and recreational facilities of all kinds.

In the mid-seventies an ideal opportunity for creating a community resource centre arose when the Cyril Jackson Primary School moved into new premises. The old school building was a fine example of Victorian craftsmanship with many rooms and halls of varying sizes. Structurally it was very sound. A local tenants' association asked the council to let them have it for a community centre. The council refused and, after leaving it empty for several years, during which time it was wrecked and vandalized, demolished it instead. Four years later the site was overgrown and still vacant. The tenants' association subsequently collapsed, its leadership exhausted and dispirited. The spark of community spirit that had been lit by the hopes of a community centre had been extinguished. Two subsequent attempts by other community organizations to secure other buildings were also thwarted by bureaucratic intransigence, despite being backed by comprehensive feasibility studies. Both buildings remain empty and derelict at the time of writing.

Symptoms 7. Private-sector Development by Remote Control

If Limehouse were in a different part of Britain, that would probably be the end of the story. But Limehouse is privileged. Since 1981 it has fallen within what is widely billed in the British property world as the largest and most successful urban regeneration project in Europe, if not the world – London Docklands. As the Port of London moved down river it left behind an eight-mile stretch of derelict docks surrounded by hundreds of acres of derelict land and a dozen or so communities very similar to Limehouse. Understandably dubious as to whether the existing local authorities could cope with the redevelopment of such vast areas when they were capable of such gross mismanagement of the land they already controlled, the government established a special new corporation to take charge – London Docklands Development Corporation. This corporation was (and is still) given vast sums of public money to invest and sweeping new powers to cut through red tape and buy land. Its main brief was to get private developers interested in investing in the area.

At that task it has been spectacularly successful, and by 1986 over £2,000m of private money had been invested in the Docklands area for an outlay of only £300m of public money. But despite having massive reserves and expertise at its disposal, the private sector has failed dismally in addressing itself to the challenges and opportunities in Limehouse.

The first development to come to public attention was on a five-acre riverside site called Free Trade Wharf, where there was a unique and historic enclave of docklands warehouses. A developer and designer, Rae Hoffenberg, who lived adjacent to the site, had drawn up a detailed and imaginative scheme for converting the warehouses for a wide range of uses which would have brought new life to the whole area. But the Greater London Council, which owned the site, sold it by means of a sealed-bid competitive tender without any conditions. The winning developer employed architects based over fifty miles away, who produced plans to demolish most of the warehouses and build an office block and two structures shaped somewhat like ziggurats, or terraced pyramids, eleven storeys high, and containing 418 luxury flats for sale. The proposals led to an outcry from the local community, the local authority and, somewhat ironically, the Greater London Council, on the grounds that it was totally irrelevant to the area's needs. But the London Docklands Development Corporation decided to support it. A five-week public inquiry into the proposals was held in 1983 and, in one of the most damning reports since 1947, the inspector strongly urged that planning permission be refused. He concluded that it was the wrong place for offices, that a broader mix of uses would be more desirable; that the design was 'totally out of sympathy with the character of the development along the river frontage'; that the housing blocks were of 'excessive height' and 'unsympathetic shape'; that they showed 'blatant disregard' for nearby buildings; and that they would 'overpower and dominate' an adjacent park, 'seriously detracting from its present quality and character and from its enjoyment by the public'.

Incredibly, the inspector's report was overruled by the Secretary of State for the Environment and, at the time of writing, the scheme is under construction. Legal opinion secured by Tower Hamlets Council on the decision argued that 'The Secretary of State has acted in an arbitrary manner to such an extent as to make the inquiry process redundant.'

But even worse was to come. At the heart of Limehouse lies one of the most interesting dock basins in London – Limehouse Basin; a twenty-two-acre site owned by a public corporation – the British Waterways Board. In 1979, when the site had been lying vacant and abandoned for ten years, a group of local citizens – some with architectural and development experience – came to the conclusion that the Basin was the key to the regeneration of the area. If it was properly developed, they argued, it could provide all the facilities lacking in the area, as well as being an exciting addition to the city in its own right. They arranged a public meeting, advertised it in the local papers, and invited all the organizations known to be interested in the area including the local authorities and landowners. At the meeting it was agreed to form a voluntary, non-party-political, democratic community organization called the Limehouse Development Group with the aim of securing 'the best possible development of the Basin'. The group's motto was 'Let's Build Limehouse Together' in recognition of the fact that the aim could only be achieved if all of those with an interest in the area worked in partnership. Consultants (prepared to work voluntarily) were appointed from a wide range of professional disciplines. An extensive survey was conducted of local needs and aspirations. Discussions were held with the authorities and landowners. A brief was then drawn up of what was required and from this a strategy was developed for achieving it, as well as a sketch scheme showing what was possible if the strategy were adopted. All stages were approved by a series of widely advertised public meetings. The outcome was a proposal for an evolutionary, mixed-use development, providing housing in mixed tenure and architectural style, and a new 'heart' or town centre for the area with a wide range of commercial and recreational facilities in and surrounding a new urban harbour.

To demonstrate the scheme's viability the group secured the backing of Bovis Homes, who guaranteed to underwrite the project to the tune of £70m. The strategy was widely acclaimed in the local, technical and national press and, later, won a commendation from *The Times*/RIBA Community Enterprise Award scheme in 1986.

The key element of the strategy was that the first step had to be for all the authorities, landowners and other interested parties to sit round a table together and discuss how to coordinate their activities. But this simple and obvious step never happened. Instead, the British Waterways Board held a limited competition without any effective brief or criteria for judgement, in which only large commercial development companies were invited to compete. All the efforts of the Limehouse Development Group were completely ignored. So too was the planning brief drawn up by Tower Hamlets Council. The winner was a Hertfordshire-based company, Hunting Gate Homes, with R. Seifert and Partners – one of the largest commercial practices in the country – as architects. The scheme, which involved filling in almost half of the water area, was for luxury housing, offices and a small marina. Predictably, there was a public outcry.

The public inquiry on the Hunting Gate scheme lasted forty-five days. After examining evidence from some of the country's leading experts on inner-city regeneration and architectural research, the government's architectural assessor concluded that it was 'a design approach which completely ignores the existing setting, and which would in fact destroy it'. The government inspector stated that the scheme reflected 'a serious degree of over-development', and that the result of building would be 'seriously to damage, even to destroy, the Basin's general amenity value . . . The scheme would not integrate into the surrounding area but would reduce the overall integration of that area.' He concluded: 'I am convinced that the scheme would not properly advance the regeneration of this particular part of Docklands.'[11] Yet his recommendation that the scheme be refused planning permission was overruled by the Secretary of State for the Environment on the extraordinary grounds that because the area was run down, *any* development would improve it and would therefore be acceptable. Effectively his decision marked the abandonment of planning.

A 17,000-word petition against the British Waterways Board's proposals was subsequently signed by the leaders of all the local community organizations, the local church leaders (one of whom organized and ran in a sponsored marathon to raise money for its publication), local councillors and local GPs, as well as the country's leading architectural critics and a host of other national figures including Dr David Owen, then Leader of the SDP, who also happens to be a local resident. (A standing joke locally is that the formation of the Social Democratic Party in Britain was a product of David Owen's observing from his windows the mess being made of his local environment by the two traditional parties.) But even this was to little apparent avail. As so often with environmental campaigns, superficial design changes were made to give the scheme a more acceptable face, but those in authority did not feel able to rectify the fundamental organizational deficiencies, even though they were now widely recognized on all sides. As the urban-development consultant Nicholas Falk told *Time Out* magazine: 'The terrible problem is that people get stuck in positions which they feel they have to defend or risk loss of face. It's like the Americans in Vietnam.'[12]

The main impact on Limehouse so far of the intervention of the London

Docklands Development Corporation and the private-sector development industry has therefore been to impose two grotesque developments, totally irrelevant to the area's needs and opposed by all sections of the local community.

The future of two of the most important development sites remaining in Limehouse – both initially owned by *public* authorities – has been determined simply on the whims of a handful of men who have no real connections with the area and who are unlikely to have any connections with it once it is built – whims that, in one case, the architectural critic for the *New Statesman*, Jules Lubbock, described as 'a back-of-an-envelope hamfisted botch'.[13] Thousands of hours of time by both professional experts and local people who know the area intimately and whose lives will be affected by its development have been wasted. No one who will live, work or play in the schemes, or who will have to manage them, has been the slightest bit involved in their preparation. And while the grandiose plans gestate, eight years after proposals were put forward for using the derelict land and water at Limehouse Basin within six months – as successfully put into practice in other places (such as Camden Lock in north London) – they still lie vacant. Every year another building is vandalized or burnt to the ground, while much of the local population remains jobless and scores are homeless.

Symptoms 8. Local-government Impotence

Local government in Limehouse has, effectively, broken down. On the main road next to the parish church stands an imposing building with the words 'Limehouse Town Hall' inscribed in the stonework. The building has long since lost that function. Ironically, for many years it contained the National Museum of Labour History. Local government powers are now held by the London Borough of Tower Hamlets. The main town-hall is half an hour's walk away and is not on a direct bus route; the Planning Department likewise, but in a different direction. Social Services, Housing and Recreation are slightly nearer but not much. So too is the Arts Office. Not a single council officer is based in Limehouse except in the library, where local people may not even display posters without sending them to the Director of Libraries at the main town-hall for approval. None of the councillors representing the ward in which most of the area falls actually lives in Limehouse.

It is no one's job within the council to think about the problems in

61

Limehouse in their totality and get to grips with them. Each officer and department deals with the area in a completely fragmented way. Furthermore, the professionals employed by the council are prevented from working creatively with the people they are employed to provide services for by a gigantic hierarchical bureaucracy. Council architects, for instance, rarely come into contact with the people they are designing buildings for and, sometimes, are specifically prevented from communicating with them. The horrendous mistakes described earlier are just part of the result. The waste of physical and financial resources is absurd; the waste of human lives grotesque. At the time of writing a recent change of political control (from Labour to Liberal) has resulted in the decentralization of many council services to seven newly created neighbourhood areas. This is undoubtedly a step in the right direction. But not a big enough step to make any significant inroads into any of the fundamental planning, architectural and property-management problems mentioned above. The boundaries of the new neighbourhood units bear no relationship to the way people perceive the area or to the tasks that need to be tackled. Limehouse has been arbitrarily lumped together with other communities up to two miles away. The community still has no direct access to the architects, planners and other professionals it needs. Instead of grasping the opportunity to evolve new systems of local government based on learning from yesterday's mistakes and today's community needs, the new system appears to be simply a truncated version of the old one.

The introduction of the London Docklands Development Corporation has not significantly improved the picture. The corporation's offices too are hard to get to, with different departments in different directions away from Limehouse. It has no officers based in the area nor any place locally where members of the public can go to find out what is going on. To inspect a planning application for a development across the street one still has to travel two miles during office hours, when many people are at work. Taking photocopies is not permitted. No one in the corporation has a mandate to look at the problems comprehensively and there are no mechanisms for harnessing local knowledge and experience positively. Participation is restricted to commercial developers and landowners, and even they often complain about the way they are treated. While the corporation may justifiably be proud of having attracted private development into docklands, it has not yet begun to grasp how to build civilized communities.

Paralysis

Decayed infrastructure and bad physical conditions generally were two of the five factors identified as signifying the nature of inner-city problems in the government White Paper *Policy for the Inner Cities* in 1977. The other three were high levels of unemployment, limited job opportunities and a concentration of people with social difficulties. All are present in Limehouse today. Deprived urban areas also tend to include a high proportion of ethnic minorities; almost 49 per cent of this population of England are believed to live in government-designated Partnership and Programme authority areas, which matches almost exactly the 48 per cent ethnic population of parts of Limehouse.

The past ten years have seen a whole panoply of government initiatives aimed at addressing the problem: Task Forces, Enterprise Zones, Derelict Land Reclamation Schemes, National Garden Festivals, Urban Development Grants, Urban Regeneration Grants and the designation of Partnership and Programme authorities, of which there are now fifty-four in England. Development Corporations are the latest flagship of the Thatcher government's approach. Limehouse, not surprisingly, is high on the list of priorities for government action and has fallen within the scope of many of these programmes. But there has been little noticeable effect on the ground.

Buildings that were empty ten years ago are still empty, yet one third of the adult population remains unemployed and one fifth of residents live at a density of more than one person to a room. Land that was derelict ten years ago is still derelict, while less than 5 per cent of residents have gardens. Canals that were dirty, dangerous and unused ten years ago are still dirty, dangerous and unused, and yet there are still no recreational facilities. Housing estates that were run down and badly managed are still run down and badly managed. Apart from a handful of successful building conversions by owner-occupiers and housing associations, the only significant construction in Limehouse for the past ten years has been for new luxury homes selling at £300,000 each – a lifetime's earnings for the average *employed* inhabitant. No wonder that there appears to be no end in sight to the vandalism, burglaries and assaults which afflict residents and businesses alike with monotonous regularity, causing many to leave if they can. Wealth differentials within the community are becoming increasingly apparent and the most catchy new slogan to appear on the railway bridges in the East End is 'Mug a Yuppie'.

Despite having a proud and distinguished history, a strong community spirit, a distinctive character, some fine buildings and natural features, and some exceptionally resourceful community groups, Limehouse in 1987 remains lifeless, resembling a morgue rather than a city. Meanwhile another generation of children have grown up deprived of the urban environment they should, and could, have.

People living in and working in Limehouse – as elsewhere – know by and large what they want and what needs to be done. Instinctively. They know because every day they experience the problems and understand what is wrong. They know, for instance, where it would be useful to have shops or play facilities; they know that a new footpath in a certain location would mean they no longer had to walk along a fume-choked pavement within inches of juggernaut lorries. Furthermore, many of them have skills which would enable them to help with the community's problems and bring it back to life.

Yet those with the power and resources to influence events in Limehouse are not drawing on this wealth of talent and understanding when they make their plans. Apart from a handful of owner-occupiers (less than 5 per cent of the population), none of the people who make decisions about land and property in the area live or work there. There is no way for local people to influence events. And when they try to take the initiative, they run up against insuperable obstacles. They cannot improve their own homes because the landlords' rules forbid it, and in many cases the buildings are so badly designed that they require major reconstruction. They cannot build new housing for themselves because they cannot get any land or raise finance. They cannot start up new businesses because there are no suitable small and well-serviced premises available. All initiatives, both individual and collective, run up against bureaucracy and inertia. Confrontation takes the place of sensible discussion. Frustration breeds a sense of hopelessness, apathy and despair.

Technical solutions to all the problems in Limehouse exist and have been employed successfully elsewhere. The housing estates *could* be redesigned to make them pleasant places to live. The derelict basement car-parks *could* be put to other purposes, such as workshops or music studios. Unused pockets of land *could* be turned into parks, gardens or playgrounds: the filthy canal *could* become a pleasant recreational amenity. The area has great potential. But the inhabitants have no way of putting these ideas into practice for two fundamental reasons: *they have no access to the technical assistance necessary to turn ideas into reality and they have no effective form of neighbourhood government through which to coordinate the community's affairs.* In short they are up against a brick wall.

None of this state of affairs can be blamed on any particular individual officers or members of the various authorities involved, or on professionals *per se.* Many of them are equally frustrated by the state of paralysis. *But they have not been trained to deal with it and are unable to find a framework of employment which would enable them to apply their skills creatively with, and in the interests of, the people of Limehouse.* Many talented planners, architects and designers actually live in Limehouse but can only find employment building office blocks and luxury housing outside the neighbourhood. *All parties are simply locked into a system which has ceased to function.*

The re-development – or rather mal-development – of Limehouse is not addressed to any community, past, present or future. It is not guided by knowledge, history, vision, theoretical analysis or practical experience. Neither is it based on open and rational discussion, weighing the evidence or reasonableness. At every level – from the management of individual homes to the planning of the neighbourhood as a whole – it is simply an architecture of neglect, short-sighted expediency and stupidity.

That, in a nutshell, is the problem.

The Crisis of the Built Environment

The institutions in Britain and many other countries do not have the ability to create, or even maintain, civilized human settlements any more.

The environmental professions and construction industry responsible – architects, planners, landscape architects, builders, developers and planning authorities – are in a state of chaos. They are making a mess. They are squandering massive resources. And they are undoubtedly creating a great deal of unhappiness, illness and social stress in the process.

What has been happening – and continues to happen – in Limehouse, might not replicate precisely what is happening elsewhere. But the pattern is the same. Similar horror stories could be recounted in every city in the country and, in less stark form, in rural areas too.

Here are some of the frightening statistics, culled from government and other official sources,[13a] which help paint a picture of the state of the built environment as it existed in 1987:

- Britain's public-sector housing stock requires immediate expenditure on repairs and maintenance of at least £18,000m.
- Britain's private-sector housing stock requires immediate expenditure on rehabilitation, improvement and repairs of £26,000m.
- More than 3·8m dwellings (84 per cent of public-sector stock) require expenditure of an average of £4,900 per dwelling.
- The backlog of repairs and maintenance to public-sector housing is growing at a rate of £900m a year.
- The number of homes in serious disrepair rose from 860,000 to 1·2 million between 1976 and 1986.
- There has been a cumulative shortfall of about 750,000 new dwellings over the last ten years.
- Birmingham City Council will need six hundred years (at the present rate of progress) to carry out the full modernization of its housing stock. Manchester can afford to repair only three hundred houses a year because of government cash limits.
- More than £2,000m needs to be spent on schools, and another £2,000m on hospitals to bring them up to a reasonable standard.
- There are 100,000 acres of derelict land in the inner cities.
- The number of people living in bed-and-breakfast accommodation increased from 49,000 to 160,000 between 1979 and 1984; there are 1·25 million people on council waiting lists for homes.
- The number of people officially classified as homeless in England doubled between 1978 and 1987 to about 100,000. This figure excludes most single homeless people and childless couples. Unofficial estimates for 1987 are 400,000.
- There are 112,000 empty council houses and flats in England, about 28,000 of them in London.
- There are 545,000 homes empty in the private sector.
- In 1986 more than 200,000 households applied to local authorities in England for housing under the Homeless Persons Act.
- Some 400,000 construction workers are unemployed (about 30 per cent of the total).

But, as we have seen in Limehouse, the real cost of physical deterioration cannot be told simply in figures. The tragedy of mental stress, physical illness, crime, economic inefficiency, wasted resources and, above all, lost opportunity, are unquantifiable. Lord Scarman, UK President of the International Year of Shelter for the Homeless, asked at its launch in January 1987:

Do people understand the misery, the squalor, the threat to health and even to life itself which homelessness inflicts upon millions of our fellow men? Does the public realize that homelessness is a critical element of the social conditions which provide the breeding ground for crime, marital breakdown, child abuse and neglect, and that homelessness destroys man's chance of developing and maintaining stable human relationships?

Scarman could – with equal relevance – have asked the same questions replacing the word 'homelessness' with 'communitylessness', 'neighbourhoodlessness' or 'citylessness'. Most would agree with the sentiments thus expressed. But few would have any idea how to translate them into a practical critique of the present system or a programme of action for change. Despite the construction industry's being worth some £30,000m per annum in Britain (about 10 per cent of gross domestic product), virtually nothing is spent on analysing the success of its output.

As a result, the industry has been largely rudderless, failing to learn from its own mistakes, let alone those of others in other places or in past times, where solutions have been evident. The industry has proceeded in a haphazard manner based on the profit motive, simplistic political ideologies (land nationalization or privatization), voguish styles (such as Modernism or Post-Modernism) and a firm belief in centralization, technology and the economies of operating on a large scale. It has been left to the community movement to start asking the right questions and indeed to start providing the right answers. As the geographer Dr Alice Coleman wrote in her book *Utopia on Trial* in 1985:

It is the natural condition of human beings to make progress by trial and error, and it is the misfortune of our age that the trial and error have been both large-scale and prolonged, with only minimal attention to the question of progress. Planners, architects, developers and housing managers have all been drawn into the same huge plausible vortex – so plausible, indeed, that none of them can be blamed for lacking the foresight to see where it would lead.

The Vicious Circle

As construction techniques, cities and society itself have become more complex since the onset of the Industrial Revolution, the proliferation of experts and specialists has been inevitable. But sadly these experts and specialists have become increasingly divorced from the environmental needs of the population they purport to serve, developing their own professions with their self-perpetuating, self-interested objectives.

To protect the public from unscrupulous or misguided experts, governments have evolved a whole new tier of bureaucrats, controls and regulations to act as mediator. This tier has become ever larger, more sophisticated and hierarchical and ever less equipped to deal with the intricate, human-scale problems of a particular building or neighbourhood.

In parallel with increasing specialization and bureaucratization has gone a de-skilling and de-education of consumers in environmental matters. Lack of involvement has led to lack of knowledge and understanding, and this has not been rectified by the formal education system, which has almost completely ignored environmental issues. So people have lost touch with their environment. They have lost the ability to solve their own most basic environmental problems, let alone those of their neighbourhood or city, through the democratic process.

The result is a vicious circle of environmental paralysis. People cannot solve their own problems because they lack the knowledge and skills and because the whole system is geared to intervention only by experts. Experts cannot solve the problems because they have been divorced from the people they are meant to serve and are not given relevant training. A web of red tape stifles creativity or innovation by both citizens and experts, leading to an environment which is increasingly mediocre, unresponsive and unrelated to people's needs.

People have been talking about this crisis in the built environment for decades. Community architecture is what is being done about it.

Chapter 4

The Pioneers
The Community Architecture Approach Explained

Everywhere we see evidence of alienation, the fraying of the social fabric, the breakdown of community. Commercial architecture contributes to these trends. Academic architecture – Post Modernism – is in retreat from these painful realities. Social architecture,* limited so far as its adherents and its armamentarium, remains to probe, to test, to propose new solutions that at once satisfy immediate needs and open up new visions of life and work . . . Rekindling the desire for architecture and for the city is the task that social architecture sets for itself.

    Richard Hatch, *The Scope of Social Architecture*, 1984

By accepting the involvement and initiative of the user as a starting-point for contemporary housing, we may begin to see a way out of the constraints in which we operate. Unsuspected possibilites emerge. Both the technological and the human sides of the housing problem can acquire new perspectives. There is scarcely any limit to the possibilities which will be opened up, and new and long-lacking enrichment of life will again be within our grasp.

    John Habraken, *Supports: an Alternative to Mass Housing*, 1961

The more people feel themselves involved in architecture, the more likely we are to get the buildings we think we deserve. An enlarged architectural conscience brought about by the greatly increased participation of more people as partial clients is more likely to lead to good architecture than the most scrupulously applied aesthetic controls. If architecture is to flourish and progress in an age when change is constant and development rapid and relentless, it must, with renewed vigour, use society as a partner in the creative process. Only then can the primary unchanging function of architecture be achieved; to provide decent surroundings for people and to help them to a wider vision of life.

    (Sir) Denys Lasdun, 'Process of Continual Cooperation', *The Times*, June 1961

---

* 'Social architecture' is a term commonly used in the United States with a meaning similar to 'community architecture'.

The best way to understand how community architecture provides a solution to the seemingly elusive task of creating humane environments is to examine case studies. Just as there is no single identifiable problem, there is no single solution. But community architecture has developed methods of dealing with environmental problems at all levels – from an individual home to a city.

Community architecture has emerged from people trying out, in hundreds if not thousands of live projects, alternative methods of obtaining the homes and neighbourhoods they want. Most have failed to achieve their objectives due to institutional or bureaucratic restraints. But some have succeeded sufficiently to provide precedents and proto- types for others to follow and learn from. These are the pioneers.

This chapter looks at a range of British pioneering projects which cover the three main categories of development: housing; social, business and industrial facilities; and neighbourhoods.

Housing

1. Rehabilitation – Private Sector

In 1972, three hundred red-brick terraced houses clinging to the hillside around Black Road, in the Pennine town of Macclesfield in Cheshire, seemed to be approaching the end of their useful life. Built for workers in the town's textile industry at the beginning of the nineteenth century, they were poky by present-day standards and lacked proper bathrooms. Many were in a poor state of repair, with rotting timber and leaking roofs. The local council responded in the manner which was standard practice at the time. Without consulting the residents, it declared their homes to be 'substandard' and earmarked the entire neighbourhood for demolition. The community would be split up and moved elsewhere.

Sixty-one of the homes were saved and refurbished over the next three years. By 1985 Black Road had become a place of pilgrimage for aca- demics, professionals, politicians, community groups – and even royalty. The scheme for restoring the houses had won numerous awards and been featured in magazine articles and television programmes in many parts of the world. Many British architects have found the 'hype' hard to stomach. What, they complain, is so special about restoring a few ordin- ary homes, particularly when there is nothing eye-catching or innovatory about the design?

What attracted international attention to Black Road was not the look of the restored buildings, but the innovative process by which they were saved and improved, and the positive effect that their restoration has had on the residents and on the community as a whole.

In a BBC Radio 4 interview in 1979, June Daniels, one of the residents, put it like this: 'It's a strong community now where we live, because we've made it so with doing the work we have done to our houses. At one time I only knew my next-door neighbours or the people that shared the yard with us. We spoke to the other people – just "Hello" and "Good morning", but now it's "Are you coming over for a cup of tea?" Everybody's friendly and it's really brought us close together as a community.'

Mrs Daniels, in her late forties, was a housewife before the renovation programme started. By the end she had become the personnel manager for a construction site for thirty-two houses. She acquired the skills and confidence for her new profession by renovating her own home and helping her neighbours with theirs.

She is not alone. Many formerly unemployed residents in the area now have work as a direct result of being involved in the scheme. Furthermore, people who were formerly renting their homes and who had no financial assets whatsoever now own those same houses, whose market value has increased from £500 to around £20,000 each. People have gained skills, confidence, security and a sense of community, as well as their own homes.

'I was electrified by the atmosphere I encountered,' Prince Charles told the Institute of Directors' annual convention after visiting Black Road and Weller Way, another community architecture scheme in Liverpool (see p. 77), in 1985. 'I hadn't come across anything quite like it before.'

What I saw of these schemes filled me with enthusiasm and I reflected a great deal on the immense possibilities they conjured up. It seemed to me that if only we could enable more people, especially in the inner-city areas, to develop the kind of self-confidence I had seen with my own eyes in the sort of places of which most authorities and agencies tend to despair, that self-confidence – from the discovery of previously hidden talents and abilities – could spill over into other regenerative enterprises.[14]

So how was it done at Black Road? The starting-point was when residents began talking amongst themselves about the demolition threat, decided that they did not want to be moved into new council homes and campaigned to stay where they were. They formed an action group and adopted the slogan: 'Keep It Up, Black Road!'

What made them different from hundreds of similar communities which had taken the same steps but whose homes eventually succumbed to the bulldozer was that one of the residents was an architect, Rod Hackney, who was prepared to take up their cause. Working closely with the action group, Hackney devised a formula with the following main ingredients.

First, the residents formed a trust controlled by a committee comprising one member from each household. This trust was given the responsibility for improving all the land around the houses and was empowered to negotiate with the authorities and contractors on behalf of individual residents. This gave the residents an efficient, legally constituted form of neighbourhood government and allowed the rationalization of the tatty backyards and backlands.

Second, the council was persuaded – by means of an intense campaign of lobbying and publicity backed up by a fifty-four page technical report – to declare the area a General Improvement Area under new government housing legislation. This meant that grants could be obtained both for renovating individual houses and for landscaping. This in turn made it easier for residents to secure mortgages and loans, by restoring confidence in the area. (Before the scheme started, nearly all the residents had bought their homes from absentee landlords and so become owner-occupiers.)

Third, a self-help programme was organized to bridge the gap between the money available from grants and mortgages and the total necessary for the construction work. Residents bound themselves legally to bring their homes up to the standards required by the Housing Acts within twelve months: but how they did it was largely up to them. A formula was decided whereby people who did not wish to do so much building work could pay others to do it, but in practice everyone pitched in, applying whatever skills they had both to their own homes and those of their neighbours. Outside contractors entered into the spirit of the project by leaving their equipment on site for residents to use in the evenings and at weekends. On average, residents cut building costs by 25 per cent on their homes, and the cost of landscaping works was cut to one third of what it would have cost to employ a contractor.

Finally, Hackney himself was appointed as architect to the Trust and set up an office on the site in a corner shop, two doors from his own home, from which to coordinate the programme. This was the essential difference from any other attempts at saving people's homes. It worked and caught the world's attention. 'There is a new type of architect, a community architect working on site twenty-four hours a day,' reported BBC 1's 'Tomorrow's World' programme in 1977. Hackney's role went way beyond that of a normal architect – mainly designing and supervising contractors, and from a distance. He worked alongside the residents and builders throughout; digging drains, repairing roofs, helping them to overcome obstacles and to make decisions. He got to know all the residents and their homes intimately and was able to advise each of them on the options available. As a result every house turned out differently, reflecting the individual wishes of each occupant. The windows and doors are different, some kitchens are larger than others, some houses are open plan, some have back extensions, and so on.

'Black Road taught me the greatest lesson of my life,' Hackney told *Woman* magazine. 'Architects, councils and government planners all have to get closer to the wishes and needs of ordinary families.'[15]

'What makes the community architect different from the traditional architect is that he's available, he's there – seven days a week, twenty-four hours a day – to feel the vibration and pulse of the community,' says Hackney. 'The architect's presence on site is essential. That very presence is wealth – not just for the architect but for the whole community.'[16] Or as Joan Reeder concluded in *Woman* magazine, 'The lesson seems to be that if you rehabilitate houses, you don't need to rehabilitate people.'[17]

2. Rehabilitation – Public Sector

For several years critics tried to belittle the significance of Black Road's revival. Such a process could only be made to work by the private sector in areas with low property values, they claimed. Surely it could be of little relevance to the vast stock of decaying public-sector housing estates in the inner cities? It took the renovation of Lea View House in Hackney, east London, to prove them wrong.

Building workers from Hackney Council's Direct Labour organization (DLO) arrived at Lea View House one morning in March 1982 to start the reconstruction of the bleak, five-storey, three-hundred-flat estate. They were greeted by a huge hoarding proclaiming 'Hello DLO!' and a breakfast party was put on for them by the tenants. It was an unprecedented event for a local-authority rehabilitation project to commence in this way; and it demonstrated the extent to which the tenants were involved and committed to the work going ahead.

The renovation of Lea View House was the first occasion in Britain where local-authority tenants were fully and effectively involved in the rehabilitation of their homes; the results were remarkable. Before the rehabilitation, Lea View House was a hard-to-let, multi-racial, 'sink' estate and it typified the social, political and environmental problems that beset much inner-city housing in Britain. It was vandalized, litter-strewn and detested. Thefts and muggings were common. People's health was poor. They only moved there if they had no other choice. Existing tenants felt trapped and helpless, resigned to a life of misery from which there was no escape; 90 per cent said they wanted to leave.

After the renovation, crime and vandalism were virtually eliminated, common areas remained spotless, people's health – both physical and psychological – improved dramatically and there was a new-found sense of community spirit. At an opening ceremony in July 1983 the leader of the council, Anthony Kendall, described it as 'a model example for us all to learn from, a pioneering scheme that shows the way forward as to how we should modernize our estates in the future, concentrating on quality rather than quantity'. Tenant Dolly Pritchard put it this way: 'I just walk around my place, I'm so chuffed with it. It's been worth every meeting, every protest. Once people fought to leave Lea View – now they're all wanting to get in . . . Before, we hardly knew anybody, now everybody is mixing and we are beginning to get a really good community once again.'

These results contrast markedly with those from conventional local-authority renovations. For instance, none of these attributes are to be found in an identical estate next to Lea View – the Wigan Estate – which was renovated just before Lea View by the same authority within the same government guidelines and cost limits, but without effective tenant involvement. Within six months the Wigan Estate had reverted to a slum. The 'improvements' are there, but the estate is still vandalized, ground-floor flats are boarded up, tenant morale is low. The architect for Lea View, John Thompson, comments:

Wandering around Wigan it is difficult to believe that there is *no* fundamental difference between the people living there, and their neighbours at Lea View. It is a vivid example of how social behaviour responds to design. Crime, vandalism, muggings have been eliminated at Lea View. They thrive on Wigan. It is also difficult to believe that Wigan is the same builiding as Lea View. Lea View is housing for people, in a new, hospitable design derived from, and responding to the needs of the people living there. Wigan is unit housing, committee housing, faceless housing, thoughtless housing, uncaring in both its execution and its management.[18]

So how did the renovation process work at Lea View? What made it special? As in Macclesfield it began with a vigorous and well-organized campaign by the tenants to get improvements and be involved in determining what form they should take. As a result the council appointed Hunt Thompson Associates, a private firm of architects, who took the unprecedented step of moving into an unoccupied flat on the estate and setting up a project office with four staff. At first the tenants were suspicious – their newsletter warned 'The architects are using Flat No. 3 . . . so beware!' But it quickly became the social focus for the estate and allowed a creative dialogue to begin between tenants and architects. Thompson reports:

As trust began to be established, the architects began to realize that the greatest resource available to them in their search for a meaningful and lasting solution was the tenant community itself, available at first hand and with detailed and highly critical knowledge and opinions about every single aspect of their own environment. If this knowledge could be tapped and the real nature of their problems understood, then the architects could start to apply their own skills as designers.[19]

After gathering information, scientifically by means of a social survey and intuitively over cups of tea, 'the architects began to perceive the inextricable relationship that existed between the physical design of the original estate and the true extent of the social and physical deprivation of the community'. It was also realized that simply making physical improvements to the flats – *even though it would satisfy the tenants' initial demands* – would be 'money wasted, for it was the underlying organization of the estate that was now the major factor in creating an unsatisfactory environment for people to live in'.[20]

The design solution which emerged from the collaboration between architects and tenants therefore addressed itself primarily to the organization of the estate: restoring identity to individual homes and groups of homes by rearranging flat layouts and access to them, facilitating management of communal areas by clearly defining public and private space, reducing fuel bills by insulation and solar-heating systems, and customizing flats for individuals with special needs.

The project team was expanded to include representatives from the construction workforce and the council's housing department, as well as tenants and architects. Visits were made to other schemes so that tenants could see physical examples of the options under discussion. As well as being involved in the general planning and design of the estate, each tenant chose their own internal decorations.

After building work commenced, tenants paid regular site visits to their new flats and were able to make last-minute adjustments. Children were involved in planting and landscaping. The tenants and workforce organized joint Christmas parties, raising money for local charity.

The end result is an estate which works well and looks good. 'We take so much pride in it, we won't allow anybody to come around and destroy it or disturb it,' says Mr Brown, one of the tenants. And all parties agree on what was the essential ingredient. 'We've been involved in everything that's happened here from the very beginning. We've made decisions that no other council tenants have ever made,' says tenant Miriam Lewis. 'Through participating, we helped to become a community, to get people to live together, to work together, to communicate together.' The deputy leader of Hackney Council, Peter Kahn, told the *Hackney Gazette*, 'The direct relationship that exists between the workforce and the tenants has produced a very high level of motivation on the site and the standard of workmanship has been excellent.'[21]

Tenants from an estate faced with similar difficulties who visited the Lea View House Tenants' Association reported: 'The families we met did not just talk about the renewal of their homes but the renewal of their community. Many of the management problems of the estate had in fact been solved by achitectural solutions. But the long-term guarantee of a successful estate will come when the community that has lived together through difficult times has helped to create the solution to their problems.'[22] Thompson sums it up: 'The process of regeneration of the estate has also regenerated the community spirit. People now know their neighbours and respect each other's territory. Once you can re-establish pride you can solve all the other problems which flow from loss of pride, loss of dignity and loss of self-respect.'[23]

3. New Housing – Public Sector

The two examples described above – in Black Road, Macclesfield, and Lea View, east London – demonstrate the effectiveness of community architecture in dealing with housing rehabilitation, whether in the private or public sectors. In both cases capital costs were the same or less than if the buildings had been converted in the conventional manner without involving the residents, and the design solutions were more imaginative and appropriate. The savings in each case were very substantial compared with the possible alternative of demolition, rebuilding and providing temporary accommodation in the interim. In addition, both individuals and communities have been significantly strengthened in ways not found when using conventional approaches.

But what about new housing? Is it possible to apply the same methods when building new housing from scratch?

Several attempts have been made to involve people in designing new public-sector housing over the last fifteen years. The best-known is in Newcastle where, in 1968, Ralph Erskine – who in 1987 was awarded the Royal Gold Medal for architecture – was invited to rebuild a slum neighbourhood of over two thousand dwellings in the district of Byker. His first step was to establish a site office in a disused funeral parlour, from which the scheme was designed with the involvement of the inhabitants. The outcome was universally praised by architectural critics and very popular with residents. But its success was the result of a unique combination of political circumstances and has not proved replicable elsewhere. The stumbling blocks have been local authorities' persistent failure to devolve sufficient power to their tenants or to allow council officers and other professionals to work properly with them.

The breakthrough was made in Liverpool. On 3 October 1982 a new estate of sixty-one houses was opened in the Toxteth district, the scene of some of Britain's worst inner-city riots only one year previously.

It was an opening with a difference. Instead of the standard pompous ceremony with the mayor being photographed handing over house keys to the first grateful tenants, it was a street party which lasted until four in the morning, with music, games and dancing, and a 'banquet' for the children. A plaque inscribed with a poem composed by one of the residents was unveiled:

> Just a bit of everyone.
> There's not much more to say.
> We gave our time and leisure,
> To show we're here to stay.

The manager of the company which constructed the houses announced that it was the first time he had ever worked on a housing project where he knew the first names of everyone who was to live there, including the children.

The Weller Streets Co-op did indeed have something to celebrate. Fighting bureaucracy and political inertia all the way, sixty-one working-class families living in some of the worst housing conditions in Europe had succeeded in obtaining £1·3m of public money to buy land in their neighbourhood and build new homes designed to their own specifications – homes which were to be owned, controlled, managed and maintained by themselves. As the *Architects' Journal* proclaimed:

Something incredible has happened in Liverpool – arguably the most important step forward in British housing for decades. Without anyone else in the country really noticing it, an era spanning sixty years of paternalistic public housing provision has quietly come to an end. In its place a new way of building publicly funded housing has taken over in which the users are firmly in the driving seat.[24]

The path forged by Weller Streets Co-op was rapidly followed by others in Liverpool, and by 1986 eight such schemes had been completed and twelve more were at various stages of design and construction. Over a thousand families were engaged in designing and supervising the construction of their own homes and the city's architectural practices had developed a whole range of new skills and working practices to help them do so. In the church halls and working men's clubs, families thrashing out the details of their new homes with their architects in design meetings rapidly became a prominent feature of Liverpool night life.

The way it works is as follows: local-authority tenants living in slum-clearance areas or deteriorating tenements organize themselves into groups – ranging from twenty to 150 families – and obtain the services of one of Liverpool's cooperative development agencies. With its assistance they register as a housing cooperative (non-equity with limited liability), locate a site and negotiate to buy it. They then select an architect; together they examine the options and then design a scheme which is submitted to a funding body (Liverpool City Council or the Housing Corporation). After obtaining the necessary approvals, the houses are then constructed by a private builder. When the houses are completed, the co-op members become tenants of the homes, paying standard fair rents, but they are also collectively the landlord, responsible for management and maintenance.

'The most important thing about it is the power-to-the-people bit,' says Alan Hoyte, first chairman of the Hesketh Street Co-op.

In general, in Liverpool people are told what they are getting, not asked what they want. But once we had established our viability by being accepted by the government for funding, we determined everything: the way we lived and who we employed to run our affairs. We did not succumb to bureaucracy.

We got the architects and builders and everybody else on our terms. We told them what we wanted and consulted right through, from day one, at every stage. Through the design committee we decided on every single aspect of the scheme right down to the sort of trees we planted.

We've proved to the council and government and anybody else listening that if people are given the reins, get the right help and are committed, they can come up with a really excellent, viable housing scheme that people *want* to live in.[25]

And so they had. The co-op schemes in Liverpool cost no more than any other public housing and took *less* time to build. Construction standards are well above average. And yet each dwelling is personalized for its occupants and there are infinite variations in layout and fittings. After occupation the schemes have been properly maintained. Once again, however, the most exciting factor has been the effect on the inhabitants and the strength of the communities. Vandalism and petty crime have been virtually eliminated, with some residents no longer bothering to lock their front doors when they go shopping. The elderly are looked after and feel secure. Drug abuse has been reduced. People have developed confidence, learnt new skills and found out how to work with each other. 'It's learnt me an awful lot in the process of doing it. When I first came on to this scheme I couldn't open my mouth I was so timid. I couldn't lobby, I couldn't sit down with an architect and learn how to read plans. I always felt I wasn't educated enough to do that. I've achieved something in my life that I never thought I would,' Maureen Doyle, a member of the Prince Albert Gardens Cooperative told *Voluntary Action* magazine in December 1985.

Many of the co-ops have gone on to undertake other projects in providing social facilities. 'It's to do with caring. People got to know each other during the design stage and we agreed things together,' says Elaine Dutton, a member of one of the Hesketh Street Co-op's design committee. Or as another co-op member put it in a letter to a local councillor: 'Apart from the ambition which comes from the very fact that we are doing things for ourselves . . . there are also prevalent feelings of being part of, taking part in, belonging to and being. It is a very healthy attitude that is positive and contagious.'[25]

For the architects too it was a valuable experience. Danielle Pacaud, architect for one of the schemes, is convinced that

working with a co-op in this way has allowed us to produce the best housing design possible. Working with co-ops is proving very enjoyable. It is the most rewarding experience in housing design that we have had as a practice or as individuals. It releases the architect's imagination from the stereotype of the building-user conceived from a housing manager's view that determines local-authority housing, as well as from the overriding emphasis on cost in developer housing. On reflection, the cooperative works so well that to return to other systems of housing production would seem for us a step backwards into contradictions whose resolution has been discovered.[25]

Cooperative Development Services, the development agency most involved with pioneering the cooperatives in Liverpool, concluded in its 1984 report, *Building Democracy: Housing Cooperatives on Merseyside*:

Liverpool has solid practical evidence that co-ops can and will meet the most acute housing need; offer value for money; and make intelligent, practical and speedy use of available expertise and funding. In short, there is tangible proof that co-ops offer one alternative that really works. The future of cooperative housing to become a major new sector for twenty-first-century housing must now be taken seriously.

Dumbfounding the sceptics, the Liverpool cooperatives demonstrate that the construction of publicly funded housing can quite safely be entrusted to the people who live in it, provided they have access to professional expertise, and that the professionals are sensitive to community concerns and have learnt to work in such a development context.

4. New Housing – Private Sector

One has to return to Macclesfield for a glimpse of the potential for involving future occupants in the construction of private-sector estates.

In theory, owner-occupation should provide an ideal form of tenure for user control. But, in practice, rules applied by mortgage companies and statutory authorities have restricted the scope of owner-occupation and ensured that the market is dominated by commercial developers. Speculative estates built by large, nationally or regionally based development companies are the main source of housing in Britain. People buy houses off the peg just like any other consumer product. The designs are based on a marketing manager's views of what the average purchaser wants, but shortage of supply often ensures that virtually anything will sell. The architects, if any are involved, are often based hundreds of miles away and never meet, let alone consult or involve, the prospective occupants. In *The Production of Houses* (1985), Christopher Alexander wrote:

Such houses are identical, machine-like, stamped out of a mould and almost entirely unable to express the individuality of different families. They suppress individuality, they suppress whatever is wonderful and special about any one family. Placed and built anonymously, such houses express isolation, lack of relationship, and fail altogether, to create human bonds in which people feel themselves part of the fabric which connects them to their fellow men. In the modern world, the idea that houses can be loved and be beautiful has been eliminated almost altogether. The task of building houses has been reduced to a grim business of facts and figures, an uphill struggle against the relentless surge of technology and bureaucracy, in which human feeling has been almost forgotten.

In 1985 Castward Homes, a company set up by Rod Hackney & Associates, advertised thirty-two houses for sale on an estate called Roan Court, at the other end of Macclesfield's Black Road from the self-help renovation scheme described earlier. The estate had been planned in consultation with residents adjoining the site but the houses had not yet been built. Purchasers could choose to buy a completed house, a serviced ground-floor slab, or anything in between, priced accordingly. Those who chose an incomplete house could call on the developer and architect to provide any advice and skills they themselves lacked in completing their house. The developer and architect – both permanently at hand in a site office, in fact the first house built – bought materials centrally to obtain maximum discounts, hired out equipment and arranged for mortgages and bridging finance. House designs included flexibility for future expansion and could be altered by the purchasers within certain limits. As well as purchasing the freehold/leasehold of their own home, the new occupants could also join an association responsible for common areas, including a proposed swimming-pool.

The advantages of the scheme compared with those of conventional volume builders are obvious:

1. People get customized houses to suit their own budgets and lifestyles.
2. Money and resources are not wasted by the developers providing unwanted finishes and gloss in order to obtain quick sales.
3. People have the opportunity to have as much physical involvement in the construction as they wish, with a highly supportive technical back-up at hand.
4. There is a built-in mechanism for evolving collective management of the common areas, making it easier to provide collective facilities – play areas, swimming-pools, etc.
5. Both individual homes and the entire estate can continue to evolve indefinitely as needs and aspirations change.

While, in practice, many of the options available were not taken up at Roan Court, the scheme provides a model for commercial housing developers.

5. New Housing – Self-build

Self-build – in which people mostly unskilled in the building trades physically construct their own homes – has grown dramatically in recent
years, to around 11,000 units, or 5 per cent of the annual number of
homes built in Britain. In 1986 this was the largest category of 'house-
builder' in the country. There are three main reasons why people opt for
self-build:

1. They have definite views about the style, layout or quality of house
    they want and cannot obtain it in any other way.
2. They have a natural instinct to build for themselves, and derive
    satisfaction from embodying their ideas and labour in their own
    homes.
3. They want to save money – up to 40 per cent can be saved on the
    mortgage value of standard houses.

Building one's own home is difficult enough at the best of times. But it
has been made much more difficult in the past fifty years by the problems
of obtaining land and finance. Land – particularly in the cities – is mostly
sold in large tracts and mortgage companies have, until very recently,
been reluctant to lend money except for completed houses. The creative
potential of self-build has also been hindered by planning controls and
building regulations which have restricted people who want to explore
unconventional designs and new methods of construction. Until recently
self-build was restricted to those prepared to construct fairly conventional
homes – usually to standard blueprint designs prepared by companies
specializing in such schemes, which arranged for land and finance to be
made available – and who had at least some financial resources of their
own.

The breakthrough was made when Lewisham Council in south London
appointed architect Walter Segal to help fourteen families, selected by
ballot from the council's waiting and transfer list, to build their own
homes. Segal developed a special timber-frame construction system, using
widely available building materials, which fits together quickly and easily.
The whole building process is simplified so that it can be carried out by
one person with easily acquired basic carpentry skills – apart from the
services and roofing.

Furthermore this system is extremely flexible, so that self-builders can
determine their own design and easily extend, change and improve it

over the years. The Segal method has opened up a new era for self-build. As Jon Broome, Segal's colleague, wrote in the *Architects' Journal* in 1986:

> The simplification of the building process enables people who are not experts to build a house, and those who are not professional architects to have a controlling influence on designing one. This approach shows how people can participate in a significant way in the housing process and enjoy the sense of satisfaction and achievement that can follow. They can have a house to suit their individual needs and wishes at a relatively modest price. Houses built in this way provide a variety and vitality so often missing from our living environments. People's individual skills, energy and creativity are given expression and other skills are acquired . . . It's an architecture of liberation.[26]

In the first Lewisham scheme, says Broome, 'No one was prevented from taking part because of their circumstances, lack of capital, income or building skills, and indeed houses have been built by people in their sixties and by a single mother.'

For those who took part, it was an exciting experience despite years initially wasted fighting bureaucrats before starting to build. Ken Atkins, chairman of the Lewisham Self-Build Housing Association, who formerly lived in a concrete tower block, said in 1983:

> The house took me and the wife eleven months to build. It was a very enjoyable experience after all the time involved in getting the scheme off the ground. It is an adaptable building, unusual yes, but extremely nice to live in. The sheer joy of putting a spade in the ground . . . well, it's an indescribable feeling . . . you finally have control over what you are doing in your life.
>
> When you build yourself a house like that, and understand what a house really is, and how anybody can do it, you get re-educated. You don't need to move or trade up; you've got your own house exactly the way you want it and you understand exactly how it went together.

Segal, who died in 1985, once said of his system: 'This is not the only way. It is merely the approach that is important. There are many other technologies and methods.'[27]

One of those methods was developed at Colquhoun Street in Stirling, Scotland. It combines self-help refurbishment and self-build homes on the same site and for the first time put home ownership within the reach of disadvantaged groups such as the unemployed, low paid, single parents and families on the council waiting list. Stirling District Council commissioned Rod Hackney & Associates to undertake the scheme of twenty-seven refurbished flats and nine new two- and three-bedroom houses on a derelict site in 1984. The Abbey National and Scottish building societies provided mortgages, with the council giving bridging loans and maximum improvement grants.

By doing most of the work themselves the self-builders are saving up to one third of the normal market cost of their homes, giving them a new house for less than £25,000 and a flat for around £15,000.

As with Hackney's other projects there is a comprehensive support system, with a community architect's office (and flat) on-site linked by computer to the Macclesfield head office to facilitate the ordering of materials. Every dwelling is different, thanks to the professional assistance on hand. Furthermore, the building societies were persuaded to accept dole payments as a normal regular 'income' for unemployed people involved in the scheme.

An apparently hopeless situation has been made to work. The rate-capped local authority could not afford to build homes for those on its waiting list. What it did have, however, was a derelict site which has now been put back into productive use. The self-builders have housed themselves, and the building societies have the risk in lending money for mortgages underwritten by the council. It is a formula which should make self-build home ownership an option available to virtually everyone in the country who wants it.

Conclusion on Housing

Political debate on housing this century has centred largely on the issue of tenure; the Right has pushed private ownership; the Left has pushed state ownership and the Centre has pushed a combination of the two. All have tended to measure success in physical terms: the amount of space and the standards of heating, plumbing and other services provided, and the number of 'units' built.

The experience of community architecture projects in housing indicates that there are other factors of importance for achieving and measuring success which have hitherto been overlooked by those shaping policy. The projects described cover different kinds of tenure and measure up favourably using any conventional criteria: the same or better physical standards have been achieved for the same or less money and in the same or less time. Yet the projects also have vital additional attributes not found using conventional methods: first, all homes have been customized to suit the needs of the occupants, thereby reducing waste and increasing people's satisfaction and sense of belonging; second, people's homes have been integrated – physically *and organizationally* – into the fabric of the immediate locality. This has resulted in the reduction or elimination of vandalism and crime and the enhancement of people's sense of community and civic pride. In all the schemes described, the people involved have gone on to tackle other problems facing their neighbourhoods, setting up projects dealing with shopping, employment, crime and the special needs of children and the elderly for instance. By providing a means for people to work together on their housing, these projects have generated the confidence, ability and organizational skills necessary to take the next step of rebuilding neighbourhoods and cities.

Four essential characteristics can be found in all the schemes and underpin the success of the community architecture approach to housing:

1. *Individuals and families are given the maximum possible control over, and responsibility for, the design and management of their own homes.*
2. *An organizational mechanism is developed for people living in close proximity to communicate with each other and take joint responsibility for common land and facilities.*
3. *Both individuals and communities are able to develop a working relationship with professionals with appropriate technical expertise.*
4. *The partnership of residents and professionals makes it its business to tackle all aspects of the residents' environment, developing both design and organizational solutions simultaneously.*

These characteristics are not, of course, only found in community architecture projects – indeed they can be found in hundreds of successful small-scale, *ad hoc* projects where people have been free to create their own environment unencumbered by legal, financial, professional and bureaucratic restrictions: in squatting communities, in rural and urban communes, in the conversion of large country estates or town houses, in some student housing schemes and above all in cooperatives. What makes the community architecture projects described here special is that they have provided prototypes incorporating these characteristics for the five major systems of housing production. They have established precedents.

At the time of writing, public-sector house building in Britain has reached its lowest ebb for half a century. But, as Colin Ward concludes in his classic book *When We Build Again: Let's Have Housing That Works!*: 'When we build again, we need not a plan for housing, but an attitude that will enable millions of people to make their own plans.'

Social, Business and Institutional Facilities

If there is anything to be learnt from past experience, it is that the best planning and architecture is usually sterile unless the planners and architects, as well as those who commission them, have a personal relationship with, and a civic pride in, the community for whom they are working. Cities can only be created by their own citizens, otherwise they just become conurbations.

HRH The Duke of Edinburgh, Foreword to *The Continuing Heritage* by Lord Esher, 1982

It isn't only the result that is important, but the way that the community feels about having achieved it. The more people feel involved along the way, the more they will identify with the finished buildings or open space, and so the more important to everyone the whole venture will have been.

Community Land and Workspace Services, *Planning a Capital Project*, 1985

There is an absolutely inevitable and unstoppable increase in ordinary people's knowledge and, in the next century, they will demand – and they will get – a say in the architecture that is presented to them and the money that is spent on it.

Edward Cullinan, quoted in the *Guardian*, 29 April 1985

These are difficult times. They demand architects grounded in history, technically prepared to build and allied to those who need them most. This is the continuing path of social architecture, and if we trace it assiduously, it will lead us to that world where aesthetic is not the quality of isolated objects, but of life itself.

Richard Hatch, in Richard Hatch, ed., *The Scope of Social Architecture*, 1984

1. Community Projects

In the summer of 1982, some young parents (mostly, but not all, women) in the Poplar area of London's East End met to discuss the difficulties of bringing up small children in isolation from other families.

They started meeting regularly in each other's flats and for a while in the local health clinic. They swapped information and experiences of being parents. The children naturally enjoyed and benefited from being with others. It also became clear that the lack of pre-school play facilities in the area was causing a great deal of hardship, particularly for single parents. There are more children in the care of social workers in Poplar than anywhere else in the country. After unsuccessful attempts to persuade the authorities to provide more facilities, the parents decided that they themselves would take on the responsibility of building a play centre. They appointed Community Land Use, a team of architects and landscape architects working with communities in London's East End, to help them find land and finance (£175,000), and then design and build what became known as Poplar Play.

When the Poplar Play Centre was formally opened four year later, Linda Bellos, chair of the Greater London Council's Women's Unit, which had largely funded the project, described it as 'the most beautiful building I have been in for a long time. This is one of the most proud and monumental examples of what the Women's Unit stood for.' Peter Polish, representing the London Docklands Development Corporation, apologized for the fact that the Corporation had not given more support and said: 'What this project is about is precisely what the Corporation is about – it's about regeneration. The only reason it happened was because of a determined group of women, a determined group of supporters and a determined group of community architects who supported their initiative.'

Poplar Play has improved the lives of many local parents and their children dramatically. Instead of remaining isolated all day in tiny flats, parents can go at any time and look after their children with other parents in a purpose-built play palace surrounded by a lush garden. Arrangements can be made to leave children in the care of trained staff, allowing people to work who would not otherwise have been able to do so. In addition, the centre can be booked for children's parties at weekends. It has become a valuable social centre for the neighbourhood. And the key to its continuing and future success is that it is run by an annually elected voluntary management committee of parents who constantly modify the way it is run to suit their changing needs.

Poplar Play is just one example of a new generation of community projects which have been built *by*, and not simply *for*, local residents who commissioned their own architects, planners and other professionals to help them. Hundreds of similar community facilities have been created in cities, towns and villages all over Britain, covering all areas of social and cultural life. Teenagers in Penzance in Cornwall, for instance, have converted a redundant warehouse into a 'drop-in' centre where they can mend motorbikes, practise music, obtain information about employment possibilities or simply meet and have coffee. Elderly people in the village of Ashill in rural East Anglia have turned a stone shack into a 'social meeting point' for the elderly, with a luncheon club, chiropody clinic and branch surgery. Residents in Cardiff have transformed a four-acre refuse tip into a city farm with a wide range of animals, a pottery workshop, a fish farm and a vegetable garden, and special facilities for the disabled.

Sometimes the motivation has come as much from a desire to make use of buildings or land lying idle as from the need to create a specific facility. Groups have formed to turn derelict plots of land into adventure playgrounds or nature parks. Rotting warehouses have been given a new lease of life by being converted into workshops, community arts centres, museums and flats. Initially most of these projects relied almost entirely on grants from charities and local and central government. Increasingly they have become more commercial, often with a careful balancing of profitable and non-profitable uses. For instance, of some three hundred case studies of conversions prepared by development consultants URBED in 1985, three quarters were in some way commercial.

Conceived, executed and then run by the people who use and benefit from them, this new generation of projects represents a radical departure from the centralized provision of social facilities, so often inappropriate, badly designed by professionals remote from the users, and ultimately abused by the people they were intended for, which has been the hallmark of the post-war welfare state. Furthermore they would not have happened had the people involved not had technical assistance from professionals – often donating much of their time voluntarily – who have been instrumental in turning dreams into reality.

The process typically works as follows:

1. People who share a concern to establish a new facility or re-use a redundant resource meet informally to discuss how it might be done.
2. They decide to set up an informal organization (a working party, steering group, etc.). They arrange a contact address, agree to meet regularly and encourage others to get involved by publicizing their intentions. They become the client group.
3. Contact is made with appropriate professionals (architects, landscape architects, planners, lawyers, etc., depending on the nature of the project), who help analyse the problem and advise on options for solving it.
4. Approaches are made (by the client group and the professionals) to the authorities and others for funds, permissions and other resources.
5. The client group formally establishes an association, trust or other

legally constituted body to manage land and resources, while at the same time being democratically accountable to the people who will use the facility.

6. Detailed design is undertaken and followed by construction, the client group remaining in charge of, and closely involved in, both.

7. After completion, the client group manages the project, undertaking further improvements as necessary.

This is a somewhat simplistic description and there are many variations. Often the project will be initiated by a community organization that already exists. Sometimes, by virtue of their experience and vision, professionals will be key instigators of projects, particularly in areas where they live or work. But the essential difference from conventional methods is that the people who will ultimately use the facilities direct the projects from inception through to construction and management.

Evidence indicates that, providing the right technical expertise is available at all stages, facilities evolved in this way will perform better than those provided by conventional means in many ways. After analysing sixty case studies of community projects (most falling in this category) in 1978, the Royal Institute of British Architects concluded:

Where residents, whether tenants or owners, have added their own efforts to over-stressed local services, these have manifested themselves in a better maintained physical environment and greater public spirit. Community projects represent good value for money by ensuring appropriate solutions and reducing maintenance and vandalism costs.

For those involved the experience is invariably gruelling but rewarding. 'It's been bloody hard work. I've cried, I've had bags under my eyes and at one time I was resigning every week,' is a typical response from thirty-eight-year-old Rose McCarton, chair of the Turkey Lane and Monsall Lane Residents Group, on a bleak council housing estate on the outskirts of Manchester; it built a £70,000 community centre with architects from Design Cooperative. 'But it's been great and we've all learnt a lot,' she told the *Architect's Journal* in 1982.[28] By then she had a new career as the completed centre's first manager.

The training and confidence-boosting effects of these projects has not been adequately studied but is undoubtedly immense. So too is the effect they have on revitalizing communities by establishing networks of communication between people with common interests and problems. For instance, as a result of working together to create the Poplar Play

Centre described at the beginning of this section, the parents involved got to know each other, became friends and embarked on other projects: a band, Saturday morning classes for two year olds, a babysitting circle.

But perhaps the most profound impact of the user-led approach is its potential for changing the very nature of the social facilities themselves. By establishing a process whereby people can group together to create their own social facilities, the way is opened up for providing facilities which could not possibly be conceived by centralized planners and which do not fit into any neat category. For instance, in the Yorkshire village of Broadbottom, a community association has converted a disused railway shed into a sports hall and a riding school for the disabled. At Greenland Farm near Glastonbury in Somerset, a community group from inner London has created a rural centre for allowing city children to experience living on a working farm in the country. And in the parish of Heaton in Staffordshire, a community group has converted a redundant village school into a multi-purpose village centre with a wide range of social and commercial facilities.

The barriers between work and living space are also being broken down. One of the most popular new prototypes is the atelier flat, where people both live and work. Opportunities are occurring for exploring new ways of living and re-evaluating the role of 'community'. It is no accident that the most popular type of community project to have emerged has been the community centre. Over one third of the applications received by the Royal Institute of British Architects' Community Projects Fund (p. 131) in its first four years of operation fell into this category. Community centres are not of course a new invention. The parish hall has an ancient history and local authorities have provided community halls for many years. But the new generation of community centres – developed by community groups in conjunction with professional enablers – is a completely new type of building providing space for a wide range of activities and continually evolving as the community's needs change and as people become aware of the possibilities.

A simple community centre is likely to include a large multi-purpose hall for sports, dances or meetings, surrounded by smaller activity rooms plus a kitchen, toilets, office and storerooms. The effect of building one in an area can have a dramatic effect on community life, stimulating new cultural, educational and social activity. In Cornwall, for instance, where community associations were formed in several villages to build new centres with architect Robert Poynton, the police reported a reduction in crime and estate agents claimed that property values were higher in those villages where centres had been built. And, once established, such centres invariably generate demand for additional facilities and may eventually become quite elaborate. For instance, the new Albany Centre, built in Deptford, London, in 1982, contains a theatre, a large central café, a bar, children's playroom, pottery, darkrooms, printing workshops, craft rooms and a large number of project rooms at ground level with shopfront entrances on to the street. The Centre's publicity advertises over seventy activities ranging from a pensioners' club to a mural workshop.

Interest in community development has been growing for many years but most of the work has been theoretical in nature. Community architecture has provided a missing link, enabling people to put theory into practice. The projects described in this section are scattered throughout the country, and are mostly small and of local signficance only. But it is clear that the new alliance between community groups and professionals is changing the social landscape in ways whose broader cultural significance is only beginning to become apparent.

2. Managed Workspaces

It is often said that stimulating small enterprises is a key to reviving the economy. Yet small firms frequently find it hard to find premises which are sufficiently small, flexible and cheap, and adequately serviced. The response of developers, funding institutions and local authorities to creating space for people to work in has generally been to build 'industrial estates', usually on isolated, out-of-town sites, or speculative office blocks in the city centre. In order to reduce management costs, only large self-contained units are provided. Small firms find the rents prohibitive; they also find such environments inflexible and unconducive to innovation.

The most successful new prototype to emerge from a community architecture approach to this problem has been the 'managed workspace' or 'working community', which gives small firms a creative and supportive environment in which to develop by providing them with a mechanism for collaborating. A vital factor is the sharing of support services which, individually, the firms could not afford. This allows the firms to concentrate on the production side of their business. In many respects managed workspaces are the business equivalent of community centres, but stimulating economic rather than social activity. They also depend on a similar combination of design and organizational skills to make them work.

Managed workspaces are set up in one of several ways. The most common is where a social entrepreneur with design, development and management skills brings together a group of small firms in a similar field looking for premises. A more unusual way is for the small firms to get together themselves to look for a building. Either way, a lease is taken on a redundant factory or warehouse and the space is divided up with movable partitions so that each firm has the space it needs and can afford – even if this is only a desk and a telephone. Common facilities – reception area, kitchen, meetings rooms, computer terminal, photo-copying, telex and fax facilities, exhibition space and occasionally a crèche, and so on – are provided and the cost shared between the occupants in proportion to the space they occupy. A limited company is set up to run the building and services, usually on a non-profit-making basis, with a paid part-time or full-time general manager and other staff as necessary. Extra facilities can be provided as and when members need and feel they can afford them. Firms can expand or contract easily by readjusting the partitions which separate them. If they leave, their successor will be selected by the owner or the remaining members. Compatible back-up businesses – secretarial, book-keeping, etc. – can easily be encouraged to move in since there is a ready market for their services.

The result is a self-generating and self-sustaining, supportive and in-novative environment for small enterprises. Firms have exactly the space they require at an economic rent and with security of tenure; capacity for growth or reduction at short notice while retaining continuity of address; better and more responsive services, equipment and machinery than they could provide by themselves; the possibility of cooperation and cross-fertilization with other firms to their mutual benefit; and the security of belonging to a big group, combined with independence and a separate identity.

Managed workspaces were pioneered in Britain by the architects Rock Townsend, who set up the first one, at 5 Dryden Street, Covent Garden, in central London, in 1972. It comprises some sixty-five firms in a five-storey building and there has always been a waiting list for places. Others followed and by 1986 there were over 250 in various parts of the country, and the concept had spread to other European countries as well. Initially most were set up by entrepreneurs – significantly not on the whole by property professionals, who almost invariably claimed the idea to be unviable – although local authorities have increasingly played a role.

There are many variations in size and organizational structure and each has chosen its own 'theme'. Whereas Dryden Street focused on firms in the design and construction industry, others have focused on arts and crafts, publishing or light industry. Initial difficulty in persuading property and financial institutions to accept such ventures as viable concerns has largely been overcome, although there is frequently resistance to accepting full user control, which means that the full benefits are not achieved, tending to lead to stagnation and loss of morale. Dryden Street remains one of the few truly user-managed workspaces where the member firms are automatically the shareholders and determine policy.

The impact on the local and national economy of managed workspaces has not been adequately studied, but by 1986 the National Managed Workspace Association (formed in 1984) felt able to state that 'it now seems to be generally accepted by politicians of all parties that managed workspaces make a valuable contribution in the start and growth of small businesses and in job creation'. Architect David Rock, who has been an active promoter of working communities since setting up and working at 5 Dryden Street, explains their success as follows:

> The sense of security that derives from belonging to a big group is a very real human need to most people: equally strong is the wish to be independent, to have a separate identity, and to be able to make one's own decisions. Being part of a managed workspace or community such as 5 Dryden Street creates the opportunity to fulfil both these fundamental human needs. The essential ingredient is that, at any time, people are free to participate or not, depending on individual requirement or morale. The individual identity, in what is virtually a mutual support group, gives confidence – in design, in dealing with clients and projects, in life and outlook generally. People feel stronger – and are stronger – because of the extra facilities and firms . . . In effect, the managed workspace provides the best aspects of large firms without the weakness of those organizations, while at the same time promoting the best of the small firm's vitality and personality without the weaknesses of small size.[29]

By 1987 the workplace concept had been developed by Rock Townsend and others to include 'pro-active' services – such as business and personnel management, advice and training; skill re-training; and marketing.

Although there are relevant historical precedents, the modern managed workspace differs from past collectives and cooperatives which were totally integrated and frequently failed because of conflicting views on what should be done. The key to setting one up and maintaining it is the blending of design, management and entrepreneurial skills with faith in user control, a combination unique to community architecture.

3. New Institutions

The breakthrough in the design of institutional buildings was made in Lambeth in south London. 'The Lambeth Community Care Centre is our hope for a National Health Service Mark 2, an important evolution of what is left of the civilized values which gave birth to the currently threatened post-war NHS Mark 1,' declared an editorial in the *Architects' Journal* when the building opened in 1985.

The Lambeth building is a combination of that fine inter-war libertarian tradition where local community-health pioneers, together with architects, transformed their separate, and then finally shared, visions of hope into reality. Their struggle to transform the former master–servant relationship between medical professional and patient, and between professional architect and user client, into one of shared knowledge and mutual dependence/independence, is the same vital struggle that personifies the Community Health and Community Architecture movements of the 1980s.[30]

The health service has suffered as much as other parts of the welfare state from a divorce between those who design and commission buildings and the public and staff who use them. Since the Second World War there has been a trend towards increasingly centralized and standardized facilities, giving neither architect nor client much room for manoeuvre and resulting in impersonal and alienating buildings. Growing dissatisfaction from consumers (and some doctors) about this and other aspects of the health service led to demands for more patient influence. In 1973, an Act of Parliament introduced community health councils, one for each district, drawn from local interests, elected and voluntary, to speak for the users.

The Lambeth Community Care project had its origins in community pressure arising from the closure of the local Lambeth hospital as part of a rationalization programme. Exhaustive consultation by the West Lambeth Community Health Council through public meetings, household surveys and discussions with councillors, tenants' associations, doctors, nurses and home helps identified the need for a new kind of facility to bridge the gap between hospital and home. People wanted a hospital that was friendly, small, within walking distance, which they still regarded as 'theirs'. After a long battle to secure funding, a detailed brief was drawn up for an 'intermediate care' centre and Edward Cullinan Architects were appointed to design a building.

Cullinan's were chosen, even though not on the NHS lists of approved architects, because of their reputation for making enjoyable and stimulating spaces and for exhaustive consultation with building users. In creating the Lambeth Community Care building the architects attended some three hundred meetings. Formally, the client was the West Lambeth Health Authority, but a special project team of fifteen was established, comprising doctors, representatives of the Community Health Council, nurses, therapists and a works officer and administrator. Working closely with this team, the architects prepared and rejected nine separate schemes before the final design was evolved.

The result was a new prototype building universally praised by patients, medical practitioners and design critics alike. It has twenty inpatient beds and thirty-five day-centre places, whose occupants are referred by GPs and have access to a wide range of services including physiotherapy, occupational therapy, speech therapy, chiropody, dentistry, dietary advice and hairdressing in addition to medical and nursing care. A more limited range of services is available without a doctor's referral, and the centre also has a role as an educational and social resource. After hours the building is used by tenants' associations and other local groups, including junior judo!

What makes the building unique, however, is the way these functions have been integrated and enhanced by the physical design; a design which could only have emerged from the creative tension between highly imaginative and talented architects and a dedicated user-client group, both with firm ideas of their own. 'The building is better than we could ever have imagined,' wrote the former secretary of the Community Health Council in *Building Design*.[31] And reviewing the building for the *Architects' Journal*, Jules Lubbock concluded:

Above all the building not only assists therapy but is therapeutic in its own right. Ward patients ask for the curtains to be drawn, look out at the trees and want to get out of bed. Its beauty and intricacy teases one to explore and encourages patients to walk and become independent . . . The building also supports patients. There is none of the depersonalization of waiting in dreary corridors. Waiting is a positive social activity. People talked of 'feeling safe here' . . . Terminal patients and their families feel suddenly free of tension, and don't feel 'put away' . . . Staff find the place makes stressful work more relaxing. They appreciate how different it is from most health buildings with their windowless rooms and fluorescent lights. They are not departmentalized – hence patients are not depersonalized – and they cannot hide behind their desks . . . And local people who supported the idea in those early public meetings feel that the building is theirs. They look after it, chase off vandals, drop in and visit the sick, bearing potted plants.[32]

For many years it was thought that community architecture had no relevance to specialist institutional buildings, since there was rarely an easily identifiable user group. By demonstrating the value of architects working closely with a team made up of representatives of the various interest groups, Lambeth Community Care Centre destroyed that myth and provided a blueprint which can be applied to factories, schools, churches and many other specialist facilities where there is inevitably a divorce between the paying client and the user client. In doing so it also provided a glimpse of the potential impact that community architecture could have on reforming the institutions themselves. Edward Cullinan told the *Guardian* on 29 April 1985:

They chose us as architects because we understood Parkinson's Fifth Law, which states that an institution begins to decline from the moment when it designs premises especially for itself. It happens because of the solidifying effect of brief writing – when you ask every person in every department to say what he wants and he looks at what he's got, puts walls around it, and adds 50 per cent. That way you don't get a more open and fluid situation, you get a larger and more closed situation, soldifying all the problems you had before.

The Lambeth Community Care Centre showed how to avoid that pitfall, a pitfall which has been a significant factor in the paralysis of Britain's institutions, itself a major contributor to economic decline.

Combining Forces

The three types of project outlined in this section – community projects, managed workspaces and new institutions – each offer new hope in their own fields. When combined, the possibilities become even more far-reaching. As experience has been gained and people have become more confident and imaginative, they have developed new types of mixed-use projects combining a range of activities and organizational models in one setting. In Glasgow, for instance, a collection of vacant historic buildings – formerly housing a fishmarket – facing demolition in 1979 had, by 1986, been transformed into a thriving new facility for the city, comprising managed workspaces, shopping, restaurants and entertainment. Initiated by ASSIST architects (who had earlier pioneered the community-controlled rehabilitation of tenements in the city) and a quantity surveyor, the £2·5m project was made possible by a complex partnership between the voluntary, public and private sectors, coordinated by a development trust formed by a local voluntary group. Similar projects are under way in several cities.

Because of rigid organizational structures and limited motivation, neither the public nor private sectors have found it easy to create mixed-use developments – where compatible and mutually supporting residential, business, social and recreational uses are combined in one building or on a single site. Rather, with a combination of zoning policies, by-laws, and lack of vision, local authorities and developers have steadily destroyed such places where they existed, leaving towns and cities lifeless and increasing people's isolation and dependence on expensive transport systems.

Community architecture has provided the impetus for reversing this trend. Barriers are being broken down and a framework is being provided developing buildings and environments which encourage and support rather than inhibit the evolution of the society which inhabits them.

Neighbourhoods

Pioneer efforts in different parts of this country and abroad have shown that the neighbourhoods which really last and give most satisfaction to people who live and work in them, are those which the residents themselves have helped to shape and manage.

Tony Gibson, Lightmore Project development officer in *Us Plus Them*, 1986

I believe there is nothing more important than weaving together our existing, much-eroded urban infrastructure. Participation of the public, working together with good designers, is one of the keys.

Richard Rogers, architect, *Building Design* 4 October 1985

The worth of viable neighbourhoods is something that most people sense when they live in one or seek community. Unfortunately it is not something most of us are highly conscious of and it is certainly not something government is conscious of. Enhancing this consciousness is the first step in ensuring the neighbourhood survival. People, planners and politicians must accept the neighbourhood as a thing of value, to be respected and protected . . . The forces ranged against the neighbourhoods are formidable: bureaucracy, politicians, local and national government, economics, apathy and parochialism. Nothing will be given freely . . . That is why neighbourhoods must mobilize individually and collectively to demand a devolution of power and a re-examination of the economic basis of land-use planning and development. Only by exercising self-determination can they gain self-determination. And only if they organize can they succeed.

Terry Christensen, *Neighbourhood Survival,* 1979

It is clear to almost all researchers in crime prevention that the issue hinges on the inability of communities to come together in joint action . . . Means must be found for bringing neighbours together, if only for the limited purpose of ensuring the survival of their collective milieu . . . Within the present atmosphere of pervasive crime and ineffectual authority, the only effective measure for assuring a safe living environment is community control . . . We see this as the only long-term measure of consequence in the battle for the maintenance of a sane urban society.

Oscar Newman, *Defensible Space: People and Design in the Violent City,* 1972

1. City Centres

During one weekend every summer, the streets of Covent Garden in central London are closed to traffic and fill up instead with musicians, dancers, clowns, jugglers, and thousands of happy people. Bunting and flags adorn the lamp-posts and for two days there are stalls, parades, games, competitions, parties, exhibitions and feasts – all organized voluntarily by people who live and work in the area. This is the Covent Garden Neighbourhood Festival which has, in the words of one of the festival programmes, become an annual 'opportunity to celebrate our community – to prove that people are more important than planners'.

Street festivals have become a symbol of a recent new determination by people to influence the future of their neighbourhoods. Dozens of new ones have been launched each year in villages, towns and cities throughout the country and, once established, they tend to grow each year, becoming more ambitious and involving more people. Providing a unique opportunity for people in a locality to discover each other's talents and work together, they are both a product of, and a catalyst for a new kind of community development.

The first festival in Covent Garden was in 1974 and marked a historic victory for a community that has become the trail-blazer for inner-city neighbourhood development. As a result of massive local and national public protest, brutal redevelopment plans for the area were thown out by the Secretary of State for the Environment, who ordered new plans to be drawn up 'with full public participation'. The outcome – fourteen years later – has become widely acclaimed as one of the most successful inner-city neighbourhoods in Britain for residents, workers and visitors alike. Covent Garden has become London's second most visited attraction for foreign tourists, and Londoners congregate there in their tens of thousands, attracted by a unique quality of street life and atmosphere. Yet few of those who now visit or work in the area realize that its success is solely due to a long-running and continuing struggle, in which many elements of the community architecture approach to neighbourhoods were pioneered. Nor that the official planning policy being pursued by the authorities was drawn up not by their own planners but by the local community.

The story starts at the beginning of the 1970s when Covent Garden was facing obliteration. The famous fruit and vegetable market was moving out and local government planners and developers attempted to seize the opportunity to restructure an area of some 100 acres, containing a mish-mash of Dickensian workshops, working-class housing, theatres, pubs, offices and warehousing. Well over two thirds of the buildings in the area were to be demolished and replaced by gargantuan office towers, high-rise flats, hotels, conference centres and commercial precincts. The intricate pattern of mixed uses was to be zoned into three tidy categories and the human-scale street pattern dating from the Middle Ages was to be swept away and, at massive expense, replaced by a new system of pedestrian walkways, urban motorways and underground access roads. The plans were typical for the period and similar to those which have destroyed the centres of most British cities in the 1960s and 70s.

A few isolated barren office blocks killing the streets around them stand in Covent Garden as a painful testimony of what that future would have been like. But, after massive public protest and a highly sophisticated community campaign, most of the planners' and developers' megalomaniac schemes were abandoned. Instead the area has evolved gradually with old buildings renovated for new uses and new buildings erected in harmony with the scale and character of those already existing. Despite land values being amongst the highest in the country (£7m per acre in 1987) the rich and balanced diversity of land use has been retained and enhanced so that it is possible for people to satisfy virtually all their basic needs – living, working, shopping, eating, entertainment and services – within a few blocks. The residential population has almost doubled from under 3,000 to over 5,400, and most of the new accommodation is for rent at low cost, making it available to people on a range of incomes and thereby maintaining a balanced community. Above all the streets and public squares have been brought back to life by pedestrianization and

99

the encouragement of pavement cafés and street artists and musicians. It is one of the few places in Britain where it is possible – and pleasurable – to eat breakfast at an outside pavement café on a mild day in midwinter.

The renaissance of the Covent Garden neighbourhood is due to the determination and skill of a few members of the local community, a handful of dedicated architects and planners who worked with them consistently over a number of years, and, eventually, a sympathetic local authority prepared to listen to them and undertake new ventures. Between them they succeeded in subduing the forces which normally destroy such neighbourhoods and establishing a system of neighbour-hood government – albeit *ad hoc* – which has provided a means for many people who lived and worked in the area to take initiative and exert some influence over the area's development. The details of how this was achieved have already been the subject of two books (by Anson and Christensen – see Bibliography). But the three essential organizational components of relevance to others treading the same path have been a community association; a neighbourhood forum; and a locally based local-authority team.

Community association

The Covent Garden Community Association (CGCA) has been the spearhead. Set up at a public meeting in 1971 it has played – and continues to play – a key role as a single-minded pressure group. It has alerted the public to proposed developments which are seen as threat-ening the community and campaigned against them. It has developed its own 'alternative' community plan which was eventually adopted by the authorities. And it has initiated and organized several practical pro-jects: a community social centre in a converted warehouse basement; several temporary gardens on derelict sites; conversion of a former market building as the country's first community-controlled sports hall; the rehabilitation of shops and housing for some sixty people; a housing cooperative; and the annual street festival. Compared with other com-munity associations, the CGCA has been fortunate by virtue of its central London location in attracting a number of talented individuals. But of paramount importance has been the close involvement of professionals – most notably architect Jim Monahan – who have provided the association with the unique capability to challenge the authorities and developers on their own terms, and to develop and implement practical and viable alternatives.

Elected forum

In 1974, the association was instrumental in establishing the country's first non-statutory neighbourhood council, called the Covent Garden Forum. It comprises thirty specially elected representatives drawn from the different sections of the community – including residential, business, churches, theatres and landowners. Although lacking any statutory powers, the forum has in practice wielded some influence in the area's development by virtue of being clearly seen as democratically representative. Significantly, however, perhaps because it has no statutory powers, its existence has not reduced the need for the pressure group tactics of the community association, many of whose members are hostile to the forum, believing it to be impotent in the face of the commercial pressures facing the area.

Local-authority area team

The third component has been the special area team established by the Greater London Council in offices in the centre of the area, and its commitment to work with the Covent Garden Forum and the CGCA. Without the sensitive use of statutory financial and planning powers and locally based monitoring of the area, much of the community effort would have been in vain. Working closely with the forum (and sometimes with the CGCA), the authorities have made an essential contribution by developing a statutory plan which endorsed local views; investing in land, specific projects and environmental improvements; protecting essential traders; imposing restrictive covenants to maintain low rent levels in its own property; and by sensitive control of planning permissions.

Although there have been many conflicts over specific issues, between them these organizations have provided a framework for balancing the myriad interests in the area and allowing all parties some influence in the area's development. They have also provided a climate in which other enterprising joint initiatives could flourish, allowing the community to initiate and implement its own development. For instance, in 1987 the £7.6m Jubilee Hall development scheme was completed by a consortium formed by the CGCA, a market traders' association, a community-run recreation centre and the community-based Soho Housing Association. The consortium formed a partnership with the Speyhawk property company and employed the Covent Garden Housing Project – established by Jim Monahan and his partner Martin Dyke-Combes – as architects. Instead of the standard office block formerly planned for the site, the

Jubilee Hall development comprises an arcaded market, restaurants and shopping at ground-floor level, a community sports hall at first-floor level, and twenty-eight fair-rent flats and 13,000 square feet of offices above. As well as being one of the most popular, attractive and sympathetic new buildings in the area, it is a unique mixed-use development of a kind not yet achieved by local authorities or a conventional commercial developer.

In 1976 Jim Monahan wrote: 'Throughout the struggle in Covent Garden it has emerged that the local community often knows more about the area and what is possible than those persons who are paid to know and that, given the chance and the funding, they could manage the future of the area much more efficiently and effectively than the local authorities.'[33] The truth of this statement has now become self-evident, although unfortunately the story has not yet ended. At the time of writing, Covent Garden is once again under threat following the abolition of the Greater London Council and a government proposal to change planning legislation, making it more difficult to maintain diversity of uses in areas with high land values. Over a million square feet of offices have been approved in the last year and a great deal more is in the pipeline. The area's popularity may be short-lived. Jim Monahan comments:

> The reason why this area is being ripped apart again is because there has been no real political transfer of power to the locality. The same forces that prompted the 1971 proposals have merely changed their spots and are doing exactly the same again. While Covent Garden might be seen as a success in some quarters . . . it also could be described as a very good example of how limited and transient community-inspired development becomes if it is not welded to legal and political control.[34]

2. Small Provincial Towns

The threat to central city neighbourhoods like Covent Garden comes mainly from increasing land values and commercial exploitation. In other areas the threat comes from inertia and stagnation. One such place was the small town of Wirksworth in Derbyshire, until a unique regeneration project based on the maximum involvement of local people turned it into a national regeneration showpiece.

With the demise of the quarrying industry on which the town formerly depended, Wirksworth, by the mid seventies, appeared to have little future. Unemployment was increasing amongst the population of 6,000 and over 50 per cent of those with jobs had to commute to neighbouring towns. Many buildings were empty and falling into disrepair and much of the housing stock was substandard. Shopping and recreational opportunities were poor. Residents complained about uncollected litter, dangerous traffic and vandalized public conveniences. They found the town shabby and depressing. Few young people stayed once they left school. In short, the town was in a state of decline and there was a degree of social deprivation arising from substandard living conditions, low wage levels and a general lack of job opportunities.

Eight years later the town had been transformed. Derelict buildings had been restored, the environment had been cleaned up, shopping had been improved, a range of new facilities and new industries had been set up and there was a range of new recreational and tourist amenities too. Several hundred new jobs had been created and over £1m had been spent on construction alone, from the public purse, from charitable sources and from the private sector. Above all there was a new atmosphere of confidence and pride amongst the citizens. In recognition of the achievements, the regeneration project received the only Europa Nostra Award given to the United Kingdom in 1982. The award citation referred to: 'The exemplary regeneration of a small country town through a broad range of self-help and innovative features which could be applied to other towns.' In a speech to the Institute of Directors in 1985 Prince Charles described the project as 'brilliantly imaginative'. It also received the 1984 Silver Jubilee Award for Planning Achievement from the Royal Town Planning Institute.

How did it work? What was it that had given the town what the *Reader's Digest* described as 'the kiss of life'? The turning-point for Wirksworth was 28 November 1978, when a packed town meeting unanimously supported proposals by the Civic Trust to set up a three-year experimental regeneration project. In contrast with most urban regeneration projects with their multi-million pound budgets, the 'Wirksworth Project', as it became known, was very modest. The budget was a mere £25,000 per year. What made it succeed was the special approach adopted. The budget was devoted entirely to employing and servicing a professional team to work in the town acting as catalysts and enablers, providing stimulus, guidance and encouragement. Architect Gordon Michell, who led the team, describes it as a 'hands-off technique'. 'The project itself didn't actually *do* anything at all apart from print leaflets. The action was always done by others. Yet absolutely nothing would have changed had it not been for the project.'

Community Architecture

The regeneration of Wirksworth was the product of many varied initiatives taken simultaneously by many organizations and individuals.
This occurred both during the three-year Civic Trust Project and afterwards when the project was adopted by the town council with support
from the district and county councils. The county council seconded its
conservation officer, Barry Joyce, to spend half his time in the town,
taking over from Gordon Michell as the project leader. Some of the key
elements illustrating the project team's role as catalyst are listed below:

Project base

The team's first act was to establish a project office in a converted stables.
As well as providing a working office for the team, it also became a
community focal point for the project. 'Surgeries' were held at which
townfolk's individual problems – technical, procedural and financial –
were sorted out by team members. Local groups held meetings there free
of charge. Small exhibitions were mounted and it provided a base for
officers from the county and district councils.

Coordination and technical aid

Discussions were held between the team and all organizations likely to
play a role, both from within the town and elsewhere. These included the
town, district and county councils, industrialists, the Chamber of
Commerce, the churches, schools and voluntary organizations such as
the Wirksworth Ladies' Group and the Rotary Club. All these organizations
were encouraged to contribute in any way they could and were given
advice on how. The formation of new voluntary organizations to tackle
specific tasks not covered by others was encouraged.

Communicating

A community information centre, which contained material on the town
and its regeneration, was created by extending the public library with
the help of a charitable donation. A regular news sheet *Wirksworth Progress
– the Wirksworth Project Newsletter* was initially published by the team to
keep people informed and generate enthusiasm. It was posted through
every letterbox by volunteers from the Civic Trust and a local school.
Later, the local newspaper was persuaded to offer half a page per month
to the project's news. Then, with assistance from the community education council, a bi-monthly community newspaper was started with a
voluntary editorial staff.

△ 1

▽ 2

The beginnings of community architecture in Britain. Byker in Newcastle
1–2. In 1968, architect Ralph Erskine abandons the conventional arm's-length
approach, sets a site office in a disused funeral parlour (1) and involves the residents
of a slum district in the design of their new homes (2). Nineteen years later – in
1987 – Erskine became the first community architect to receive the Royal Gold Medal
for Architecture

△ 3

▽ 4

The birthplace of the community architect movement. Black Road, Macclesfield
3–4. In the early seventies, architect Rod Hackney (left in 3, centre in 4) helps residents in the street where he lives save their homes from demolition by the council and restore them through mutual aid and self-help (3) to their individual requirements
5. A visit by the Prince of Wales in 1985 focuses public attention on the scheme and on Rod Hackney, who was elected President of the Royal Institute of British Architects after a fierce internal battle less than two years later

△ 6

▽ 7

A completely new approach to public-sector housing rehabilitation. Lea View House, London

6–9. Architects Hunt Thompson Associates, employed as consultants by Hackney Council in the early eighties, set up a site office (6), involve residents in all aspects of the design and implementation – including a planting weekend (7) – and evolve a scheme which not only gives the buildings a facelift (8) but also rejuvenates the community spirit

The nearby Wigan estate (9, top right), rehabilitated conventionally for the same cost, without involving residents, becomes a slum again within a year of completion because none of the underlying organizational and design problems are dealt with

8

10

The breakthrough in the design of new publicly funded housing: cooperatives in Liverpool
10. Members of Liverpool's Hesketh Street Housing Cooperative proudly stand alongside their architects (Innes Wilkin Ainsley Gommon – front right) in front of the houses they have planned, designed and now manage, 1984

△ 11

▽ 12

More scope for self-build – timber-frame houses
11–12. Residents on Lewisham Council's housing waiting list build new homes for themselves using a flexible and economical timber-frame design by architect Walter Segal, 1980

△ 13

▽ 14

A new generation of community projects conceived, designed, part-built and managed by the users with professional assistance
13–14. Parents and toddlers celebrate the first site visit with their architects (Community Land Use) to the Poplar Play Centre for under-fives in east London in 1985 – and using the finished product in 1987
15. 'The Snake' play structure at Stonebridge Park, east London, designed by Free Form Arts Trust with local children, who did the mosaic work themselves, 1985
16. Elderly residents in the village of Ashill, East Anglia, in front of the stone hut which they converted into a 'social meeting point' and branch surgery, 1986

△ 15

▽ 16

△ 17

Revolution in health care
17–18. Lambeth Community Care Centre in south London and the team of architects (from Edward Cullinan Architects), doctors, nurses, administrators and members of the Community Health Council who participated in its design, 1985

▽ **18**

△ **19**

▽ **20**

Participatory planning
19. Planning Aid workers from the Town and Country Planning Association use a flexible cardboard model to help residents of King's Cross, London, plan leisure and recreation facilities on a derelict site which became known as the Calthorpe Project, 1982
20. Starting work on Lightmoor, a pioneering new community in Shropshire being created on 22 acres of land by prospective residents themselves with help from the Town and Country Planning Association, 1987

PLANNING FOR REAL

Taking on the city

21. Residents of Swindon plan a future for their town using a large 'Planning for Real' model, where buildings and other elements can be moved around, 1985

22. Covent Garden, London, the closest yet to an inner-city neighbourhood shaped by its people. Street artists and pavement cafés regain streets from traffic. New buildings like the Jubilee Hall in the centre background (p. 101) have been designed to fit in and enhance the streetscape, 1987

22

23

Community architecture overseas
23. The controversial '*zone sociale*' of the Belgian Catholic University of Louvain Medical School designed by architect Lucien Kroll and students in the early seventies. Dubbed 'anarchist architecture' by the university administration, which disliked it and fired Kroll when the students were on holiday, the building contains a vibrant mix of living spaces, shops, offices, restaurants, theatres, workshops, infant schools and cafés

24. A neighbourhood and workshop in Otranto, Italy, in 1979, organized by architect Renzo Piano to encourage local involvement in the design and execution of low-key restructuring projects in the town

25. Full-scale models in an exhibition in Copenhagen in 1987 which can be used to try out innovative designs for housing – one of the most effective new tools for design participation

26. Environmental education at the Nottingdale Urban Studies Centre, London, 1986 – the key to a better built environment in the future

27. A cartoonist's view. 1985

△ 26

▽ 27

Feasibility studies

Expert consultants were appointed by the team to examine specific problems and their solution. For instance, a firm of landscape architects was commissioned to examine the potential for improving the look of the town and based on this work the Civic Trust produced a leaflet 'How Wirksworth Looks', emphasizing the opportunities for improvement. A research consultant was commissioned to carry out a survey of the attitudes and needs of the townspeople. Based on a series of in-depth discussion groups it provided an invaluable starting-point and was widely circulated. Several architectural practices were commissioned to study the potential for refurbishing particular derelict buildings for new uses and their findings were used by the team to attract builders and developers.

Heritage

Several initiatives were taken to raise awareness of the town's heritage, its special qualities and the potential for tourism. A set of postcards of picturesque views, a wall poster with pen and ink drawings by a draughtswoman in the planning department and a 'Town Trail' with two guided walks were published by the Civic Trust for sale in local shops. An independent study into the feasibility of establishing a heritage centre was commissioned from the Centre for Environmental Interpretation at Manchester Polytechnic. Funding for the study came from many quarters including a bank, a building society, the English Tourist Board and local businesses. The study led to the Civic Trust's attracting further funding from a wide variety of public, private and charitable sources, establishing a special limited company, and creating a heritage centre in a redundant mill. A Stone Centre Study Group was established by the project team, drawing together a wide range of interested parties and creating a National Stone Centre in the town, capitalizing on the former importance of quarrying in the area.

Environmental projects

Practical projects were undertaken by various agencies to improve the appearance of the town: the local Civic Society undertook the cleaning and restoration of a monument, repair of the church gates, the repair and decoration of a bus shelter, the planting of dozens of trees and shrubs, and the clearing and reinstatement of footpaths leading into the surrounding countryside. The town council was encouraged to set up a new Environmental Care Committee which initiated a number of projects, including the resurfacing of pavements and the rationalization of street signs, in conjunction with the statutory undertakers, and the launching of a 'Clean Up Wirksworth Campaign' in conjunction with schools, voluntary groups and businesses; each agreed to adopt certain areas of the town and keep them clean and free of litter. Public competitions were organized by the team to stimulate ideas for difficult sites.

Children

Schools were encouraged by the team to develop educational programmes relating to the local environment, many with a practical outcome. To help with this a Wirksworth Heritage Education Group was set up. It was sponsored by the local education authority, and included the heads and staff of the four Wirksworth schools. Groups from the two infants schools visited and studied the market and the fire-station. One class established a garden in the school grounds. A group of sixth-formers carried out a survey of the town's clubs and societies, and published their results in the form of a town guide. Another school mounted proposals for re-designing and equipping a vandalized playground at the town library. A local-studies centre for second-year pupils was established in one school. Based on all this activity, an exhibition 'Our Town, Our Schools' was mounted in the parish church, attracting a stream of visitors, and measures were taken for turning one of the schools into a 'community school', sharing its facilities with the townspeople.

Restoring property

Property owners were helped by the team to restore and improve their buildings, with advice on obtaining grants and on design and technical matters. Part of the town had already been declared a General Improvement Area, enabling owners to secure grants for a proportion of the work. The existence of the project increased people's awareness of what could be done and increased the uptake of grants. Additional grant sources were made available by setting up a special Town Scheme funded jointly by county, district and central government. Also, the town's Conservation Area was extended, making a greater number of buildings eligible for grant funding. Building societies and banks were persuaded to make mortgages and loans available for projects which would not normally be eligible. Once grant-aided schemes were under way, other property owners not eligible for grants began to improve their property, stimulated into action by the activity around them. A schedule of particularly important 'buildings at risk' was compiled by the team to focus attention on them. Responsibility for updating the schedule was later taken over by the Derbyshire Historic Buildings Trust, which secured funding for setting up a revolving fund for safeguarding some of the most threatened. A materials bank was started for recycling building materials.

Attracting employment

Discussions between the team, the Chamber of Commerce, the government's development agency (COSIRA) and local firms led to several initiatives to increase job opportunities. COSIRA developed a scheme of small factory units on the edge of the town. A managed workspace scheme for small firms was established by the Derbyshire Historic Buildings Trust. A 'surgery' for small businesses was held. Several new firms have been attracted to the town.

Shopping

A 'Support Your Local' shop campaign was started through the project's newsletter. Discussions between the team, the Chamber of Commerce and local shopkeepers led to improved opening hours, redecoration and the attraction of new complementary shops. Gaps in the market were identified by the team and entrepreneurs willing to fill them identified and encouraged. Traders were asssisted with business advice from the Derbyshire Business Venture. The Women's Institute was encouraged to undertake a shopping-basket survey, which demonstrated that once travel costs were taken into account, it was cheaper to buy basic groceries in Wirksworth than in superstores elsewhere.

Taken in isolation, none of these initiatives would have had much effect. But as a package they created a snowball effect. Each new initiative (not of course taken in the order listed above) strengthened the one before it and provided the starting-point for the next one. Once under way, regeneration became self-sustaining. Not only was the town improved physically but the process by which it was improved strengthened the hand and resolve of all kinds of people and agencies. The architectural benefits were a by-product of analysing and improving the whole social and economic structure of the community, rather than the result of the normal facelift approach.

City Building

Covent Garden and Wirksworth are poles apart in most respects, Covent Garden being a neighbourhood under pressure in the heart of one of the world's most prosperous capital cities, and Wirksworth a small country town. Yet their rejuvenation has four common elements which characterize the community architecture approach to neighbourhoods and make it radically different from conventional town planning and urban management:

1. *All sections of the community are positively encouraged to be actively involved in the improvement of the environment.* People are not simply 'consulted' in the abstract. Instead they are encouraged – individually and through a variety of specifically focused representative and entrepreneurial mechanisms – both to undertake specific projects relating to their own immediate needs and to take responsibility collectively for analysing and devising solutions to the problems facing the neighbourhood as a whole.
2. *Partnerships are formed between the public, private and voluntary sectors.* Instead of competing with each other and jealously guarding their own spheres of influence, the public, private and voluntary sectors recognize their interdependence and dovetail their activities. Each undertakes the tasks to which it is best suited. New structures of government emerge tailored to the needs of each neighbourhood.
3. *Professionals act as catalysts, providing vision, advice and coordination.* Instead of simply being advocates for one sector of the community and attempting to impose solutions on their behalf, professionals – or at least some professionals – act as independent enabling agents. They stimulate others to take action, coordinate the aims of the various parties and take innovative initiatives to make things happen. Instead of remaining aloof they become vital participants in their own right and, hopefully, trusted members of the community, just like local teachers or doctors. A variety of professional skills is harnessed in recognition of the complexities of neighbourhoods and the wide range of skills needed to make them work. Participation of residents is the central theme; the support of professionals gives their participation power.
4. *Neighbourhood development is treated both incrementally and comprehensively.* Instead of being seen either as a series of unrelated initiatives or as the product of a grand masterplan, neighbourhood

planning and construction is guided by a process which allows the whole to emerge gradually from specific local projects. At the same time a mechanism is established for constantly monitoring and coordinating these projects, and for identifying and filling in the gaps. The experience of each project provides lessons for the next.

This formula has been explored in neighbourhoods throughout the country, albeit with variations in the methods employed, the organizations involved and the nature of the catalysts. Success has generally been limited, due to the difficulty of simultaneously securing the necessary commitment from the public, private and voluntary sectors and the lack of expertise where it is needed. Progress has also been hindered by bureaucratic red tape and outdated and irrelevant party political dogma. The pioneers in Covent Garden managed to break through by sheer persistence over many years and the skilful exploitation of the neighbourhood's prime location. Wirksworth's unique success was largely due to securing – for the first time – commitment to the project from all significant parties.

Spirited attempts have also been made to apply the formula to the creation of new settlements and major redevelopment schemes but, with a handful of exceptions (such as the Town and Country Planning Association's Lightmoor Project in Shropshire, which started on site in 1986 and won the top award in the 1987 *Times*/RIBA Community Enterprise Award Scheme), they have mostly failed to get off the ground. None have reached the stage where the results can be properly assessed.

Cities for the Twenty-first Century

The importance of neighbourhoods is slowly being rediscovered. Modern communications and transport systems have not reduced their relevance as much as it was once assumed. There is increasing understanding that the quality of life is immeasurably improved by neighbourhoods which function properly – where the streets are safe for women and children to walk alone, where convenient shopping and social facilities are near at hand, where people know their neighbours, where there is a sense of community and mutual support, and so on. Yet there is great confusion over the concepts of 'community' and 'neighbourhood' and little understanding about what makes them tick.

Neighbourhoods are extremely complex organisms, comprising

networks of large numbers of different people and different private organizations with vastly different ideas and purposes. The conventional development industry and systems of government are not geared to deal with this complexity and indeed hardly acknowledge the concept of neighbourhoods at all. In 1961, the architect John Habraken made the following observation:

> The conditions which are most favourable for the formation of communities – communities, that is, which are more than a collection of families or individuals – are richly worth studying. We are probably quite capable at the moment of stocking an aquarium in such a way as to create a biological equilibrium, but we have hardly begun to inquire what conditions are necessary for the creation of towns or districts in which *social harmony* may develop. We have not progressed beyond realizing vaguely that this must be a question of organization.[35]

Little has changed on the ground in the intervening quarter of a century. But a growing tide of expert knowledge and grass-roots instinct has built up a powerful case for radical change in the way we manage our neighbourhoods. Practical progress has been frustrated because, as architects Rock Townsend commented in their RIBA exhibition 'Making Things Happen' in 1987, 'The would-be regenerator faces a no man's land of apathy, demoralization, ignorance of what real change is really possible and uncertainty about how it can happen.'

The community architecture pioneers have succeeded in breaking through the vicious circle and have created important precedents for others to develop and follow. The successes in Covent Garden and Wirksworth demonstrate that, despite the odds, regeneration and enhancement are possible nearly everywhere. It simply needs communities willing to get things started, experts willing and able to help them and, above all, a development process which harnesses and builds on the complexity of neighbourhoods instead of ignoring it.

The implications of pursuing the community architecture approach to neighbourhoods are far-reaching. Where communities begin to take control of their own destiny in partnership with professionals, they tend to create *complete* neighbourhoods, containing all the facilities necessary for daily life within walking distance and reducing the dependency on the private car. The special characteristics of each place and its people tend to be reinforced rather than subdued. The emphasis tends to be on human-scale streets and public spaces. Neighbourhoods tend to become self-sustaining and increasingly self-sufficient. A new future is posited for urban society. As Pier-Luigi Cervalleti, architect and chief planner for

Bologna, wrote in 1984: 'Through the involvement of the citizenry, through public participation, it is possible to set in motion the revolutionary project – not revolutionary in the technical and methodological sense, but in the sense of a challenge to all those forces that would destroy urban civilization . . . The people understand that only through the reconquest of space can they transform quantity into quality, the quantity of urban activity into the quality of life.'[36]

The pioneering projects described in this chapter – in housing; social, business and institutional facilities: and neighbourhoods – provide between them a powerful armoury for improving dramatically the prospects for our villages, town and cities, and all who live and work in them. Yet it is still early days. Those involved have all had to fight every inch of the way to achieve their objectives and in the heat of battle many corners have had to be cut. Those who follow will have more scope to explore the creative potential of the precedents established, drawing on a wealth of talent – of both laymen and professionals – which has hitherto had no outlet for expression. The real adventure of community architecture is only just beginning.

Chapter 5

Why Community Architecture Works
The Natural Laws Governing the Relationship between Human Beings and the Built Environment

When dwellers control the major decisions and are free to make their own contribution to the design, construction or management of their housing, both the process and the environment produced stimulate individual and social well-being. When people have no control over, nor responsibility for, key decisions in the housing process, on the other hand, dwelling environments may instead become a barrier to personal fulfilment and a burden on the economy.
    John F. C. Turner, *Freedom to Build*, 1972

They have made themselves solid in the world. They have shaped the world as they have shaped themselves. And they live now in the world they have created for themselves – changed, transformed, opened, free in their glory, stamping their feet, watching the water trickle through the common land, looking after their neighbours' children, waiting now to help friends take part in the same kind of process – on this piece of land or in another corner of town. They have become powerful, and are powerful, in a way that takes the breath away. They, they themselves, have created their own lives, not in that half-conscious underground, interior way that we all do, but manifestly, out there on their own land. They are alive. They breathe the breath of their own house.
    Christopher Alexander, on the construction of five houses in northern Mexico, *The Production of Houses*, 1982

While architects plan physical structures which communities use, it is the inhabitants who build communities.
    Ralph Erskine, architect, in *The Scope of Social Architecture*, edited by Richard Hatch, 1984

> I hear and I forget
> I see and I remember
> I do and I understand.
>   Chinese proverb

Why is it that community architecture works? What is it that enables community architecture to succeed where conventional approaches have so often failed? The success stories outlined in the last chapter are extremely varied, both in the problems tackled and the means used to achieve socially desirable and environmentally effective results; but they have three fundamental characteristics in common:

1. *People willingly take responsibility for their environment and participate both individually and collectively in its creation and management;*
2. *A creative working partnership is established with specialists from one or more disciplines;*
3. *All aspects of people's environmental needs are considered simultaneously and on a continuing evolutionary basis.*

When these three principles are applied together it makes human settlements more successful. They could perhaps be called 'the Laws of Community Architecture'. They are not, of course, a new discovery – rather a rediscovery of essential truths. They have been understood at various stages of history, if often instinctively, which is why so many historic settlements have a sense of harmony and well-being absent from so much of the recently created environment. They are also applied, mostly, subconsciously, in many squatting communities and other places (such as Third World cities) which are unaffected by the official system of planning and development controls. Since the industrial revolution they have generally been lost or ignored because of the intervention of third parties – the professions, bureaucracies, speculators – in the planning, development and construction process. Only recently have they been rather slowly, and painfully, rediscovered. They can now be explicitly stated.

The effect of applying these laws is summarized on p. 24–5, in the table comparing conventional and community architecture. The rest of this chapter explains the logic behind them and how they derive from human nature, the natural characteristics of the built environment and the relationship between the two.

1. User Participation in the Environment

There are two main reasons why people should be able to participate in the creation and management of their environment.

(i) *Creating an environment that fulfils the needs of the user*

The first reason is pragmatic. It improves decision-making. Whether dealing with a house or a city, the built environment is incredibly complicated. It is made up of thousands of physical objects with varying strengths and lifespans. The way in which these are put together determines the spaces which people inhabit. Yet different people use even almost identical spaces differently, as can be seen in the varied arrangements inside flats in a mass housing project, for instance. And the way people use spaces changes constantly according to their needs, as better ways of arranging things are devised and as lifestyles and social relationships change. To create and manage the built environment successfully demands an intricate knowledge and understanding both of how its physical components relate together *and* of how the end result will relate to the *specific* people who inhabit them. Every part of the built environment is essentially unique and specific to location.

Of course, there are rules of thumb – based on experience – which tell us that some arrangements *generally* work better than others. For example, having the kitchen next to the dining-room is *generally* better than having it at the opposite end of the house. Houses with gardens on the ground are *generally* more popular than flats in tower blocks, especially for families with young children. Locating shops together in one street or square is *generally* better than having them scattered all over the neighbourhood.

Such rules of thumb can be very useful. Indeed, many are enshrined in planning legislation. But they should only be used as a framework for action, never as blueprints. Examples of the inflexible application of such rules may be seen across the world, especially in the system-built housing of the 1960s and early 1970s. They will always need modifying to fit the unique attributes of each location and its inhabitants. They are part of a process, never an edict. And there will always be exceptions. In certain places, and for certain people, tower blocks will prove to be more popular than houses with gardens on the ground, for instance. Rules of thumb can never be a substitute for a detailed understanding of each place and its inhabitants.

Environmental designers and managers – who include architects, planners, landscape architects, developers, housing managers, etc. – can gain valuable insights by analysing statistics, conducting surveys and simply observing. But based on this alone, their perception is bound to be limited. It takes years to understand the qualities of a particular environment and what makes it tick – how people use it in different ways, their lifestyles and relationships. And the only people who have that 'expert' knowledge are the inhabitants – the 'users'. They are the real experts (or 'inperts' as Tony Gibson has dubbed them). Unless their knowledge and wisdom is tapped, any intervention is likely to be insensitive and unrelated to the needs and aspirations of the people it is intended to serve.

In short, the participation of 'users' is essential in order to gain the necessary knowledge to ensure that any additions or improvements to their environment will attain the intended objectives in the most efficient way.

(ii) *Creating a strong, participating community*

The second reason for participation is the positive effect it has on the participants themselves and on the strength and vitality of society. As Richard Hatch wrote in a paper to the Second International Design Participation Conference in 1985:

> The paramount purpose of participation is not good buildings, but good citizens in a good society. Participation is the means, and the richer the experience – the more aspects of the total architectural project opened to involvement, the higher the degree of participant control, the more comprehensive the education that surrounds participation – the greater the impact on alienation will be and the greater the recovery towards health.[37]

Creating one's own home and immediate surroundings makes one more confident and self-fulfilled. It helps to satisfy the fundamental human need to be in control over one's own environment. Helping to shape one's neighbourhood with other members of it improves people's ability to work together and strengthens the community. Involvement leads to understanding, which in turn leads to the ability to act, both individually and collectively.

The most obvious effect is that people take a pride in their surroundings. Environments are cared for and looked after, and respond to people's needs and aspirations. Less immediately obvious are the new skills and abilities learned by people, which can lead to personal fulfilment, and self-sustaining, creative communities in harmony with their surroundings and even new long-term, socially useful employment.

The results of users not participating in the creation and management of their environment can be seen everywhere. Where it has been left purely to the 'experts', the results have often been economically wasteful and socially inept, sometimes disastrous. The grand objectives and visions have rarely been attained, even where money has been no object. The more remote the process from the end-users and the lower the budgets, the less successful the top-down approach has been.

Ultimately, people should learn to take responsibility for their environment just as they do for their health. Environmental experts, just like doctors in the health service, have a vital role, but cannot exercise it effectively unless the patient willingly takes responsibility and participates.

The importance of people participating in the creation and management of their environment is widely recognized. The demand for it has been the central cry of hundreds of thousands of community organizations all over the world for many years. The principle (but not the practice) of it has been enshrined in planning legislation in many parts of the developed world. Its importance is continually being stressed by academic, political and church leaders.

Yet the potential has seldom been realized because of an unwillingness to devolve enough power to the participants. Early official attempts at public participation did not allow people to make a real contribution; this led some officials and professionals to conclude that it is an expensive waste of time. Participation without power is a frustrating and empty process. Only when people are given real responsibility do they respond most effectively. Only if their input is taken seriously will they take the trouble to understand the issues and examine the options available thoroughly. Only then does participation realize its full potential as a positive, creative force.

Citizen participation works at various levels, likened by American sociologist, Sherry Arnstein, to a ladder with eight rungs:

Citizen control

Delegated power

Partnership

Placation

Consultation

Informing

Therapy

Manipulation

The higher up the ladder one gets the more power is given to the user and the more fruitful the outcome is likely to be. There is also a threshold of involvement below which the exercise is likely to be counterproductive. Precisely where the threshold lies depends on the nature of the project. Evidence suggests that it is only at the top two or three rungs of the ladder – where some form of commitment or contractual relationship exists to ensure accountability of professionals to users – that real benefits come about. So far in Britain, only a handful of projects – like some of those described in Chapter 4 – have ever attained this level. Climbing the ladder of citizen participation has not been easy; but few of those who have experienced it are likely to settle for anything less again.

2. The Creative Working Partnership

A common misconception about user-participation is that it somehow compromises or rejects professional expertise. On the contrary – specialist knowledge and expertise are essential, and the service needed is, if anything, more 'professional' than it would be conventionally.

The built environment is so complex that few of us will ever be able to comprehend more than a small part of it. The building of an efficient kitchen, for instance, demands a working knowledge of cooking, interior design, plumbing, electricity, gas, joinery and the acquiring of materials and appliances. Building a housing estate must be at least ten times as complex – a neighbourhood, perhaps one hundred times – a city, perhaps a thousand times.

To create and manage the built environment successfully demands a vast range of specialist skills – in design, planning, construction, landscaping, transport management, administration, communication, politics, history, art, law, health and research – to name but a few. The issue is not whether specialist expertise is necessary, but rather how it is brought to bear on any particular problem. Since the industrial revolution specialists have become increasingly introverted, each developing their own objectives, ideologies, jargon and self-serving professional institutions. Simultaneously, ever-multiplying tiers of bureaucrats, controls and regulations have been introduced by governments to mediate between the experts and the consumers. Taken in isolation the reasons for both may seem entirely logical. But the machine has got out of control. And the cumulative effect is a cumbersome professional environment industry divorced from people's needs and numbingly frustrating for those who have to work in it. The mechanism has to be short-circuited.

What is needed is *a close and creative alliance between experts and users.* People should, individually and collectively, have direct access to the right environmental experts as and when they need them, just as they do to medical experts in the National Health Service and to lawyers in the

Legal Aid system. Furthermore, a *working relationship* must be developed between them.

Whether the task is to build a house extension, solve a neighbourhood's traffic problems, or build a community centre, the optimum solution will only emerge from a *creative dialogue* between all sections of the community affected and those with expertise. Experts have to tap the knowledge of the people they are working for and gain an empathy with them. Users need to gain a better understanding of the environmental and technical issues involved, and the options that are available to them.

Establishing a creative working relationship between users and experts can be done in many ways. But experience shows that it is easier if the experts are directly accountable to the users – even if the users are not paying the fees. And, to create the necessary trust and commitment there must be a proper contractual relationship between the parties. It is also essential that the experts work – and preferably live – in the communities for which they are working. Having experts based locally makes it easier for people to get access to them and develop a relationship with them. For the experts, being on the spot is the best way – and often the only way – to get in tune with the environment and the people they are working with. As Alison Ravetz says, the environment is something to work *in*, not *on*. There is no substitute for actually being in a place; observing, listening, sensing, feeling, moving forward step by step, and being accessible at all times to the users.

3. An Evolutionary Approach

In an attempt to deal with the complexities of the modern built environment, rigid compartmentalized hierarchies have been established by governments and the development industry. A multitude of different specialists, landowners and building owners and agencies are responsible for different aspects and parts of it. Coordination is rarely adequate. So areas of vital concern to users end up as the responsibility of nobody at all.

Hierarchies cannot deal effectively with complexity, so they oversimplify their response. As a result, beautiful new buildings may be vandalized, because the designers failed to communicate with those who end up managing and maintaining them; heating systems sometimes have to be switched off because those who specified them did not understand the budget limitations of those who would use them; homes are senselessly demolished by one arm of government while another is cramming the homeless into expensive bed-and-breakfast accommodation and hostels nearby; housing estates are built without the most basic facilities such as shops and community centres because the planners have no contact with those who might provide them and developers do not believe that it is commercially viable to build shops speculatively.

The built environment is too complex and inter-dependent to be fragmented in this way. It has to be treated as a total system. The key to solving the problems of a run-down housing estate may not be demolition or even physical renovation, but starting a residents' association, organizing a carnival or opening a shop. The key to making outdated terraced housing more desirable may be less to do with plumbing than with the reorganization of property boundaries. The key to housing unemployed homeless people may be a live training programme in self-build rather than a crash municipal house-building programme. The key to providing community facilities may be to make better use of existing buildings rather than erecting new ones. The optimum solution will only emerge if the problem is seen as a whole.

The environmental needs of individuals and communities must be tackled comprehensively – and continuously. Making the environment work is an evolutionary process. It is never-ending. Like a motorcar, the built environment needs continual maintenance, the occasional overhaul and eventually some replacement. If a person is responsible for its upkeep, the chances are that he or she will ensure that it is regularly serviced, parts are changed as necessary and that it is kept in good running order. Design and management systems must be structured to respond accordingly.

Getting the Process Right

An understanding of the principles outlined above explains why community architecture is concerned more at present with the *process* of development than with the end *product*. The present difficulties we find ourselves in are not primarily due to individual failure – either by designers, planners, politicians or tenants. They are the result of getting the *process* of development wrong; the wrong decisions are taken by the wrong people at the wrong time. Community architecture aims to get the process right first. Only when this has been achieved is it possible for all parties involved to explore their talents creatively and produce a better product.

Chapter 6

Making It Happen
**The New Organizational Frameworks,
Techniques and Roles**

The Age of Professions will be remembered as the time when politics withered,
when voters, guided by professors, entrusted to technocrats the power to
legislate needs, renounced the authority to decide who needs what, and suffered
monopolistic oligarchies to determine the means by which these needs shall be
met.

    Ivan Illich, *Disabling Professions*, 1977

The environmental professions in this country, supported by their institutes,
will, I hope, learn to identify their real clients, the users of their work, and
provide a responsive service. New standards of professional service are required.

    H R H The Prince of Wales, speaking at the Royal Institute of British
    Architects, 13 June 1986

To make our cities work, an effective 'Partnership' is needed between all sectors
– public, private, professional, voluntary and lay. But for the community to play
an active role in the 'Partnership', it is not just a matter of *more* financial
resources and better coordination of policies – essential as these are, and long
overdue – but communities must have access to professional advisers whom
they can trust and rely on.

    Neil Wallace, Chair, Association of Community Technical Aid Centres, 1986

To be successful, participation must be an on-going dialogue, extending over a
considerable period of time, based on individual commitment and respect
between all the interested parties, drawing out the best from each other in a
constant and ever-questioning search for better ways of doing things. It is a
team effort and there can be no weak links in the chain.

    John Thompson, *Community Architecture: The Story of Lea View House,
    Hackney,*1984

Putting community architecture into practice involves a radical restructuring of the development industry. The organizations and institutions most closely concerned with its evolution are having to adopt new
approaches to solving traditional problems. The participants – whether
community groups, technical advisers, political administrations or

funding agencies – are having to devise new roles and responsibilities. A new breed of organizations is emerging; new techniques and even new technologies are being introduced.

These changes have been taking place over a number of years and more will undoubtedly follow. This chapter looks at the main trends: in client organization; in professional services; in participatory design techniques; and in the roles of the participants.

1. Community Developers – the New Clients

The main client at present in community architecture is the voluntary sector – an expanding, complex and little understood part of society in which citizens band together voluntarily to undertake some specific task outside the statutory framework of government and not motivated by personal financial gain. Although few statistics are available, it is clear that the number of voluntary organizations concerned with the environment has increased dramatically over the last twenty years. Membership of local environmental organizations alone now exceeds that of all the political parties put together, according to Michael Barker, editor of *The Directory for the Environment*.

The voluntary sector comprises a diverse range of organizations operating at national, regional and local level. At one end of the spectrum is the National Trust, with over one million members and assets of land and property worth over £100m. At the other end are community groups in virtually every town, village and city dealing with local affairs at neighbourhood or street level. In between are numerous pressure and amenity groups focusing on specific issues, buildings or activities.

The voluntary sector has many advantages over the public sector – traditionally the main client in the development process – and these are increasingly being recognized. A government White Paper on the inner cities in 1977 stated: 'Voluntary organizations have particular strengths which enable them to cut across functional divisions in central and local government. They can attract funds, labour and skill from a range of sources not available to statutory institutions. They can also serve as a channel of communication between the local population and official bodies.' They can also have considerable advantages over the private sector, removing the speculative element and ensuring that development is appropriate to the needs of those it is intended to serve.

Over recent years the voluntary sector has proved increasingly effective at stopping, or securing modifications to, development by both public and private sectors. But, until comparatively recently, it has proved less effective at acting positively; of implementing development itself. The reasons for this include not being taken seriously by authorities, lack of finance, difficulty in getting – or not being able to afford – the right technical assistance and, above all, inappropriate, usually too informal, organizational structures.

To overcome these problems and become capable of acting as a client for development, groups have increasingly found it necessary to adopt more formal organizational structures. The precise nature varies depending on the project in hand – for instance, building a group of houses, regenerating a neighbourhood or building a community centre. But three requirements are common to all of them: they should be as representative as possible of the users themselves so as to internalize any potential conflicts of interest; they should involve as many people as possible and provide means for educating people about the development process; and they should be organized in such a way as to operate efficiently and consistently, and must be legally constituted to handle land and finance.

The three most successful models have proved to be housing cooperatives, special project groups and development trusts.

(i) Housing Cooperatives

The recent growth of housing cooperatives is one of the best-kept secrets in the industrial world. Over nine million people in eighteen nations now live in housing cooperatives, most of which have been developed since the Second World War. It is an expanding form of tenure across the globe in countries with widely differing political, economic and financial systems. In Britain the number of housing cooperatives increased from twelve in 1973 to 464 in 1985, housing 23,600 people.

A housing cooperative is a group of people who join together to provide and/or manage their own housing. At present it is the only form of tenure which allows people unable to afford to buy their own homes to have direct control over the provision of their own housing while at the same time receiving public subsidies. It also provides an ideal mechanism for residents to manage their immediate neighbourhood collectively as well as to cooperate in other ways.

The birth of the modern co-op movement is widely ascribed to the founding of the Rochdale Equitable Pioneers Society in 1844. Many of the founders of the society were mill workers living on a pittance in appallingly bad conditions. Among the stated objectives was 'the building of a number of houses in which those members desiring to assist each other in improving their domestic and social conditions may reside'. Like many other initiatives depending on self-help and mutual aid, cooperatives went out of fashion during the first half of the twentieth century as political creativity – on both Left and Right – was devoted almost entirely to developing the concept of the centralized state as the sole provider of social welfare. The movement's recent re-emergence is due largely to the failure of both public and private forms of housing tenure to allow individuals adequate choice and control over their immediate environment and to create a sense of community. So far the cooperative model is the only framework within which a real transfer of responsibility has taken place.

Housing cooperatives transform the relationship between users and professionals, since the users are firmly in control. As architect Michael Hook wrote in the *Architects' Journal* in 1977:

It can confidently be assumed that the processes to which architects have long been accustomed when working directly for public housing authorities, private speculators or individuals, will bear little relationship to the situation likely to be confronted when serving a cooperative. The architect will come face to face with a group client whose members are the consumers. He will have to work within similarly rigid controls but in financial terms these will now affect directly the rent levels of his individual clients within a cooperative. The architects' accountability takes on a new dimension.[38]

This new dimension has proved very productive and creative both for architects and their clients, as with the Liverpool co-op already described (see p. 77). Perhaps the most exciting product has been the way housing cooperatives have developed a wide range of shared facilities as an extension of those contained within individual homes – communal gardens (occasionally on rooftops), workshops, children's playgrounds, swimming-pools and saunas, for example. Such facilities can add much to the quality of life and, although beyond the means of most individual householders, can be relatively cheap to provide and run if the cost is shared. The essential ingredient is a form of organization which allows this to happen, while at the same time providing a sensitive, evolving means for management in accordance with the changing needs of residents.

The basic principles of cooperatives as outlined by the International Co-operative Alliance in 1966 can be summarized as follows:

1. Voluntary membership open to all who can make use of its services and are willing to accept the responsibility of membership;
2. A democratic organization where one person has one vote;
3. A limited rate of interest on share capital, if any;
4. Equitable distribution of earned surpluses or savings of the cooperative decided by the membership and applied to the development of the business of the cooperative, the provision of common amenities and services, or the payment of a dividend;
5. Continuous education for cooperative members in cooperative principles and in techniques of cooperation, both economic and democratic;
6. Cooperation among cooperatives at local, national and international level.

In practice there is a bewildering variety of different types of cooperative and new variations are being developed all the time. Also, many other organizational models for managing housing are emerging with the same essential characteristics of giving occupiers maximum control over their own dwellings while at the same time providing a means for collective control of common areas. One of these is the condominium system, which is widespread in many countries and gaining in popularity. Dwellings within a condominium building or complex are purchased by individuals who then automatically become members of an owners' association and are joint owners – with other dwelling owners – of the commonly used parts of the building or complex. This may include hallways, stairways, parking areas, gardens, swimming-pools, saunas and children's playrooms. Members of the owners' association decide how to manage the common facilities and pay a monthly service fee to cover the costs.

(ii) Special Project Groups

To develop a project such as a community centre, a play facility or an urban farm requires an organization specifically created for the purpose. Initially the impetus for the project may come from an organization set up with wider aims. Or it may come from an individual or group of individuals. Either way the development of a properly constituted, legal entity eventually controlled by the project's users is the end objective and its creation is an integral and vital part of the community architecture process.

The type of organization selected will depend on the nature of the project and will be worked out in conjunction with legal advisers. There are four main categories: an association, society or club; a trust; a company limited by guarantee; and an industrial and provident society.

(iii) Development Trusts

Development trusts are emerging as the most effective type of organization for involving communities in their own development at a neighbourhood or town level. As with housing cooperatives and special-project groups there is a wide variety of different types of development trust; but essentially they are charitable voluntary organizations which bring together in one partnership all the interests necessary to solve an area's environmental problems. Their unique and essential essence is in combining an entrepreneurial function with social responsibility. Partnership Ltd, which was commissioned by the Department of the Environment in 1986 to evaluate the success of development trusts, defines them as 'independent, not-for-profit organizations which undertake physical development to provide or improve facilities in an area. They have significant community involvement or control, bring together a wide range of skills and interests and aim to sustain their operations at least in part by generating revenue.'

The growth of development trusts in Britain has been significant. The first ones were formed fifteen years ago and by 1986 there were over seventy in existence. Most have been formed since 1980 and are still at an early stage of development. They are largely a product of voluntary groups gaining experience of running successful projects and moving on to larger programmes, combined wth an increasing realization by institutions of the need for multi-disciplinary and comprehensive approaches to urban renewal. Already many development trusts have proved exceptionally successful at regenerating areas where other methods have failed and in generating a sense of pride and community spirit. A similar concept of 'not-for-profit' development corporations in the United States has also proved successful in revitalizing places, such as Baltimore, where traditional methods have failed.

Development trusts are unique both in the projects they do and in the way that they do them. Their essential characteristics are:

1. The legal structure is usually a company limited by guarantee. They may also be a charity or have an associated charity to which they convenant profits. They are therefore able to handle large amounts of money but the individuals involved do not stand to gain financially.
2. The trust is locally based and its aims are socially useful and in the public interest. The key aim is to benefit the local community.
3. Membership of a development trust can vary to suit the nature of the task in hand. The trustees, directors, or council of management – depending on what legal format is adopted – will be carefully balanced to be acceptable to all interest groups. Typically this might include representatives of landowners, local authorities, residents, traders, industry and the churches. By combining all interests within one partnership the normal conflicts based on lack of communication between public, private and voluntary sectors are avoided.
4. They are independent; not merely an arm of the business sector, local authority or development corporation. This can be vital for raising resources from a range of organizations, to ensure support from all sections of the local community and to ensure continuity regardless of changes in political power at local level.
5. They are generally controlled by local people. Although activities may be generated by staff, the direction is provided by local people. They therefore tend to have a strong community development function, concerned not only with physical change but also with increasing confidence and skills.

These characteristics enable development trusts to take a unique approach to development, harnessing all the energy required to create successful places and ensuring balance between conflicting forces. Although at an early stage of evolution, they would appear to be the most promising vehicle for development in the future.

(iv) Neighbourhood Forums

One cannot leave discussion of the new clients without mentioning the neighbourhood forum. It has become increasingly clear that there is need for a new tier of government at neighbourhood level, particularly in urban areas, to deal single-mindedly with the needs of a small area. Calls for a comprehensive system of neighbourhood councils to be set up have come from many quarters and in 1982, the Public Participation Working Party of the Royal Town Planning Institute recommended the setting up of Community Planning Councils with certain statutory powers including development control.

Some community groups have effectively tried to fulfil the role of a neighbourhood council. In several areas neighbourhood forums have been set up as elected bodies with a constitution which guarantees representation from a cross-section of the community. But while often providing a useful function, such initiatives have been hampered by not having any statutory authority, and it has been difficult to assess their potential.

To be effective, any advance in this area would require a fundamental decentralization of power by government. In the meantime neighbourhood forums will still have an important role to play.

2. Enabling – the New Professional Services

While community groups have been gearing themselves up to take on the role of developers, environmental professionals have been exploring ways of helping them. This has involved changing the organizational structures in which they have traditionally worked – private consultancies and local authorities – as well as creating new professional aid services and community technical aid centres. Here we look at each in turn.

(i) Private Consultancies

Many of the first community architecture projects in the early seventies were started by professionals – mainly architects – responding to needs they could perceive in the communities where they lived or worked. Some of these professionals went on to establish private consultancies. Most remained small but by the mid-eighties several sizeable private consultancies – mostly architectural – had developed which specialized in community architecture. Rod Hackney & Associates was the largest; in just over ten years, Hackney had expanded from being a one-man band operating from his living-room to a large concern with twelve offices throughout the country employing over seventy staff. Several private consultancies formed themselves into workers' cooperatives, believing it

127

to be a more suitable organizational form for dealing with community clients and a more satisfying way of working for the professionals and other staff involved.

The main difficulty faced by private consultancies has been making community architecture pay, as it is very labour- and time-intensive. Professional fees are normally an agreed fixed percentage of project costs and the recommended fee scales (recently abandoned) did not allow for the additional work necessary in involving users in the process. Competitive fee bidding can make matters even worse, since there is pressure to skimp on time spent involving the community. Hunt Thompson Associates, one of the most experienced consultancies, estimate that the involvement of tenants in a relatively straightforward refurbishment project adds 20 per cent to the architect's costs. To make matters worse, much of the work required by community groups is project development and the preparation of feasibility studies, for which funds are not commonly available at all unless the project comes to fruition. Based on an assessment of sixty studies where community groups were receiving professional help, the Royal Institute of British Architects found in 1978 that 'architects have received no more than one sixth of the fees to which they are entitled'. It concluded: 'Few practices, especially small ones of the kind best suited to this kind of work, can afford to offer a full-time service. Accordingly, professional input is either reduced to a point at which it is barely effective, or is carried out on a part-time basis, which in the end benefits neither the community nor the profession.'[39]

As a result, private consultancies have only been able to undertake community architecture if committed to the approach and able to subsidize it with more profitable work from other sources. In order to do this some have teamed up with developers or become developers themselves in order to gain control over more of the development process and be able to take a more entrepreneurial role. Those that have made a success of it have tended to specialize in a particular area of work in order to reduce costs by benefiting from their own experience. By virtue of their single-minded determination and freedom to manoeuvre, these firms have tended to be the pioneers, establishing the precedents for others to follow. But, through no fault of their own, private consultancies have been unable to cater for the overwhelming general demand by voluntary organizations for assistance.

(ii) Professional Aid Services

In the absence of effective professional services at local level, aid schemes established at national level by professional and charitable institutions have filled an important gap. The most effective and well-developed has been Planning Aid.

Planning Aid is the provision of free and independent information and advice on town planning to groups and individuals unable to afford consultancy fees. It was first started by the Town and Country Planning Association (TCPA) in 1972, and adopted by the town planners' professional body, the Royal Town Planning Institute, three years later. Between them, these two organizations sponsored and supported over four hundred volunteers throughout Britain by 1986.

Planning Aid grew out of the demand for more participation in planning decisions, from residents and community groups reeling from the massive city-demolition, redevelopment and road-planning schemes of the sixties. Although the 1971 Town and Country Planning Act introduced new public information and consultation requirements for dealing with planning applications and for drawing up land-use plans, the Act only served to highlight the lack of advice services available to help residents and local groups understand the planning system and marshal their own ideas and proposals.

The Town and Country Planning Association's idea for filling this gap has been simple and effective. Using a network of planning experts from local authorities, private practices and the voluntary sector, a National Planning Aid Unit, based in London, coordinates requests for help. General inquiries about the planning system are dealt with centrally by telephone or letter. More complicated issues and those of a local nature requiring site visits, research and advocacy briefings are farmed out to volunteers. The TCPA argues that since town planning is something that many people are and should be involved in, planning aid can be provided by a wide range of experts. Specialist planners and lawyers, surveyors, landscape architects, politicians and voluntary groups can all offer advice based on their planning experiences.

In 1974 the Department of the Environment published an interim *Review of the Development Control System*. Its author, George Dobry, QC, recommended setting up a network of Planning Advice Centres and a 'Planning Aid Scheme' similar to that of Legal Aid. Though this was never acted upon, the Royal Town Planning Institute (RTPI) responded by launching its own version of Planning Aid. Today, all but one of the

129

institute's fourteen regional branches have active Planning Aid groups. Regional branches contribute to the administrative cost of running the local aid networks. Local aid groups define their own areas of work and the criteria on which chartered town planners will provide help.

With more than sixty volunteers, South Wales Planning Aid is one of the most active and innovative of the local groups. Dealing with up to three hundred cases a year, it can help with:

- applying for planning permission
- contacting the right person in the council
- appealing against a refusal of planning permission
- making your voice heard when plans are drawn up
- appearing at a public inquiry
- advice on carrying out surveys
- planning law
- obtaining information about planning problems and making the best use of it.

South Wales Planning Aid also promotes professional 'swop shops' to compare and encourage initiatives in public relations and consultation procedures. More recently, it has joined Community Design Service, a local group of architects, designers and landscape architects, to offer a more comprehensive environmental advice service. This development mirrors the evolution of the TCPA's Planning Aid service, which in 1975 set up Manchester Community Technical Aid Centre – the first multi-disciplinary environmental aid service in the country.

'Pioneering work by Planning Aid volunteers and groups has helped to change the way professional planners and planning authorities operate,' says Marc Dorfman, a planner for Southwark Council and a member of the TCPA executive. 'Planning Aid is now seen as an essential ingredient for good planning.' Many local authorities now fund planning aid groups in their own areas and some have set up planning resource centres, places where trained planners and community development officers offer independent and 'out-reach' services on local planning issues.

Planning Aid techniques of 'working with' local communities have more recently been adopted by planning authorities. The London Borough of Ealing, for instance, in 1986 created a new post of 'popular planner'; the job being to help the authority improve its working relationship with local residents, businesses and with other council departments. 'Planning Aid has helped break down the myth that professionals alone can plan our towns and countryside, our neighbourhoods,' says Dorfman, 'and above all it has helped professionals and local councils realize that there is more to representative democracy than elections and land-use plans.'

Other professions have also established aid schemes, the most notable being the Community Projects Fund set up by the Community Architecture Group at the Royal Institution of British Architects in 1982. This allocates funds, partly from the Department of the Environment, to community and voluntary organizations, to enable them to employ professionals to carry out feasibility studies for building or environmental improvement projects. Professional feasibility studies are often the key to getting projects off the ground, yet newly formed groups find it hard to obtain the necessary funding.

The fund has proved an extremely effective catalyst for community projects. Between 1982 and 1986, £123,840 allocated to 240 projects triggered over £6m in capital funding.

(iii) Community Technical Aid Centres

Community technical aid centres are one of the most important organizational models to have emerged from the community architecture movement. The concept is simple. They are places where individuals and community organizations can go to obtain all the technical assistance they need to undertake environmental projects of all kinds. Since the skills required for such work are many and varied they are multi-disciplinary. The term *technical* aid is used to overcome traditional professional divisions: to be successful, the community's objectives must be achieved whether the process involves the help of an architect, landscape architect, quantity surveyor, planner, structural engineer, financial adviser or community worker. And since the people requiring such a service generally have few resources – at least at the outset – they must be subsidized. In short, community technical aid centres are the environmental equivalent of law centres or medical general practitioners.

Community technical aid centres have developed to fill the gap between the services provided by the private sector, local authorities and professional aid schemes. They provide environmental services to people who would otherwise have no access to them. Because no systematic means of funding them has been available, their development has been pioneered by about a hundred experimental centres around the country since the early seventies. Each has had widely differing organizational structures, sources of funding, and methods of operation, determined by the resources available and the particular needs of the local area. But they have proved beyond doubt the value of such facilities and shown a glimpse of the potential if they were to become more established and widespread.

A typical community technical aid centre is staffed by a multi-disciplinary group of professionals such as architects, landscape architects, planners, surveyors, interior and graphic designers, ecologists and environmental educationalists. This enables it to deal with virtually all the environmental problems facing the community, and to deal with them comprehensively. For instance a technical aid centre will not only design and supervise the construction of a new facility but will assist groups to secure land and finance and set up the necessary legal and management arrangements. Indeed, up to 75 per cent of a centre's time is likely to be devoted to organizational and research work not normally considered to be part of a conventional architect's role. A list of services provided by a sample of forty technical aid centres is shown in Appendix 1 (p. 159).

Clients are asked to pay fees if they can afford them but services will be provided cheaply or free if not. This is one of the essential differences between community technical aid centres and services provided by private-sector consultants; technical assistance is made available to the poorest sections of the community who need it most but who have previously had no access to it.

Where centres have been set up they have invariably been overwhelmed with requests for assistance of all kinds. Their existence has had a catalytic effect, stimulating a vast number of environmental improvements, most of which would not otherwise have been undertaken. Appendix 2 lists the projects undertaken in one year by one community technical aid centre and makes fascinating reading. As Roger Kirkham of Manchester's Community Technical Aid Centre told the *Architects' Journal* in 1982: 'Once you've done something in the neighbourhood and got known, you get deluged with requests for help. People are increasingly looking for direct technical help to assist them in the design and management of all aspects of their environment.'[40] A study by Sharples and Woolley for the Department of the Environment in 1987 found that technical aid centres were experiencing a growth in demand for their services of 30–40 per cent each year.

Two things make community technical aid centres essentially different from services provided by local authorities. First, all the professionals involved work in the same place as a team, preferably in the local area where the services are required. Second, there is a commitment to user control. The Association of Community Technical Aid Centres (ACTAC), the umbrella organization representing and promoting community technical aid centres (see p. 169) states in its first report, published in 1986, that while community technical aid may be provided by a wide range of organizations, 'it is essential, however, that such organizations should be financially and operationally accountable to the community for their actions'. It continues: 'The participation process is about the user and the centre working together on the design process and developing the decisions jointly. Throughout this process the centres advise upon technical options and limitations, helping to facilitate the user's ideas and desires into practical options. The main role is that of enabler.'

All community technical aid centres encourage user participation in their projects. A growing number have been established on the basis of user-control of the service itself, a move encouraged by ACTAC. The first was Community Technical Services Agency (COMTECHSA) Limited in Liverpool in 1979. More recently the Technical Services Agency was set up in Glasgow in 1984; it is seen by ACTAC as a model for this kind of service. Reflecting the demand for its services, it had, within two years of formation, become one of Scotland's largest voluntary organizations, with a membership of over 160 tenants' and community organizations. A management committee elected annually from the membership directs all aspects of the work of the centre, which is staffed by four architects, a development worker, administration officer and typist. The main source of funding is Urban Aid via Strathclyde District Council.

Lack of adequate funding has proved the main barrier to the more rapid spread of such centres. Only 14 per cent of the running costs of ACTAC's members came from clients' fees, according to the latest figures compiled in 1985, the remainder being made up mostly by grants. Most of the first centres in the seventies were funded by charitable foundations. In the early eighties central government funds were a key source via the Manpower Services Commission and the Urban Initiatives Fund. But local authorities increasingly became an important source as they began to appreciate that technical aid centres are complementary to their own services, not simply an alternative. Public funding is clearly essential for community technical aid centres. One of the crucial issues over the coming years will be whether this comes from central or local government and on what terms.

One of the most fascinating aspects of the growth of technical aid services has been the development of organizations with specialist skills. For instance, the Free Form Arts Trust and Cultural Partnership in London specialize in incorporating art and drama into the environment; Heatwise in Glasgow specializes in home insulation and has fitted more than 17,000 houses with draught-proofing, claiming heating-cost savings to tenants in excess of £100,000; Matrix in London is committed to supporting women's environmental initiatives; Landlife in Liverpool focuses on ecology and bringing nature into the city.

All such groups have added a new dimension to the environment in which they work and an ever-expanding horizon for community technical aid in the future.

(iv) Local Authorities

One of the greatest disappointments to advocates of community architecture has been the inability of local authorities to reorganize their large technical departments to provide a more effective service to their electorates. Indeed, much of the energy of community organizations has been spent fighting against proposals put forward by professionals in their own local authorities, while the professionals themselves have become increasingly demoralized at their isolation from their real clients. As Colin Ward wrote in 1978: 'The reason why Rod Hackney, and others like him, have been elevated to hero status is because they have been living out the dreams of all those frustrated local-authority architects, separated from the site, builders and the users by a mountain of procedural bureaucracy.'[41]

But various initiatives taken by authorities up and down the country have shown that the problem is not insoluble and that local authorities can play a vital enabling role. Three distinct approaches have emerged: the setting up of specific projects at local level; general decentralization of services; and the adoption of policies aimed at strengthening community organizations. Below we look at some examples.

Specific projects

Isolated community architecture projects have been set up by several local authorities over the past few years. For instance, Wolverhampton Council in 1980 set up a team of architects and housing managers in a house on an outlying estate known as The Scotlands, then described as 'one of the most difficult to let'. From their site office the team coordinated a £9m programme of improvements, in which residents' involvement was the central objective. Shortly afterwards, Brent Council appointed an in-house community architect to assist community organizations wishing to undertake building projects. And in 1985, Westminster City Council embarked on a showpiece community architecture project on the Martlett Court Estate by providing consultant architects Lazenby & Smith with an empty flat to work in and giving them a brief to work for the tenants.

The immense scope for local authorities to set up specific projects is well illustrated by Southwark Council in London, which has formed a unique alliance with local community organizations. While the council structure has remained the same, participation has become the cornerstone of policy. Initiatives undertaken over the past decade include the following:

1. The council's Planning Committee grant-aids two voluntary organizations (the North Southwark Community Development Group and the Rotherhithe Community Planning centre) to help local residents with planning advice and local campaigns.

2. The Planning Department has established an urban studies centre to complement the local planning aid services. Its motto is: 'Get together, get involved, get things done'. The centre was designed and built by the council's architects to the specifications of a voluntary management committee drawn from a cross-section of the community.

3. Southwark Council's architects and planners have recently provided a local action group with all the technical support required to draw up plans for a seven-acre housing scheme and to campaign for its development in the face of private developers' plans to build luxury homes. Architectural aid has also been offered to a Muslim association hoping to build a mosque.

4. In 1981 the Planning Department changed the way it devised its capital spending programme. A new Facelift scheme offered community organizations a chance to plan three years' of environmental improvements and the opportunity to work side by side with the council's architects, planners and landscape architects. A borough-wide participation exercise organized by the department's newly appointed consultation team, produced over three hundred sugges-

tions for environmental works. Each suggestion was treated as an application and the sponsoring community group was allocated a landscape architect and a planner to carry out feasibility studies and work out development briefs. Project ideas ranged from play parks and nature gardens to allotments, under-fives' play areas and community buildings. Consultation on the choices for environmental improvements subsequently led to greater participation in the actual development and maintenance of sites by local people.

5. Southwark Council has also pioneered the idea of 'community action teams' to make a concerted attack on small areas with a large number of environmental, social and economic problems. These 'target' areas are used to focus council resources from a number of different departments. Community consultation exercises are used to select the target areas, whose improvements are then managed by community action teams made up of councillors, officers and representatives for local community groups and businesses.

6. Guided by the strength of community commitment and participation resulting from one-off planning and development projects, the alliance with voluntary organizations extended into the creation of the local land-use plan for the north of the borough. A steering group dominated by members of voluntary organizations not only developed the initial guidelines for the plan, but also prescribed the consultation arrangements, the planning research programme and the policy proposals, dealt with objections and revisions, and determined the design and wording of the final document. For the first time in the history of British planning, that same steering group dispensed with the services of a lawyer at the public inquiry into the local plan, presented the proposals themselves and carried out their own cross-examination of objecting witnesses. By 1986 the steering group was overseeing the plan's implementation.

Restructuring and decentralization of services

Many councils have attempted major decentralization and restructuring in recent years to make their planning and architecture services more accessible and area-based. Birmingham was one of the first – in 1975 – to set up a network of area-based urban renewal teams with a brief to stimulate resident participation as well as to undertake improvements. Leicester developed the model by incorporating a housing association, architectural consultant and council officers all in one office. Other authorities, like the London Borough of Haringey, have restructured their entire technical divisions into multi-disciplinary teams, largely area-based, to try and provide a simpler and better service to the community and make it easier to deal with user-clients.

The dramatic restructuring of local authorities currently taking place in Britain goes beyond the scope of this book. But from the limited information readily available, it appears that most of the main decentralization ('Going Local') programmes have not begun to get to grips with the requirements of community architecture and planning, concentrating instead on more superficial aspects of social service delivery. In the London Borough of Islington, for instance, the planning function was rated as the fifteenth priority service and the new neighbourhood council offices completed in 1986 do not include architects or planners. But an exciting new initiative at the end of 1986 was the Joint Social and Economic Initiatives for Drumchapel and Greater Easterhouse, two districts of Glasgow. Three local authorities – Strathclyde Regional Council, Glasgow Area Health Authority and the City Council – have pooled their resources to try and regenerate a community in the heart of one of Britain's most depressed inner-city areas. A joint authority report entitled *Building a Sure Foundation* explains: 'It has been acknowledged that a lasting success will depend on the development of robust and confident community groups capable of assuming responsibility in the management or control of local services and resources . . .' The report goes on to outline the conditions of community involvement that are required: participation should be wide and open; forms of involvement should be appropriate to the potential of local communities; community development staff should assist and enable local residents and groups to articulate their views; specialized technical aid and resources should be available to local groups as required; material prepared by the local authorities should be accessible and easy to understand.

The Drumchapel and Easterhouse Initiative aims to rebuild the structures of local government on the basis of a new joint working and participative approach to the relationship between those providing the services and those using them. It is effectively starting from scratch.

Strengthening community organizations

A third way in which local authorities have stimulated community architecture is by adopting specific policies aimed at strengthening community organizations. The last Labour administration at the Greater London Council (GLC) provides the most spectacular example. Its

137

chairman of planning, George Nicholson, described it as 'the biggest top-down enabler ever'.

The cornerstone of its community planning strategy was the Community Areas Policy which emerged from a series of public planning forums throughout inner London. Between 1982 and 1985 the GLC made grants of £18 million for community centres, environmental improvements, land purchase and general community support. This went hand in hand with funding for sixteen community architecture, planning and technical aid services throughout London. A GLC monitoring report in 1983 outlined the authority's rationale:

[The GLC] believes that technical aid organizations would:
– help community groups play a fuller part in the planning of their areas;
– act as pump primers in the development of scarce and under-used land and buildings;
– harness the skills and enthusiasm of local community groups;
– be able to target help to 'usually excluded' sections of the community;
– provide community organizations with a comprehensive service including community development, fund-raising and project management.[42]

The GLC dubbed its approach as 'Popular Planning'. According to a report to the council's Industry and Employment Committee, the phrase 'popular planning'

implies a challenge to the monopoly which professional planners and managers have of the overview and coordinating role necessary to planning, a monopoly that relegates to the public the passive role of merely assenting or dissenting to plans already drawn up. The council's support for popular planning expresses a belief that working people have the capacity for a more creative role than this.[43]

Paternalistic attitudes, hierarchical and federal power structures, bureaucracy and their monopoly position can make local authorities a formidable barrier to people participating in their own environment. It need not be so. Much depends on the attitudes and imagination of individual officers, departments and councillors.

(v) Assistance Teams

One of the most interesting recent initiatives was the launch, in 1985, of the CUDAT (Community Urban Design Assistance Team) programme by the RIBA; a concept adopted from a programme in the United States known as R/UDAT (Regional and Urban Design Assistance Teams). The idea is to send a team of 'experts' into an area for an intensive brainstorming long weekend to act as a catalyst in stimulating local action and releasing blockages in the development process. Preliminary research is carried out for several months in advance of the brainstorming, in which the local groups, councillors and their technical officers take part.

In the United States the R/UDAT programme is considered to be a great success. It first emerged in 1967 when the President of the Chamber of Commerce of Rapid City, South Dakota, described to the American Institute of Architects (AIA) the urban problems developing there. After some discussion, the AIA suggested that if the city would foot the expenses bill, it would coordinate a small group of appropriately experienced professionals to travel there, meet government officials and citizens and draw up a report and recommended plan of action.

Before they set off, the professionals were furnished with a briefing package – maps, aerial photographs, demographic information and so on. The visit lasted for three days. In that time, meetings were held with the mayor and council, local architects, local businessmen and citizens. At the end of the third day, a public presentation was made. A week later, a written report and list of recommendations (together with a bill for expenses of $900) was sent to Rapid City. The city subsequently adopted the recommendations and a planning commission was formed to act upon them, with full and open public debate of the issues as an essential part of the process.

Since then, the AIA has been asked to send teams, assembled under its R/UDAT programme, to more than eighty urban communities in all parts of the country. $4m worth of professional services have been volunteered and more than a tenth of the nation's urban population has been affected. The essential pattern of citizen initiative and citizen participation has become a widely accepted ingredient of the planning process.

Each R/UDAT is slightly different. But, in general terms, the following principles apply to them all:

1. A R/UDAT team only visits a community at the request and invitation of that community.
2. A team consists of about eight people, some of whom will have previous R/UDAT experience, some of whom will not.
3. Team members come from more than one discipline and will be chosen for their expertise and ability to tackle particular types of problems and to work in a team.
4. The team will be briefed on local issues and essential background and technical details prior to departure.

5. Team members volunteer their time; only travelling, food and accommodation expenses are reimbursed and no commissions for work arising from the R/UDAT plan may be accepted by any team member.
6. Students from the nearest schools of architecture, planning and urban design commonly join the team.
7. The team's visit lasts four days and includes: a tour of the locality; meetings with representatives of the city council, business sector and community groups; a town meeting; one-to-one discussions with more vocal, influential or in some way prominent members of the community; a twenty-four-hour session report writing; report printing; and a second town meeting and press conference at which a presentation of the findings and recommendations is made.
8. Preparation for the four-day visit can take up to a year and commonly involves many preliminary meetings when relevant issues are discussed and background information assembled.
9. Follow-up visits can be arranged. These are usually seen to be helpful to the community in the implementation process and are also beneficial to the R/UDAT programme in gaining feedback.

The American Institute of Architects claims that its R/UDAT programme has led to a rediscovery of cities and the importance of urban design. A major review of the programme edited by Peter Batchelor and David Lewis in 1986 concludes:

The impact of the R/UDAT programme on the nation's cities is unequalled by any other urban design activity over the past decade ... Born in an atmosphere of crisis in the sixties, the growing and deepening impact of urban design is one of the most exciting developments in recent years in architecture and related professions, bringing new enlightenment and dedication to the people of our cities. The civil rights movement taught us to listen, and to hear those whose voices had gone unheard for generations. The bicentennial [anniversary of the United States of America] taught us to see in our cities a history and tradition that is strong and uniquely American. R/UDAT has taught us how to turn the aspirations of citizens, and their descriptions of urban value, into action.

The first CUDAT in Britain took place in the St Mary's area of Southampton in June 1985. Although some positive changes occurred in the area as a result, it did not prove as successful as its promoters had hoped, largely due to cynicism from many quarters, including the local authority, which, unlike the American authorities, perceived it as a threat to its autonomy. A second CUDAT planned by the RIBA for Hull in 1986 had to be called off after opposition from community groups who said they had not asked for it. Given the entrenched attitudes which prevailed at the time, it is not surprising that the first attempts to mount CUDATs in Britain faced difficulties. Nevertheless, important lessons have been learned and the idea may yet take root.

3. Participatory Design – the New Techniques

Regardless of what organizational models are adopted, the key to making community architecture work effectively is a range of new techniques for enabling professional and lay people to work creatively together. These techniques are known as participatory design. Here is a summary of those which have been found to be the most useful over a decade or so of experimentation in Britain and abroad.

Social surveys
Before embarking on any project a survey is undertaken of all future users and interested parties to determine their needs and aspirations. Both clients and professionals collaborate on the survey, which provides essential briefing material and is likely to prove invaluable in deflecting pressure from those who claim falsely to represent the views of others. It also provides an excuse, if one were needed, for knocking on doors and generating public interest in a project.

Public meetings
Public meetings can be useful for informing a large audience about proposals, generating preliminary interest and setting things up. But they have limited value, since even with elaborate audio-visual equipment, for example, it is hard to communicate the details of a project. Constructive dialogue can be difficult at first since participation is restricted to those who are confident in public speaking.

Design meetings
Design meetings, where the hard work is done, are the basis for participatory design. On most projects they will occur weekly or even more often at the peak of activity. They are most effective with a small number of people and there must be continuity of membership. Groups will usually appoint a subcommittee of members to take part in design meetings or split up into several groups working in parallel. Minutes can be published in a simple newsletter to keep those not attending in touch.

It is essential that the client group appoints one of its number as co-ordinator of design meetings. On complex projects, groups may decide to have separate committees dealing with different aspects, such as landscaping.

Visits to other schemes
Visits by coach or train to other completed projects – both good and bad – are invaluable both before and during the design process. They bring people face to face with the reality of construction and give client and architect a common vocabulary from which to generate their own ideas. Wherever possible people should talk with those using the projects, who are invariably the most perceptive about what works or does not work well. Many community architects believe such trips – which can also be enjoyable social occasions – to be the single most important aspect of participatory design.

Slide shows
Showing pictures of other projects can be helpful in demonstrating the possibilities; but they can also be very misleading. The seductive power of photographs, particularly in design magazines, can give false impressions, particularly since wide-angle lenses make it difficult to appreciate the reality in three dimensions. Groups have often found that schemes which looked exciting in pictures were disappointing in reality. 'Before' and 'after' photographs, however, can be a very useful way of helping people to see the possibilities.

Project offices
An open and accessible project office is almost invariably the best way for people to be involved on a continuing basis. On many projects this will be best located on site, allowing the professionals to immerse themselves in the environment they are dealing with and making it easier to supervise construction work. People have access at any time and in some cases the 'community architect' literally lives 'over-the-shop' and is available all day and every day, seven days a week.

Models
Models are useful for helping people to visualize designs in three dimensions and for bridging the communication gap between lay people and professionals. They need not be glossy presentation models (although these may be useful for attracting funding) and in fact effective models

can be made very quickly with cardboard. Models should in any case be flexible so as to enable people to test alternative design solutions. Education for Neighbourhood Change at Nottingham University has developed a special kit system for model-making, called 'Planning for Real', which has been successfully employed by many groups (see p. 172).

Full-scale mock-ups

Full-scale mock-ups of rooms and flats can be helpful for both users and professionals in perfecting designs. Cost usually precludes this from being done except on large schemes, although in some European countries full-scale modelling laboratories have been constructed to allow people to experiment with designs. Nothing of this kind is available in Britain yet, which is surprising, since the cost is small compared with the huge sums invested in construction.

Computers

Computers (now capable of elaborate three-dimensional modelling) can be useful as a design tool, particularly where there are repetitive designs with minor variations, e.g. a block of flats or a large estate of houses of different floor plans. Word-processing is invaluable in allowing untrained typists to produce newsletters and other material quickly and easily.

Drawing

Despite the benefits of more sophisticated techniques, many groups have found that sketching with felt-tips is one of the most effective ways of exploring ideas.

Videos

Videos are rapidly becoming one of the most effective tools for showing examples of other projects and for recording the progress of projects in hand. Building and environmental projects can often take many years to complete and the same people will not be able to be involved at all stages.

Site visits

Regular visits to site during construction are useful for keeping people in touch with progress when there is not much for them to do. It also helps people to understand the physical difficulties involved in construction. It is essential for at least the coordinator of the design committee to attend site meetings, to avoid conspiracies developing when design changes have to be made due to unforeseen circumstances (which invariably happens). Site meetings can also be beneficial for construction workers to meet the people they are building for, giving them a greater sense of purpose, which is likely to result in higher standards of workmanship.

Self-help and self-build

Entire projects can be physically constructed by the users (see p. 82). More often people will be involved in only a few aspects such as clearing the ground, landscaping or decorating. Physical involvement, however little, is extremely good for morale and for getting people working together. Very often a self-build group will include specialist trades, such as a bricklayer, carpenter and electrician; people with craft skills may be able to construct elements of the project such as gates or seats. Involving children in planting, making mosaics or painting murals can be particularly productive and ensure their commitment to the end product.

Ceremonies

Ceremonies or celebrations marking key points in the development process are a good way of helping people to gain a sense of common purpose and progress, and are a boost for morale. Such occasions are likely to include: securing funds; 'breaking ground' or starting construction; 'topping out' or completion; opening. All those involved – users, professionals, construction workers, local-authority representatives – are usually invited, and sometimes local dignatories too. Community arts groups have developed fascinating techniques for making these events theatrical and great fun, for instance by introducing street theatre and music.

Pattern language

Pattern language, developed by the architect and writer, Christopher Alexander, in the United States, is based on the premise that people can only participate effectively if they know the issues and choices, and that optimum solutions to most environmental problems have already been discovered and that there is no need for each group to reinvent the wheel. It comprises more than two hundred solutions to environmental problems (patterns) and these are used as a basis for new designs. In a sense it is a kind of 'teach yourself' architecture, enabling untrained people to design their own buildings and cities in accordance with timeless principles of good design. Although the language has not found more than token acceptance from the design professions, it is very popular with users.

Several practical applications (for instance, housing at Mexicali in Mexico) indicate that it has great potential for wider application.

Supports and infill
The supports and infill concept is a system of design, management and construction developed by Nicholas Habraken at the Stichting Architecten Research (SAR) unit at Eindhoven Technical University in the Netherlands. It aims to distinguish between collective and individual areas of responsibility and develop building and management systems accordingly. It is widely used by public housing authorities in the Netherlands, giving tenants freedom to modify the internal arrangements of their own dwellings. The best single example is probably the Molenvliet housing complex in the small town of Papendrecht. The system has also been used and modified in other countries, for instance, the PSSHAK – Primary Support Structures and Housing Assembly Kits – project at Adelaide Road in London in the late seventies.

Competitions
Competitions can be a good way of stimulating imaginative ideas and solutions to complex problems. Traditionally, competitions have been restricted to, and judged by, members of the professions, but there have been several successful examples recently – for instance, Manchester City Council's 'Manchester Once More' competition – where they have been opened up to members of the public, with lay judges and categories for all age groups including children, and where the ideas that have emanated have led to practical action.

Festivals
Neighbourhood festivals have become a symbol of neighbourhood revitalization. They provide unique opportunities for all sections of a community to participate in a collective effort and meet one another in an informal setting.

Publicity
Publicity and promotion is a vital part of most projects, since success depends on people knowing what is happening and supporting it. Self-published leaflets and newsletters are valuable at certain stages, but one of the easiest ways is to make projects newsworthy, thereby attracting local – sometimes national – media attention.

Television

As well as a medium for publicity, television can be a powerful design tool in its own right. It has not been used for this purpose in Britain to date but in Roanoke in the United States a series of live design shows with facilities for viewers to call in with comments and suggestions proved to be a valuable tool for involving people in the revitalization of the city. Chadwick Floyd, an architect, writes of the experience: 'Not only has it helped us reach richer solutions to urban design problems, it has demonstrated a power to strike the collective imagination of a community and focus disparate energies towards a common goal'.[44] The introduction of cable television is likely to increase the extent of such techniques.

Maintenance manuals

Building manuals, much like those for cars, are an important way of ensuring that buildings and landscaping are properly maintained. They should be in simple language comprehensible by all those who are likely to take responsibility for it. Compiling such a manual at the design stage is also a useful discipline for ensuring that future maintenance problems are kept to a minimum.

4. New Roles and Attitudes

Two key new roles have emerged in the community architecture process: the *professional enabler*, a person with technical expertise who uses that expertise to help people do things for themselves; and the *social entrepreneur*, a person who makes things happen by taking initiative on behalf of his or her community rather than for private or personal gain.

The search for a new role for professionals has lain at the heart of the crisis within the professional institutions (described in Chapter 2) and has been the subject of much soul-searching and has given rise to a number of metaphors. In 1985 John Habraken, an architect, compared the new professional role of gradually 'cultivating' the built environment to that of the gardener tending plants.

To have a good garden we sometimes must make an infrastructure: dig the soil, make paths and provide water. Sometimes we must reorganize the distribution of plants. Sometimes we must feed and stimulate. Sometimes we must weed and trim. At all times we must propose forms, suggest forms, help forms to come about. The gardener is in touch with physical things, working with his hands, but he also understands life and knows he cannot make plants but can only help them grow and become healthy . . . The new practitioner is the one who accepts the fluid movements of the everyday environment and rejoices in them. He knows that life is rich, unpredictable and ever-changing, and that buildings and cities are part of life: are the product of life itself.[45]

The editor of the *Architectural Review*, J. M. Richards, wrote in 1970 that architects should become the equivalent of the family doctor, developing an intimate knowledge of his patients.

Architects should similarly have a long-term relationship with one area for which they should feel wholly responsible and to whom anyone with a building problem in the area should automatically turn because of their involvement in its history . . . Like the family doctor, who knows everyone's history, this local architect should be familiar with every street, every tree, every lamp-post, every sign, every boundary wall . . . Again like the doctor, he should – ideally – live there as well as work there.[46]

The writer Colin Ward argued in 1976: 'If architects have a professional future at all it is as skilled understanders enabling people to work out their problems.'[47] Rod Hackney said in 1983 that the new professionals should have a 'missionary role' – 'going in where it hurts, getting their hands dirty and sticking with it, even if it is a bit of a killer . . . The community architect cannot be protected by the arm's-length, so-called "professional" approach which most architects adopt.'[48] And for architect David Rock, it is simply a matter of the architect *reverting* to his traditional role: 'A top-class "enabler" tied into, and aware of, society and culture, its problems, potential and needs.'[49]

However, while acquiring these attributes, professionals cannot abandon their traditional specialist technical skills, as architect Berthold Lubetkin reminded the RIBA in a speech on 11 June 1985. 'After consulting all the pundits, however exalted or however humble, architects will not be able to evade their responsibility to create an architecture that evokes the promise, and so provides the action for, a more sane society to come. Only then are they likely to deserve and therefore receive the confidence and respect of the public they so assiduously seek.'

The community entrepreneur on the other hand need not have any specialist technical skills at all. His or her role is simply to make things happen by taking initiatives and communicating with all the parties involved, so as to bring all the necessary skills and knowledge to bear on the problem at hand. The credentials necessary are commitment, determination, energy and, above all, local knowledge. Michael Middleton, former director of the Civic Trust, described the role as follows:

He, or she, must believe totally in what he is doing; be prepared to work all hours; must be as knowledgeable as the professionals and officials and community leaders with whom he will have to deal. Above all, he – or she – must be responsive to human beings – patient with Mrs Buggins while helping her to fill out her grant application; sensitive to political nuances when mediating between two local authorities; good humoured when the owner of the fish shop changes his mind and pulls out of the operation half-way through; enthusiastic and encouraging at all times. He or she must, quite simply, like people.[50]

Frequently the two new roles – the enabler and the social entrepreneur – overlap. And there are many variations on the themes. As yet the new roles are not formally taught in schools or universities and are not formally recognized by the professional institutes. But, as architects Rock Townsend concluded in the introduction to the exhibition 'Making Things Happen' in 1987:

The people who can make things happen are currently forging a new profession. It is one which is not preoccupied with its dignity and status, one which does not pretend that it knows the whole conspectus, one which is actively prepared to work with all kinds of relevant expertise and with clients. It is a profession of people who apply themselves to current, human environmental problems from the practical position of the real world – not from that of the ivory tower of theory; people who understand that traditional funding routes don't work any more, and that frequently traditional paths to regeneration don't either. They are people who understand that alternative, non-standard routes have to be found and sometimes devised if things are to happen in the regeneration of our environments. They are the professionals of the Third Force: broader, wider and longer in their perspectives than the traditional professionals could ever be.

Conclusions

Over the last decade the development field has changed dramatically. Fifteen years ago it was the exclusive preserve of local authorities, commercial developers and specialist private consultants in the traditional fields of architecture, planning and so on. Now there is a multiplicity of organizations geared to tackle the problems in a variety of new and different ways.

There has been a great deal of controversy, particularly in the pages of the professional press, as to whether one approach is better than another. Because of the diverse nature of environmental problems it seems that a great many approaches are valid, particularly in the present stage of transition between the old paradigm of architectural, planning and development practice, and the new.

Chapter 7

The Way Forward
What Needs to be Done Next

Our ability to survive will depend, in part, upon the extent to which we can create 'appropriate places', that is, places to which people can relate satisfactorily and which fit emerging patterns of work and lifestyle.
  David Cadman, Fitzgerald Memorial Lecture, 1984

At this very moment, millions of pounds are being spent on improving the country's housing estates. The majority of these are still 'package' improvements doomed to failure. The scandal of the eighties will be how we failed to put it right when we were given a second chance.
  John Thompson, partner of Hunt Thompson Associates, February 1987

If ever we are to have a time of architecture again, it must be founded on a love for the city. No planting down of a few costly buildings, ruling some straight streets, provision of fountains or setting up of stone or bronze dolls is enough without the enthusiasm for corporate life and common ceremonial. Every noble city has been a crystallization of the contentment, pride and order of the community.
  W. R. Lethaby, 1857–1931

The real purpose of community architecture can be seen as twofold: first, architects using their skills to enable people to achieve better conditions for themselves; and second, giving such people direct experience of controlling their own futures . . . The crucial point is that once given a taste of responsibility, such groups will not willingly give it up; and therein lies the real future for democratic change.
  Charles McKean, secretary, Community Architecture Working Group, RIBA (*Architects' Journal*, 23 November 1977)

Architecture is too important to be left to architects alone. Like crime, it is a problem for society as a whole.
  Berthold Lubetkin, RIBA President's Invitation Lecture, 1985

Community architecture has come to the end of its pioneering phase. A decade of protest and isolated experimentation has been followed by a

149

decade of consolidation in built projects and organizational development. There are now numerous precedents for further action and a growing number of experienced practitioners.

Yesterday's radical alternative has become part of today's conventional wisdom. The community architecture movement is now supported and promoted by people from all walks of life and from across the political spectrum: by anarchists, libertarians, the traditional and radical Left, the Green Movement, social democrats and free marketeers.

By the summer of 1987 there was a new spirit of optimism in the air. Partnership and realism were the words on everyone's lips. New alliances were sprouting up between the parties involved – between central and local government, the private-sector construction and development industry, the environmental professions and community and voluntary groups. A consensus appeared to have been reached that community architecture worked, and that it could no longer be written off as some apocalyptic or subversive activity promoted by extremists or some loony fringe. And with the cost of repairing Britain's decaying built environment – estimated at as much as £85,000m, or more than £1,500 for every man, woman and child in the country – it was becoming widely accepted that the task could only be dealt with effectively by adopting new approaches such as those offered by community architecture; and through a partnership of all sectors – public, private, professional and community.

Inevitably some cynics remain unconvinced; but they seem increasingly irrelevant in the face of the obvious practical achievements. The political extremists, who initially saw the movement as part of a class revolution, have been left on the sidelines. They could never reconcile themselves to the apolitical way in which community architecture developed. Some on the extreme Left still see it as a palliative to the working classes which will delay a popular uprising against the capitalist 'oppressors'. Some on the extreme Right still see it as the thin end of the wedge in transferring too much power to the people.

Surviving the flack from all sides, the community architecture movement has in fact grown stronger as a result of the bureaucratic obstructions and political vendettas which have marked its painful birth. Through a combination of social commitment, tactical skill and good fortune, its members have always seemed to manage to be in the right place at the right time. Its opponents, who initially convinced themselves that it could be defeated or ignored, have been out-manoeuvred at every turn, and they have been weakened and disorientated in the process. The energy and stamina of social entrepreneurs and their professional enablers have made them the victors, not the vanquished. The movement has emerged as a formidable force for change.

But despite the spectacular advances made over recent years, conventional methods still prevail in many areas of the development industry, continuing to frustrate those who are trying to put community architecture into practice. The main difficulty is that because the development system is so complex and interdependent, any new approaches are difficult to implement effectively without changes in methods and attitudes by a wide range of different organizations simultaneously. Before the full creative potential of community architecture can be explored, a great many changes are needed at all levels. Many of these have been spelt out on different occasions by others. Below we summarize them, adding some of our own thoughts, in the form of a manifesto for the next phase of community architecture.

A Manifesto for Community Architecture

1. Voluntary Sector

- Voluntary organizations – representing geographical communities and communities of interest – should willingly demand and accept more responsibility for the creation and management of the environment and should strengthen and restructure themselves in order to become more effective as developers and property managers.

- Community organizations should have access to sufficient funds to employ the varied technical expertise they need to implement environmental projects.

- Special emphasis should be put on encouraging the formation of housing cooperatives, special project groups, development trusts and neighbourhood forums.

2. Government

- Central and local government should learn to trust community organizations and should actively assist them in their formation and development. There should be a fundamental policy shift from 'providing' to 'enabling'.

- Government affecting the built environment should be devolved to the smallest identifiable group practicable and the formation of new statutory tiers of estate and neighbourhood government encouraged.

- Most central and local government staff should be decentralized to multi-disciplinary neighbourhood offices to assist communities in handling their neighbourhood affairs. In urban areas no one should be more than a few minutes' walk from such an office.

- A national network of community-controlled, publicly-funded multi-disciplinary technical aid centres should be established.

- Accountability procedures for the receipt of public funds should be redefined to encourage community initiatives and provide voluntary organizations with consistent, long-term funding, to facilitate forward planning.

- Democratic planning policies should be strengthened but handled by a more appropriate (usually more local) tier of government. Bureaucratic procedures and red tape should then be minimized and controls which inhibit and delay development, especially zoning, relaxed. Planning legislation should be rewritten in straightforward language.

- Pragmatism should replace outdated dogma. Development policy, whether for housing or other social, commercial and industrial provision, should be 'depoliticized' in party political terms and the construction industry should cease to be used as an economic regulator.

- Derelict land and buildings (both public and private) should be made available for community-led initiatives and be made the subject of a punitive tax to encourage its productive use.

- All relevant social and environmental issues should be considered in planning appeals, public inquiries and local planning decisions, and the recommendations of public-inquiry inspectors should not be overturned by central government except for overriding reasons, such as national security. Community groups should be given access to the necessary resources to present their case effectively.

- Planning policies should encourage incremental, evolutionary development with large development sites broken down into smaller packages.

- Land ownership should be public information, always kept up to date, and land in public ownership should be sold to those wishing to develop it for the most socially desirable ends rather than automatically to the highest bidder.

3. Development Industry

- The development industry, including the professions, should enter into creative partnerships with community organizations and the public sector. As with government, there should be a fundamental shift from 'providing' to 'enabling'.

- The construction process should be de-mystified, wherever possible using methods and materials which are easily understood and usable by lay members of the community, and construction methods which are labour- rather than capital-intensive and flexible for future adaptation. All buildings and landscaping projects should have simple maintenance manuals.

- Recommended professional fee scales should be adjusted to take account of the extra time needed to involve end-users.

- The curricula of architecture and planning schools should be radically changed so as to include relevant training for professional enablers and social entrepreneurs. Special courses should be established at all schools as an initial step.

- Locally based building activity should be encouraged so that the economic benefits of development stay within the community. The employment of local labour, particularly the unemployed, should be a prerequisite and training local people in building skills should form part of any contract.

- The public sector should be prepared to do more to underwrite private-sector risk, through tax breaks and other mechanisms, to encourage business and the financial institutions (including banks, building societies and insurance and investment funds) to invest in urban regeneration. At the same time private-sector developers should enter into legally binding contractual partnerships with community groups to ensure that the community is involved in planning new development and secures major benefits from it. Independent environmental impact studies should be made publicly available for all major projects before approval.

4. Research and Communication

- Far more resources should be devoted to research on the built environment by government and the development industry to avoid making the same mistakes over and over again. Research and development programmes should be undertaken on the long-term cost effectiveness of different approaches – in the UK and overseas – and the results widely disseminated. Special attention should be directed towards the development of techniques in participatory design.

- Information systems should be established to make data about successful examples of community architecture and development widely available. Programmes should be established to encourage more exchange of experience between the various groups involved in the process – public, private, professional and voluntary.

- Environmental education programmes for the public should be expanded so that people learn how the built environment works and how they can take part in improving it. Environmental education should form part of every primary- and secondary-school curriculum, and a national network of urban and rural studies centres should be established covering all areas of the country.

- The media should be encouraged to give far more prominence to environmental issues. The technical press in particular should develop greater investigative capacity and take a more positive role in promoting change.

- Methods should be devised for exchanging information internationally so that relevant lessons may be learned and action implemented in the shortest possible space of time.

Such a programme of action could be easily adopted by any and all of the major political parties as well as the other individuals and organizations involved. It will clearly have to be fleshed out and the changes obviously cannot take place overnight. Some aspects will require drastic modification to working practices. Others will require legislative change. But the most profound change of all required is a change in attitudes. On all sides – and this applies to community groups as much as to experts and politicians – there needs to be a determination to make things happen, a willingness to be open-minded to new ideas, a tolerance of those with different backgrounds and experience, and a preparedness to believe that the seemingly impossible can be achieved. As Theodore Roszak wrote, in *Where the Wasteland Ends*: 'I can think of forty reasons why none of these projects can possibly succeed and forty different tones of wry cynicism in which to express my well-documented doubts. But I also know that it is more humanly beautiful to risk failure seeking for the hidden springs than to resign to the futurelessness of the wasteland. For the springs are there to be found.'[51]

A New Renaissance

It is important to see the development of community architecture in the context of the fundamental restructuring of society which is currently taking place. A predominantly industrial society based on manufacturing industry is giving way to something new. We are in a period of unprecedented diversity, change and uncertainty marked by a plurality of new approaches both to new and conventional problems. Community architecture – combining previously separate technical and organizational skills – is one such new approach. And it exhibits many of the trends which most futurists believe to be essential if life on this planet is to remain tenable: decentralization rather than centralization; self-help rather than dependency; participatory democracy rather than representative democracy; networking rather than hierarchy; setting long-term objectives rather than short-term. It cuts across yesterday's political and organizational boundaries.

In this respect it can be no accident that community architecture first emerged as a *conscious* movement in Britain. As has often been said, Britain, the first industrial society, has also become the first post-industrial society, exhibiting more clearly than many other countries the tensions of the transition from the old to the new order.

Community architecture is developing the spatial infrastructure required for the new order. It is providing a means for creating the homes, neighbourhoods and cities in which other necessary changes – in lifestyle, work patterns, transportation and so on – can take place. The failure of the development industry to respond more quickly to societies' new needs has been a major factor in the frustration faced by innovations in other areas and thus in the decline of Britain and many other industrial nations. In this respect community architecture provides the missing link; it provides a means for people to give form to their rapidly changing lives and cultures.

The challenge posed by the necessity to create humane settlements is awesome. According to United Nations estimates, one billion people around the world lack adequate shelter, water supplies, sanitation and services. At least 100 million are thought to be literally homeless. Quite apart from coping with the decay and recent mismanagement of our existing cities there is a staggering demand for expansion. An extra 600 million homes are likely to be needed worldwide in the next thirty-five years, a total that will amount to the creation of 3,500 new cities of a million people. Just three hundred such cities currently exist. Unless the development industry can put its house in order relatively quickly, misformed, wasteful and socially divisive human settlements are likely to become the major problem in the twenty-first century.

Community architecture does not yet have all the answers. But it has begun to provide the practical, theoretical and, above all, *political* framework within which they can begin to be worked out. Until its emergence, all those with vision trying to design, plan and build better buildings and cities had become exhausted and demoralized due to being isolated and permanently struggling against the tide. Even the most brilliant creations of modern architects and euphoric community victories appeared as drops in the ocean when compared with the systematic decay and cancerous malformation of the everyday environment taking place all around. The architectural profession had become so demoralized that it was even supporting government proposals to make cuts in its numbers instead of changing direction and urging the massive increase so obviously called for to meet the need. Community architecture has provided a new and effective focus around which all parties can come together and campaign for change.

There are undoubtedly many dangers ahead. Not least that short-sighted politicians and impatient private commercial interests will attempt to gain the advantages of community architecture without accepting its principles or playing their part in making it work.

But one of the hardest battles – that of turning round the architectural profession – has already been fought and won. The combination of Rod Hackney's simultaneous Presidency of the Royal Institute of British Architects and of the International Union of Architects, and the gathering momentum of the Association of Community Technical Aid Centres, will ensure that the environmental professions will never be the same again. The ghosts of the degenerate inheritors of the Modern Movement in architecture and planning – whose paternalistic, technocratic and dehumanizing influence for the last fifty years has made it the single most disastrous episode in the whole history of the built environment – can finally be laid to rest. A new era has been opened up in which the creativity of professionals can once again be directed towards enhancing the lives of the population as a whole.

No one will ever know whether this sea change could ever have been possible without the assistance and influence of the Prince of Wales. Certainly it would have taken much longer. But his recent outspoken and continuing support for community architecture has been one of the most welcome and remarkable events of the 1980s and has given a new significance to the role of royalty in a modern democracy. In his choice of unorthodox advisers like Hackney, Prince Charles has leapfrogged the many bureaucrats and sycophants surrounding him and forged a link with a new generation who want to speed up the pace of change before it is too late. He has used his unique position to focus, articulate and publicize popular views and then to help to secure changes in society for which there was a broad popular consensus but for which the conventional political machinery was inadequate.

For the man who would be both king and philosopher there is clearly a link between his support for community architecture and his searching for the meaning of life as when he disappears into the Kalahari desert with his friend and mentor, Sir Laurens van der Post. The communion of man with his environment and immediate neighbour is of great importance to the Prince. It is reflected in his belief in the importance of the individual and the individual's contribution to the community. As he told delegates to the First International Conference on Community Architecture, Planning and Design in November 1986:

One of the main reasons why I believe that the community architecture approach makes sense is because I believe in the individual uniqueness of every human being.

157

I believe that every individual has a contribution to make and a potential to achieve, if it can be brought about. There are of course exceptions, I do realize, but I [also] believe that individuals tend to operate best within a community of other individuals; within an environment that is based on a human scale and which is designed to create a sense of belonging rather than of alienation and anonymity.[52]

The Prince used his speech on that occasion to call for 'a new renaissance in architecture' and 'a major campaign to save our heritage and to stimulate a whole host of local initiatives to promote community and economic development'. And he ended with an uplifting call to arms which should be the rallying cry for all those struggling to create and manage their own environment:

Can't we try therefore to make mankind feel grand? Can't we raise the spirits by restoring a sense of harmony; by re-establishing human scale in street patterns and heights of buildings; by re-designing those huge areas of what is euphemistically known as 'public open space' between tower blocks which lie derelict, festering and anonymous? Can't we restore people's pride; bring back self-confidence; develop the potential and very real skills of individual people in this island? This may all be a tall order, I realize, but how can any country survive and prosper unless it has an aim and an inspiration? So, let's make 1987, if we possibly can, the start of a new renaissance for Britain – from the bottom up.[52]

Services Provided by Community Technical Aid Centres

This table shows the wide range of services currently provided by community technical aid centres, and their diversity (see pp. 131–4). Information compiled by the Association of Community Technical Aid Centres (ACTAC) in October 1985 based on a survey of forty centres.

	Services provided	*Number of centres providing the service*
1.	Building feasibility study	20
2.	Design and supervision of building	17
3.	Landscape feasibility study	10
4.	Landscape design and supervision	14
5.	Planning advice and advocacy	12
6.	Construction work, buildings/landscape	6
7.	Development/maintenance of plant nurseries	1
8.	Rectifying housing defects	14
9.	Rectifying other building defects	11
10.	Other technical assistance	14
11.	Art and graphics	14
12.	Employment generation and training	4

Workload of a Community Technical Aid Centre

Projects undertaken in just over a year by Community Land and Workspace Ltd (CLAWS), London, September 1983 to October 1984.

Funded by the Greater London Council, CLAWS employed six staff: a project co-ordinator and information officer, an architect, an architectural assistant, a landscape architect, and two workspace development officers.

Information supplied by CLAWS.

Client	*Project Description*
Barnet Arts Workshop	Advice on basement conversion for arts educational use
Old Barn Youth and Community Centre	Sketch design and costing for a BMX track
SANGAM	Feasibility work and costing for new-build Asian women's centre
Brent Voluntary Service Council	Feasibility work and costing for refurbishment and conversion of terraced houses
Purves Road Over-sixties' Club	Advice on proposed allotments for elderly and disabled people on wasteland
Stonebridge City Farm	Technical advice for a new city farm
Calthorpe Project	Advice on project implementation for a community garden
Hillview Estate	Feasibility study and costing for conversion of flats to workshops in a mixed refurbishment scheme
IDRUM Project	Advice on repairs and alterations of premises for an African-drum workshop
Croydon Pastoral Foundation	Financial advice for building acquisition
Bush Hill Park Community Project	Advice on grant application for mixed community project
Hawksley Court Tenants' Association	Improvements to community hall to provide new kitchen, toilets and fencing

Holly Street Estate	Feasibility work and costing for community hall, outdoor sports space and related landscaping
Lincoln Court Tenants' Association	Provision of small community hall
Union of Turkish Workers	Advice on use of building as a centre
Crisp Road Residents Association	Creation of a community garden
Old Oak Primary School	Playground improvement feasibility study to create a school garden
MIND	Advice and technical report on building conversion work
Tottenham Green Under-fives' Centre	Conversion of school building into an under-fives' day nursery and drop-in centre
Honeybun Residents' Association	Feasibility work for new-build centre
Woodlands Community Association	Feasibility work for new-build community centre
Hounslow Council for Voluntary Service	Advice on making grant application
Claremont Islington Mission	Advice and costing for cleaning building facade
Grafton School	Development of a wild garden in the playground
Islington Voluntary Action Council	Feasibility work for seed-bed workshop development
Sunnyside Gardens	Creation of a garden for people with disabilities
Allen Edwards Oasis	Measured survey of community garden; advice on services and asbestos in their building
Brass Tacks Palace Road Site	Feasibility report and costings for public open space and nature reserve
Brixton Housing Co-op	Feasibility study for an ecologically based horticulture scheme
Brixton Music Development	Feasibility study, costings and business plan for converting a car-park into a recording studio and community radio station

Harleyford Road Community Garden Association	Development of community garden on wasteland
Lambeth Intermediate Treatment Centre	Office refurbishment and renovation work
Lambeth Youth Training Service	Advice on office modifications and renovation work
Mount Herman Church of God	Feasibility work and costing of building repairs and conversion for use as meeting-hall and community restaurant
South London Single Parents' Group	Building survey and lease evaluation
Stockwell Good Neighbours	Survey and costing for building conversion work
Women and Training (South London)	Conversion of a garage
The Deptford Drop-in Centre	Advice on new-build day centre for homeless people
Dumps Adventure Playground	Feasibility work and costing for building to be used as a storeroom
Federation of Independent Self-Help	Feasibility study, costing and business plan for mixed development (retailing, sports club, community advice centre)
St Andrew's Church Hall	Investigation of damp problem in a club for teenagers; advice on converting existing church into workshop units
Silwood Tenants' Association	Advice on condition of building and cost of improvements
Spare Plot of Land Action Group	Feasibility of including an under-fives' nursery in a joint ILEA/council development
Wandle Industrial Museum	Technical and financial feasibility work on renovation of listed and other buildings on Liberty Mill site to create a museum and historic craft centre
Newham Allotments and Wasteland Group	Feasibility work and costing of refurbishment for a city farm building
River Boat for People with Disabilities Project	Feasibility work and costing for converting a river boat for use by people with disabilities

Umoja Eats	Financial advice on taking out a lease
Richmond and Twickenham Friends of the Earth	Feasibility study and costing for restoration of listed building for a nature-reserve centre on Crane Island
Alleyn Community Centre	Feasibility work and costing for new-build community building
Lyndhurst School Association	Phase two of school playground improvements
Elephants Jobs	Feasibility work and costings for a new day-centre for single homeless people
St Giles Day-centre	Feasibility studies and surveys of potential premises for a day-centre for homeless people
Association of Island Communities	Feasibility study and business plan for landscape-maintenance, plant-nursery and garden-centre employment scheme
Weavers Youth Group	Feasibility work and costings for refurbishment and conversion of alternative buildings for use as a community centre by Bangladeshi youth group
First Neighbourhood Cooperative Nursery	Conversion of a church hall into an under-fives' day nursery and drop-in centre
St Margaret's Parochial Church Council	Advice on making further grant application for refurbishing church hall for community use
Battersea Boatyard	Technical and financial feasibility studies of the suitability of the Wandle River Basin for community recreation and employment projects
Black Action Group (Wandsworth)	Building survey
Sherfield Gardens Tenants' Association	Feasibility work and costing for new community centre
West Hill Project	Advice on condition of community hall and estimate of repairs
Fitzrovia Greenwell Street Site	Perspective drawing for possible community garden
The London Green Centre Association	Advice on setting up a London Centre for Green Movement resources and activities

Concise History of the Community Architecture Movement

1950s Professionals start working with urban poor on self-help schemes in developing countries.

1960s Architects and planners in the United States start working from shop fronts in low-income neighbourhoods and launch the 'advocacy planning' movement.

Dramatic growth worldwide of community-based voluntary groups protesting about the anti-social effects of conventional architecture and planning.

Influential writers and academics begin calling for citizen participation in the environment.

1969 The Skeffington report *People and Planning* is published in Britain; it is the world's first official government inquiry into public participation in planning.

Architects, planners and artists begin working for community groups in several parts of Britain and start pioneering new approaches and working practices: Shelter's Neighbourhood Action Project (SNAP) installs resident architect in Liverpool; Ralph Erskine establishes local office at Byker in Newcastle; Interaction and Free Form Arts Trust formed as independent environmental aid agencies committed to working with community organizations.

Government begins switching emphasis from new-build to rehabilitation.

1970 European Conservation Year focuses public attention on the built environment.

1971 First International Design Participation Conference held in Sheffield.

First development trust set up in north Kensington, London.

1972 First managed workspace set up at Dryden Street in London.

ASSIST formed in Glasgow to involve residents in the rehabilitation of tenement blocks; it pioneers community-based housing associations.

Award-winning Pruitt-Igoe, St Louis, public housing estate in the United States dynamited after it proved to be a social disaster. Claimed by many as signalling the death of the Modern Movement in architecture and planning.

1973 Planning aid scheme launched by Town and Country Planning Association, making planning expertise available to community groups.

Government scraps gargantuan redevelopment plans for Covent Garden, London, in response to community pressure.

1974 Completion of Britain's first self-help General Improvement Area at Black Road in Macclesfield.

First local-authority neighbourhood project offices set up in Birmingham.

First non-statutory neighbourhood council established in Covent Garden, London.

1975 Community Action in Europe network launched to exchange grass-roots experience between countries.

1976 Community Architecture Working Group formed within the Royal Institute of British Architects to examine the relationship between the profession and the community.

United Nations International Habitat Conference in Vancouver focuses worldwide attention on human-settlement problem and stimulates international exchange of information.

1977 RIBA launches Architectural Aid scheme with architects holding 'surgeries' in Citizens' Advice Bureaux and Architectural Workshop programme to stimulate environmental education.

Community architecture featured on national television for the first time in BBC's *Tomorrow's World* programme.

1978 RIBA unsuccessfully presses government for a National Community Fund to make architectural expertise as available to the public as medical and legal expertise.

Model provincial town regeneration project launched by the Civic Trust at Wirksworth in Derbyshire.

1979 The first community technical aid centres open in Manchester and Liverpool, providing multi-disciplinary professional assistance to community groups.

1980 Launch of European Campaign for Urban Renaissance focusing public attention on cities.

1981 Completion of the first Lewisham self-build housing scheme.

Chartered Surveyors Voluntary Service scheme launched.

Community architecture the main theme of the Commonwealth Association of Architects general assembly in Nairobi.

Inner-city riots in Brixton, Birmingham, Bristol, Liverpool and Manchester.

1982 Community Projects Scheme launched by the RIBA to provide grants for community groups to employ their own professionals.

First national conference on community architecture held at the RIBA.

First of new breed of new-build cooperative housing schemes completed in Liverpool.

Architects' Journal launches regular series on community architecture.

1983   Rod Hackney attacks anti-community-architecture lobby in RIBA and threatens to form a breakaway community architecture institute.

Association of Community Technical Aid Centres launched with all-party support to service the growing number of multi-disciplinary agencies providing technical aid.

Completion of first public-sector rehabilitation project involving tenants at Lea View House, London.

1984   Prince of Wales endorses community architecture for the first time at the RIBA's 150th anniversary celebrations at Hampton Court. National media takes a serious interest in community architecture for the first time.

The government establishes a Special Grants Programme for funding voluntary organization promoting community architecture nationally and regionally.

First new settlement planned and managed by its occupants gets the go-ahead at Lightmoor in Shropshire.

Coin Street Community Builders secure site for multi-million community development on prime London site after long battle with office developers.

1985   Government approves £6.5m community planned and managed mixed development by the Eldonian Housing Association in Liverpool despite opposition from the local authority.

Prince of Wales visits community architecture projects in Macclesfield and Liverpool, and asks RIBA to prepare a report on the inner cities.

Community Urban Design Assistance Team (CUDAT) programme introduced into Britain with a pilot project in Southampton.

Community Enterprise Award scheme launched by *The Times* and RIBA to focus attention on community architecture projects, with the Prince of Wales as patron.

Groundwork Foundation launched to promote Groundwork Trusts at national level.

Model community care centre completed in London by Edward Cullinan Architects.

Inner-city riots in Bristol, Birmingham and London. A policeman murdered and 240 injured on the Broadwater Farm estate in London.

'Divided Britain' controversy erupts when Rod Hackney says the Prince of Wales is fearful of becoming king of a divided nation with no-go areas.

Archbishop of Canterbury endorses community architecture, followed by leading politicians of all main parties.

Government launches Urban Housing Renewal Unit – later renamed Estate Action – to help local authorities involve tenants in the improvement of run-down estates.

International Union of Architects organizes 'Architect as Enabler' Competition and receives entries from forty-four countries.

1986   National Community Partnership of over twenty national voluntary organizations formed to increase the pressure for funding for professional technical assistance for community groups.

Community Architecture Resource Centre established at RIBA headquarters in Portland Place, London.

Prince of Wales visits community architecture projects in east London, Burnley, Cardiff and Stirling, and the Hull school of architecture; commissions community architects to work on Duchy of Cornwall properly; presents top 1986 Community Enterprise Award to the Derry Inner City Project and calls for 'a new renaissance for Britain – from the bottom up'.

Building Communities, the First International Conference on Community Architecture, Planning and Design, held in London, attracts over a thousand delegates and unprecedented media coverage.

Inner City Aid (with Prince of Wales as patron) and National Community Aid Fund launched to raise funds for bottom-up community development.

Rod Hackney elected as the next President of the RIBA.

1987
(to
Aug)
United Nations International Year of Shelter for the Homeless focuses attention worldwide on the problems of human settlements and emphasizes the importance of the 'bottom-up' approach. British launch held at the RIBA.

Ralph Erskine becomes the first community architect to be awarded the Royal Gold Medal for Architecture.

Community Networks launched; the first national publication for the community architecture movement.

Rod Hackney takes office as RIBA President and is elected President of the International Union of Architects.

Habitat International Coalition of non-governmental organizations launched to campaign for community architecture worldwide.

Conservative Party wins third term of office and pledges to focus resources on regenerating the inner cities. Within weeks of the election Rod Hackney is called in as government adviser.

Prince of Wales presents top Community Enterprise Award to the Town and Country Planning Association's Lightmoor Project and calls for a 'crusade' to speed up the pace of change.

Directory of Information Sources

This selection of more than fifty organizations focuses on those providing information and advice, which operate nationally or internationally and, between them, cover the community architecture spectrum. To obtain details of organizations operating at a local or regional level readers are advised to contact the Association of Community Technical Aid Centres, the Community Architecture Resource Centre at the Royal Institute of British Architects, the Planning Aid Unit at the Town and Country Planning Association or their local authorities. Organizations are listed alphabetically.

Alternative Arts
1–4 King Street
Covent Garden
London WC2E 8HN
  01–240 5451
Organization developing open-air and public entertainment. Provides programmes of street performers and information services on performers and performances in Britain and overseas.

American Institute of Architects
1735 New York Avenue, NW
Washington DC 20006
USA 202 626 7300
Provides information on a range of programmes in the United States, including R/UDATs (Regional/Urban Design Assistance Terms).

Art and Architecture
Dunsdale
Forest Row
East Sussex RH18 5BD
  034–282 2704
Non-commercial organization devoted to encouraging collaboration between artists and all those involved in influencing the form of urban landscape. Organizes conferences, seminars and workshops.

Arts Council of Great Britain
105 Piccadilly
London W1V 0AU
  01–629 9495

National body for promotion and funding of the arts. Provides information about community arts.

Associated Housing Advisory Services for Alternatives in Habitat for Another Society (AHAS)
PO Box 397
London E8
　01–249 5869
Company providing worldwide consultancy and information services on community-based local development.

Association of Community Technical Aid Centres (ACTAC)
The Royal Institution
Colquitt Street
Liverpool L1 4DE
　051–708 7607
A national umbrella organization for the community technical aid movement. Registered charity. Publishes directory of its member organizations (over 100 countrywide) and the services they provide. Provides information and referral services.

Building and Social Housing Foundation
Memorial Square
Coalville
Leicestershire LE6 4EU
　0530 39091
Independent research and education institute focusing on sustainable forms of housing. Runs award schemes for imaginative user-controlled projects.

Building Communities Bookshop
c/o T. C. Farries
Irongray Road
Lochside
Dumfries
Scotland DG2 0LH
　0387 720755
Worldwide mail-order and distribution service for books and audiovisual material on all aspects of community architecture, planning, development and technical aid. Regularly updated and annotated catalogue available on request.

Business in the Community
227A City Road
London EC1V 1LX
　01–253 3716
Agency set up to assist commerce and industry play a part in community development. Information and advice available.

Calouste Gulbenkian Foundation
98 Portland Place
London W1N 4ET
    01–636 5313
Charitable foundation focusing on self-help, community development and inner
cities. Publications and information on grants available plus arts and educational
programmes.

Chartered Surveyors Voluntary Service *see* Royal Institution of Chartered Surveyors

Civic Trust
17 Carlton House Terrace
London SW1 5AW
    01–930 0914
Charity with wide-ranging brief for encouraging the protection and improvement
of the environment through conferences, practical projects, films and publications.
Information and advice to local amenity societies.

Community Architecture Information Services (CAIS) Ltd
5 Dryden Street
London WC2E 9NW
    01–240 2430
Consultancy specializing in community architecture. Media specialists and
organizers of Building Communities; the First International Conference on
Community Architecture, Planning and Design in London, November 1986.

Community Architecture Resource Centre *see* Royal Institute of British Architects

Community Projects Foundation
60 Highbury Grove
London N5 2AG
    01–226 5375
National agency for establishing innovative community development projects.
Information, consultancy and publications.

Community Technical Aid Centre
11 Bloom Street
Manchester M1 3HS
    061–236 5195
Community technical aid centre operating in the Manchester area. Establishing a
computerised information database on self-help action in the environment funded
by the European Commission.

Constructive Individuals
53 Adys Road
London SE15 4DX
    01–870 8764

Company offering design, management and training services for people wanting to build their own home.

Co-operative Development Agency
20 Albert Embankment
London SE1 7TJ
  01-211 3000
Set up by Parliament to support the development of cooperatives. Advice and information on cooperatives.

Co-operative Development Services
39–41 Bold Street
Liverpool L1 4EV
  051-708 0674
and
140–42 Stockwell Road
London SW9
  01-737 3572
Information and consultancy on establishing housing cooperatives.

Council for Environmental Education
School of Education
University of Reading
London Road
Reading RG1 5AQ
  0734 875234 ext. 218
Provides advice and information on educational aspects of environmental projects. Publications available.

Councils for Voluntary Service
26 Bedford Square
London WC1B 3HU
  01-636 4066
Independent local agencies to promote effective voluntary service and community based activity. Contact national office for local branches.

Decentralization Research and Information Centre
School of Planning
Polytechnic of Central London
35 Marylebone Road
London NW1 5LS
  01-486 5811 ext. 318
Research and information centre on local-authority decentralization. Regular newsletter and various other publications available.

Department of the Environment
Inner Cities Directorate
Inner Cities Division 3
Room P2/102
2 Marsham Street
London SW1P 3EB
  01–212 3515
Runs special-grants programme which provides funds for management and project grants for bodies in the environmental field at national and regional level. Information available.
and
Architectural Policy Directorate
Room N3/07B
2 Marsham Street
London SW1P 3EB
  01–212 6422
Provides information on various programmes including architecture competitions, art and architecture and free-form arts.

Directory of Social Change
Radius Works
Back Lane
London NW3 1HL
  01–435 8171
Educational charity providing information and training to the voluntary sector. Leading publisher of guides and handbooks.

Ecological Parks Trust
c/o The Linnean Society
Burlington House
Piccadilly
London W1V 0LQ
  01–734 5170
Information and advice on urban nature areas.

Education for Neighbourhood Change
School of Education
University of Nottingham
Nottingham NG7 2RD
  0602 506101
Research and development unit focusing on communication techniques for helping people to get involved in changing their environment. Wide range of resource packs available by mail order.

Free Form Arts Trust
38 Dalston Lane
London E8 3AZ
  01–249 3394
Community arts organization which works with community organizations to improve their environment. Information and advice on community arts.

Friends of the Earth
377 City Road
London EC1V 1NA
  01–837 0731
Campaigning organization promoting policies to protect the natural environment. Information and advice.

Groundwork Foundation
Bennetts Court
6 Bennetts Hill
Birmingham B2 5ST
  021–236 8565
Charitable body promoting groundwork trusts which bring together all agencies, whether in the public, private or voluntary sectors, to promote environmental action. Provides information, advice and support.

Habitat International Coalition
c/c IULA
39–41 Wassenaarseweg
2596 CG – The Hague
Netherlands
  (70) 24 40 32
International federation of non-governmental organizations concerned with human settlements. Policy-making pressure group and advisory body. Range of publications and information available.

Healthy Cities Campaign
c/o World Health Organization
Regional Office for Europe
8 Scherfigsvej
DK 2100. Copenhagen 0
  (1) 29 01 11
and
Department of Community Health
Liverpool University
Medical School
Ashton Street
Liverpool L69 3BX
  051–709 6922 ext. 2894

Campaign launched in 1986 for promoting healthy cities. Information and advice.

Housing Rehabilitation Research Unit
Department of Architecture and Building Science
University of Strathclyde
131 Rottenrow
Glasgow G4 0NG
    041–554 4400
University resource base providing academic back-up in the fields of community technical aid and design participation.

Inner City Aid/The Inner City Trust
8 Bedford Row
London WC1R 4BA
    01–430 0524
Fund-raising registered charity. Provides grant aid, in cash and in kind, for capital building projects generated through self-help community initiatives in deprived urban areas and outer estates. Patron: HRH The Prince of Wales.

Institute of Advanced Architectural Studies
University of York
King's Manor
York YO1 2EP
    0904 24919
Research and educational institute. Runs courses and seminars relating to community architecture.

Inter-Action
Royal Victoria Dock
London E16 1BT
    01–511 0411/6
Group of associated not-for-profit companies involved in social enterprise. Provides training, advice and consultancy in a wide range of fields.

International Union of Architects (UIA)
51 rue Raynouard
75016 Paris
France
Organization representing 900,000 professionals in ninety-eight nations. Organizes conferences, awards and competitions.

Landlife
The Old Police Station
80 Lark Lane
Liverpool L17 8UU
    051–728 7011

National charity aiming to protect and encourage wildlife in cities and rural areas. Works with local groups in active projects. Information and advice.

National Centre for Environmental Interpretation
Manchester Polytechnic
John Dalton Building
Chester Street
Manchester M1 5GD
  061–228 6171
National centre for countryside and urban interpretation. Provides short courses, seminars, conferences, bulletins, advice and information.

National Community Partnership
c/o National Federation of Community Organizations (see below)
Partnership of over twenty national voluntary organizations formed to coordinate their services to help community groups. Runs National Community Aid Fund which raises money for enabling community groups to employ their own professional advisers.

National Council for Voluntary Organizations (NCVO)
26 Bedford Square
London WC1B 3HU
  01–636 4066
Membership of more than 500 national voluntary organizations, public bodies and professional associations. Provides a wide range of professional advisory services to voluntary organizations and has extensive publications programme. A special Urban Unit supports the interest of urban voluntary groups.

National Federation of City Farms
The Old Vicarage
66 Fraser Street
Windmill Hill
Nedminster
Bristol BS3 4LY
  0272 660663
Mutual support and development organization with a membership of city farms and community garden groups. Provides services to members, new groups and the general public.

National Federation of Community Organizations
8/9 Upper Street
London N1 0PQ
  01–226 0189
National body for community organizations. Provides practical advice and support, organizes conferences and publishes guidebooks and information packs.

National Federation of Self-Help Organizations
150 Townmead Road
London SW6 2RA
  01–731 4438/9
Coordinating body for self-help organizations. Provides advice and support and publishes regular newspaper.

National Managed Workspace Group
c/o Richard Allsop
11 Newark Street
Leicester
LE1 5SS
  0533 559711
Coordinating and promoting body for managed workspaces. Organizes conferences, provides information and advice, and publishes quarterly newsletter.

Open House International Association
Centre for Architectural Research and Development Overseas
School of Architecture
The University
Newcastle upon Tyne NE1 7RU
  091–232 8511 ext. 2024
Association of institutes and individuals aiming to spread information about housing and planning with a special focus on encouraging local initiatives by ordinary people. Publishes quarterly journal, *Open House International*.

Participation Network
c/o Stephen Klein
Context
10 West 86th Street
New York, NY 10024
United States of America
International network of people concerned with public participation in environmental change. Publishes newsletter.

Partnership Limited
19 Pelham Square
Brighton BN1 4ET
  0273 677377
Specialist publisher and consultant producing material which helps people to enjoy their surroundings, and to take action to improve them.

Planning Exchange (The)
186 Bath Street
Glasgow G2 4HG
  041–332 8541

Independent non-profit organization providing information services on economic development, housing, planning, urban development, public finance and management.

PRATT Institute Centre for Community and Environmental Development
275 Washington Avenue
Brooklyn, NY 11205
  USA 212/636 3489
Advocacy architecture and planning office with important role in development of community design centres in the United States.

Royal Institute of British Architects (RIBA)
66 Portland Place
London W1N 4AD
  01–580 5533
Professional institution for architects. A range of referral and information services available from its Community Architecture Resource Centre. Runs the Community Projects Fund, providing grants to community organizations for feasibility studies, and the Community Enterprise Award Scheme (jointly with *The Times*). Also has an environmental education unit. Can supply lists of architects experienced in community architecture projects.

The Royal Institution of Chartered Surveyors (RICS)
12 Great George Street
Parliament Square
London WC1P 3AD
  01–222 7000
Runs Chartered Surveyors Voluntary Service. Advice and information service for tenants, landlords and householders unsure how to obtain the services of a surveyor.

Royal Town Planning Institute (RTPI)
26 Portland Place
London W1
  01–636 9107
Professional institute for town planners. Coordinates planning aid network. Advice and information on town-planning matters.

School for Advanced Urban Studies
University of Bristol
Rodney Lodge
Grange Road
Clifton
Bristol B58 4EA
  0272 741117

Teaching and research centre in the field of urban policy. Reports and information available.

Society of Self-Builders
Chelston House
Flower Lane
Amesbury
Wiltshire
  0980 22933

Offers information and other services to self-builders and self-build groups. Publishes regular newsletter.

Stichting Architecten Research (SAR)
Postbus 429
5600AK Eindhoven
Netherlands
  (40) 433616

Research unit at the Eindhoven Technical University concerned with developing the architectural and technical means for facilitating participation in urban housing and neighbourhoods. Many publications available.

Streetwork
c/o Notting Dale Urban Studies Centre
189 Freston Road
London W10 6TH
  01-968 5440

Promotes urban studies in schools with a view to helping children to learn how to become more involved in changing their environment. Runs seminars, conducts research, produces resource packs and publishes the Bulletin of Environmental Education. Runs the Council for Urban Studies Centres.

Town and Country Planning Association (TCPA)
17 Carlton House Terrace
London SW1Y 5AS
  01-930 8903

Britain's oldest voluntary group working to enhance both the built and the natural environment. Provides information and advice, particularly on community planning, planning aid and urban studies centres. Also runs full-time Planning Aid service and sponsors experimental projects. Range of useful publications available. Publishes several regular magazines and bulletins.

United Nations Centre for Human Settlements (UNCHS)
PO Box 30030
Nairobi
Kenya
Africa
  Nairobi 333930

United Nations agency dealing with housing, building and planning. Secretariat for International Year of Shelter for the Homeless 1987. Information and advice, particularly for developing countries.

URBED (Urban and Economic Development) Ltd
99 Southwark Street
London SE1 0JS
  01–928 9515
Provides information and assistance on economic development and re-use of re-dundant industrial and commercial buildings. Range of publications available. Runs training courses.

Walter Segal Trust
6 Segal Close
Brockley Close
London SE23 1PP
  01–690 5882
Trust dedicated to continuing the pioneering work in self-build housing of the architect Walter Segal.

Glossary

Community architecture introduces a wide range of new concepts and programmes. Developing the language of community architecture has been part of the process of developing the activity itself and much of the controversy surrounding the movement has been over semantics. This glossary explains the most commonly used terms.

Adventure playground: Playgrounds that encourage children to construct and manage their own environment.

Advocacy planning: Term popular in the United States in the early 1970s to describe the work of professional planners working as advocates for the poor.

Appropriate technology: Construction materials and techniques geared to local social and economic needs, possibilities and sources of materials. Sometimes referred to as user-friendly.

Architecture workshop: Centre established to provide environmental education, particularly relating to building design; usually for children. Frequently tend to evolve into community technical aid centres.

Balanced incremental development: Development process undertaken in stages that lead on from one another. Allows schemes to evolve organically.

Barefoot architect: Term used in the Far East to describe architects who work in the villages helping people construct their homes. Same meaning as *community architect*.

Building cooperative: Cooperative building contractor. All members usually receive equal rates and decisions are made collectively.

City action team: Programme set up by the government in 1985 to coordinate the policies of various government departments relating to inner-city areas at local level.

City farm: Working farms in urban areas run by a voluntary committee of local people. Their primary role is educational rather than for food production.

Client: Individual or organization which commissions buildings (see also *user-client*).

Community: Used in many ways. Usually refers to the group of users on a particular project or those living within a small, usually ill-defined geographical area.

Community action: A process by which the deprived define for themselves their needs and determine forms of action to meet them, usually outside the prevailing political framework.

Community architect: Architect who practises *community architecture.*

Community architecture: Architecture carried out with the active participation of the end users. Term also used to describe a movement embracing *community planning, community landscape* and other activities involving *community technical aid.*

Community art: Visual and performance art addressed to the needs of a local community. Often related to environmental issues.

Community-based organization (CBO): Voluntary organization operating at a local level. Term increasingly used at international level. Similar in meaning to *community group,* a term more popular in the UK.

Community business: A trading organization owned and controlled by the local community which aims to create self-supporting and viable jobs for local people and to use profits to create more employment, provide local services or support local charitable work.

Community design: Term sometimes used instead of community architecture, especially in the United States.

Community design centre: Place providing free architectural, engineering and planning services to people who cannot afford to pay for them. Term most commonly used in the United States. Similar concept to a *'community technical aid centre',* the term most commonly used in Britain.

Community development: Promotion of self-managed, non-profit-orientated, projects to serve community needs.

Community development corporation: Non-profit-orientated company undertaking development for community benefit. American concept similar to the British *community development trust* (see below).

Community development trust: Independent, not-for-profit organization which undertakes physical development to provide facilities in an area. It will have significant community involvement or control, will bring together a wide range of skills and interests, and will aim to sustain its operations at least in part by generating revenue.

Community enterprise: Enterprise for the benefit of the community rather than private profit by people within the community.

Community garden: Publicly accessible garden or small park created and managed by a voluntary group.

Community group: Voluntary organization operating at local level.

Community landscape: Landscape architecture or design carried out with the active participation of the end users.

Community planning: Planning carried out with the active participation of the end users.

Community planning council: Umbrella organization at neighbourhood level with powers to deal with planning matters. Concept developed and recommended by the Royal Town Planning Institute in 1982. Councils would be made up of representatives from various sectional voluntary interests.

Community politics: A style of political action through which people are enabled to control their own destinies. Identified with an on-going political movement which seeks to create a participatory democracy.

Community project: Facility for the local community, created and managed by a voluntary committee, elected or unelected, from that community.

Community Projects Fund: Fund established by the Royal Institute of British Architects for making grants to community groups for employing professionals to undertake feasibility studies on environmental projects. Part funded by the Department of the Environment.

Community technical aid: Multi-disciplinary expert assistance to community groups enabling them to play an active role in the development of land and buildings. The term 'technical aid' is used to cover the diverse range of skills likely to be necessary including architecture, planning, landscaping, surveying, ecology, environmental education, financial planning, management, administration and graphics.

Community technical aid centre: Centres staffed by a multi-disciplinary group of experts who work for voluntary groups, helping them to undertake any project involving the development of building and land. Will provide whatever assistance is needed – design, planning, organization, decision-making, management – from conception to completion.

Community Urban Design Assistance Team (CUDAT): British version of American RUDAT programme. See *Regional/Urban Design Assistance Team.*

Cooperative: An enterprise conducted for the mutual benefit of its members. A business that is democratic, each member having one vote irrespective of capital or labour input. Any economic surplus belongs to the members – after providing for reserves for the development of the business.

Co-ownership: Tenure arrangement in which property is partly owned by the occupier, the remaining portion being gradually purchased during the period of occupation.

Defensible space: A design approach which inhibits crime by creating the physical expression of a social fabric that defends itself.

Direct action: Exertion of political pressure by tactics other than voting at elections. Usually used to refer to strikes, squatting or occupations.

Disabling: Non-participatory form of service which renders the user unable to have a say in the process.

Enabler: Professional or other person with technical expertise or in a position of authority who uses it to help people to do things for themselves. The term can also be used to refer to organizations which behave likewise.

Enabling: Professional and other services that consciously encourage or allow the user to participate.

Enterprise agency: Non-profit-making companies whose prime objective is to re-spond to through practical action to the economic, training, social and en-vironmental needs of their local communities. A principal activity is providing free advice and counselling to support the setting up and development of viable small businesses. Mostly public sector led in partnership with the private sector, but there are many exceptions.

Enveloping: Programme where a local authority renovates the outside of all houses in a terrace without the need for anyone to move out.

Environmental education: Programmes aimed at making people more aware of their environment and the forces which shape it.

Equity sharing: Similar form of tenure to *co-ownership*

Forum: Non-statutory body for discussing a neighbourhood's affairs and acting as a pressure group. Members may be publicly elected – usually in sectional categories (e.g. residents, traders, churches, etc.) – or be nominated by organizations entitled to be represented under the constitution. Effectively a non-statutory *neigh-bourhood council*.

General Improvement Area: Area designated under government legislation as priority area for renewal. Government grants available.

Habitat: The social and economic, as well as physical, shelter essential for well-being.

Homesteading: Programme in which property owners (usually local authorities) offer substandard property for sale at low cost to householders who will work on it in their own time, doing basic repairs and renovation to standards monitored by the original owners.

Housing association: Association run by an elected management committee which uses government money to provide housing in areas and for people which the government believes to be a high priority. Building-society money is also increasingly used to fund housing associations.

Housing cost yardstick: Financial limits applying to different required items in public-sector dwellings built to government standards and cost limits.

Low-cost housing: Housing affordable by people on low incomes.

Managed workspace: Communally managed building for individual, and independent, enterprises sharing common support facilities and services. Sometimes known as a 'working community'.

Mutual aid: Where people help each other without any formal organization.

National Community Aid Fund: Fund established in 1986 by the National Community Partnership (which consists of over twenty national voluntary organizations) to enable community groups to pay for technical assistance for environmental projects.

Neighbourhood council: Elected body at neighbourhood level with certain statutory powers. Urban equivalent of the parish council and effectively a mini local authority.

Non-governmental organization (NGO): Term commonly used at international level referring to voluntary and non-profit-distributing organizations promoting and supporting community-based development. The difference between an NGO and a CBO (*community-based organization*) is that an NGO is organized and sponsored from outside the local communities in which it operates.

Participation: Act of being involved in something.

Participatory democracy: Process which involves people directly in decision-making which affects them, rather than through formally elected representatives such as councillors or MPs as in representative democracy.

Participatory design: Method of design which uses special techniques to allow users to be involved.

Partnership: Arrangement for joint working on a project. Usually between local authorities and the private sector but increasingly with the voluntary sector as well.

Pattern Language: Method devised by Christopher Alexander in the United States to enable untrained people to design their own buildings and cities in accordance with well-tried principles of good design.

Planning aid: The provision of free and independent information and advice on town planning to groups and individuals who need it and who cannot afford consultancy fees.

Planning for Real: Method enabling people to plan their own neighbourhoods using simple and flexible models which can be supplied through the post in kit form. Devised by Tony Gibson at Education for Neighbourhood Change (see p. 143).

Popular planning: Term coined by the Greater London Council to describe planning from the bottom up.

Priority Estates Project: Experimental government programme to give council tenants a chance to exercise more control over their homes and neighbourhoods by establishing estate-based management systems. Set up in 1979.

Regional/Urban Design Assistance Team (R/UDAT): Programme developed in the United States in which a multidisciplinary team of experts is invited into an area by community leaders to spend a weekend brainstorming session with all sections of the community, examining environmental problems and devising programmes of action to solve them. British version of the programme known as a *Community Urban Design Assistance Team* (*CUDAT*).

Resource centre: Place designed to provide community groups with the facilities they need to make the most of their energies and enthusiasm. No two centres are exactly alike, but will provide some or all of the following: information, office equipment, professional advice and support, meeting facilities, equipment for meetings and fund raising, training courses and opportunities for groups to meet and share ideas.

Self-build: Construction (or repair) work physically undertaken directly by future (or present) occupiers on an individual or collective basis.

Self-help: Where people take responsibility, individually or collectively, for solving their problems.

Self-management: Where a facility is managed by the people who use it.

Self-sufficiency: Reduction of dependence on others, making devolution of control easier and encouraging self-reliance.

Shell housing: Construction system where only floors, walls, roofs and services are provided, leaving occupiers free to build their own interiors.

Short-life housing: Use of empty property on a temporary basis, usually by a voluntary organization.

Site and services: Provision of a serviced site for self-builders. Usually by government, but increasingly also by the private sector.

Social architecture: Similar concept to community architecture. Term commonly used in the United States.

Social entrepreneur: Person who makes things happen by taking initiative in the interests of his or her community rather than for private or personal gain.

Squatting: Unlawful occupation of land or housing.

Supports and Infill: Concept of design, management and construction which aims to distinguish between individual and collective areas of responsibility. Developed at the Stichting Architecten Research in the Netherlands (p. 178).

Sweat equity: Where an individual or community acquires an asset by expending labour rather than money.

Third wave: Revolution transforming society following the industrial revolution (i.e. the second wave – the first wave was the agricultural revolution). Based on growth of high technology and information systems. Term coined by Alvin Toffler.

Town development trust: 'A people's entrepreneurial organization (probably taking the form of a charity owning a trading company), created by a local community – whether that be a street, part of a town, a whole town, a village or part of a region – to revitalize, by rebuilding or renovating, that community's physical surroundings and, in so doing, the community spirit itself' (David Rock, 1980). Similar to *community development trust*.

Urban aid: Government funding intended for community development in urban areas.

Urban design: Emerging discipline which studies the built form of streets, neighbourhoods and cities, not just buildings.

Urban studies centre: Centre of *environmental education*, usually focusing on the immediate surroundings.

User: Actual or future occupier of a building or neighbourhood or beneficiary of a service. (See also *user-client* below.)

User-client: People who are the end-users of buildings and are treated as the *client*, even if they are not technically responsible for paying the bills.

Voluntary sector: Organizations controlled by people who are unpaid, and usually elected, but do not form part of statutory government. Ranges from national to local organizations. Increasingly the divisions between the public, private and voluntary sectors are becoming blurred.

Working community: See *managed workspace*.

Notes

Full details of publications referred to can be found in the Bibliography.
AJ = Architects' Journal.

1. Lord Scarman, *The Scarman Report*, 1981, 6.7, 6.42(iii).
2. Nick Wates, 'The Hackney phenomenon', *AJ*, 20 February 1985, p. 50.
3. *Oxford English Dictionary.*
4. From his speech to Building Communities, the First International Conference on Community Architecture, Planning and Design, November 1986; published in Jim Sneddon and Caroline Theobald, eds., *Building Communities*, 1987.
5. Quotations from Colin Ward, *Tenants Take Over*, 1974, p. 43.
6. Transcript available from Buckingham Palace or the RIBA.
7. *Manchester Evening News*, 23 October 1985.
8. Cooperative Development Services, *Building Democracy: Housing Cooperatives on Merseyside*, rev. ed., 1987, p. 2.
9. Interview with Charles Knevitt, quoted in *Building Design*, 31 January 1986.
9a. 15 June 1987.
9b. 12 June 1987, p. 1.
9c. *Building Design*, 15 July 1987, p. 6.
10. *Observer*, 23 August 1981.
11. Report to Secretary of State for the Environment by S. A. E. Reese, Inspector, 15 June 1984.
12. *Time Out*, 16–22 April 1986, p. 9.
13. *New Statesman*, 11 January 1985.
13a. Sources: Department of the Environment, *House Condition Survey*, 1981 and 1986; Association of Metropolitan Authorities, 1986; Audit Commission, 1986; Building Employers' Confederation, *Neglected Britain Report*, 1987; Department of the Environment, *Housing Policy Review Estimate*, 1977; Building Employers' Confederation, *Nationwide Survey*, 1986; UK Section, International Year of Shelter for the Homeless, 1987; Union of Construction and Allied Trade Technicians, 1987.
14. Transcript available from Buckingham Palace or the RIBA; speech given on 5 January 1987.
15. Joan Reeder, 'The Pied Piper of Black Road', *Woman*, 20 October 1982.
16. Nick Wates, ibid., p. 48.
17. Joan Reeder, ibid.
18. In a letter to the authors.
19. John Thompson, *Community Architecture*, 1985, p. 4.
20. ibid.
21. *Hackney Gazette*, 15 May 1984.

22. *Hillview Community News*, May 1984.
23. In a film sponsored by British Gas, 'Housing solutions: the story of Lea View House'.
24. 'The Liverpool breakthrough', *AJ*, 8 September 1982.
25. Patrick Hannay and Nick Wates, 'Co-op dividends', *AJ*, 18 July 1984.
26. Jon Broome, 'The Segal method', *AJ*, 5 November 1986.
27. ibid., p. 33; *Guardian*, 15 January 1986.
28. Nick Wates, 'Shaping a service in Manchester', *AJ*, 4 August 1982.
29. David Rock, *The Grassroots Developers*, 1980, p. 46.
30. Jules Lubbock, 'Lambeth Community Care Centre, a patient revolution', *AJ*, 16 October 1985.
31. Susan Freudenberg, 'Responding to Cullinan', *Building Design*, 21 November 1986, p. 27.
32. Jules Lubbock, ibid.
33. Peter Hain, ed., *Community Politics*, 1976, p. 190.
34. In a letter to the authors, May 1987.
35. N. J. Habraken, *Supports: an Alternative to Mass Housing*, 1972, p. 38 (first published in Dutch in 1961).
36. In Richard Hatch, ed., *The Scope of Social Architecture*, 1984, p. 252.
37. 'Towards a Theory of Participation in Architecture', in Tom Woolley, ed., *The Characteristics of Community Architecture and Community Technical Aid*, 1985, p. 15.
38. Michael Hook, 'Housing cooperatives', *AJ*, 29 June 1977.
39. RIBA, *The Practice of Community Architecture*, 1978, p. 5.
40. Nick Wates, 'Shaping a service in Manchester, *AJ*, 4 August 1982.
41. *New Society*, 18 May 1978.
42. 'Review of Technical Aid Organizations', GLC Transport and Development Department, 29 July 1983.
43. Quoted in an article by Kevin McGovern in *Going Local* (Newsletter of the Decentralization Research and Information Centre), No. 7, March 1987, p. 17.
44. Richard Hatch, ibid., p. 287.
45. Beheshti, M. R., ed., *Design Coalition Team*, 1985, vol. 1, p. 6.
46. In 'Conservation conspectus: architect at the local level', *Architectural Review*, December 1970, pp. 367–8 and 375–6.
47. Unpublished lecture.
48. *AJ*, 20 February 1985, p. 50.
49. David Rock, *The Grassroots Developers*, 1980, p. 11.
50. Wirksworth Project, *The Wirksworth Story*, 1984, p. 82.
51. Quoted in Rock, ibid., p. 77.
52. Transcript available from Buckingham Palace or the RIBA.

Bibliography

This bibliography contains the theoretical and descriptive writings, reports, case studies and speeches of most relevance to the development of community architecture. The items starred are those that the authors recommend as of most interest to the general reader. Restricted to English language material only. Most can be consulted at the RIBA Community Architecture Resource Centre (see Appendix 3).

BOOKS, PAMPHLETS AND REPORTS

Adams, Eileen, and Ward, Colin, *Art and the Built Environment*, Longman, for the Schools Council, 1982.

*Alexander, Christopher, *The Linz Café*, Oxford University Press, 1981.

*Alexander, Christopher, *The Timeless Way of Building*, Oxford University Press, 1979.

Alexander, Christopher, *The Production of Houses*, Oxford University Press, 1982.

*Alexander, Christopher, *et al.*, *A Pattern Language*, Oxford University Press, 1977.

*Alexander, Christopher, *et al.*, *The Oregon Experiment*, New York, Oxford University Press, 1975.

Ambrose, Peter, and Colenutt, Bob, *The Property Machine*, Penguin Books, 1975.

American Institute of Architects, *R/UDAT Handbook*, Washington, AIA; regularly updated.

Anson, Brian, *I'll Fight You for It! Behind the Struggle for Covent Garden*, Jonathan Cape, 1981.

Armor, Murray, *Building Your Own Home*, Dorchester, Dorset, Prism Press, 1978.

Armstrong, Dave, ed., *Miles Better, Miles to Go: The Story of Glasgow's Housing Associations*, Glasgow, Housetalk Group, 1986.

*Association of Community Technical Aid Centres (ACTAC), *Working with Local Communities: National Directory of Community and Technical Aid Centres*; first published 1985 (regularly updated).

Association of Community Technical Aid Centres, *First Report*, ACTAC, 1986.

Association of Community Technical Aid Centres, *A Community Technical Services Agency for Knowsley*, ACTAC, 1986.

Bailey, Ron, *The Squatters*, Penguin Books, 1973.

Barker, Anthony, *Public Participation in Britain: A Classified Bibliography*, Bedford Square Press, in association with the Royal Town Planning Institute, 1979.

Barker, Michael J. C., *Directory for the Environment*, Routledge & Kegan Paul, 1984.

*Batchelor, Peter, and Lewis, David, eds., *Urban Design in Action: the History, Theory and Development of the American Institute of Architects' Regional/Urban Design Assistance Teams Programme (R/UDAT)*, North Carolina State University School of Design and the American Institute of Architects, 1985.

Beheshti, M. R., ed., *Design Coalition Team*, Vols. 1 and 2 (Proceedings of the International Design Participation Conference), Eindhoven, University of Eindhoven, Department of Architecture Building and Planning, 1985.

Bishop, Jeff, *Building Design for Non-Designers: an Innovative Distance-learning Pack*, Bristol, School for Advanced Urban Studies, 1987.

Bishop, Jeff, *Voluntary Sector/Local Authority Collaboration on Environmental Improvement*, University of Bristol, School for Advanced Urban Studies 1983.

*Blake, Peter, *Form Follows Fiasco: Why Modern Architecture Hasn't Worked*, Boston, MA, Little, Brown and Company, 1974.

Boericke, Art, and Shapiro, Barry, *Handmade Houses: a Guide to the Woodbutcher's Art*, London, Idea Books International, 1975.

Bowman, Anna, *Homelessness – Shortlife Answers*, National Federation of Housing Associations, 1986.

Breakell, David, The *RIBA Community Architecture Working Group and Architectural Education* (Paper for NAM Education Group Meeting, Cardiff, London), 1978.

Broady, Maurice, *Planning for People: Essays on the Social Context of Planning*, London, Bedford Square Press, 1968.

Butcher, H., Collins, P., Glen, A., and Sills, P., *Community Groups in Action: Case Studies and Analysis*, London, Routledge & Kegan Paul, 1980.

Cadman, David, *Changing Places* (The Fitzgerald Memorial Lecture 1984), London, Polytechnic of the South Bank, Faculty of the Built Environment (Occasional paper), 1985.

Caird, David J., *Alternative Practice: a Major Study for the Diploma in Architecture*, Oxford, Oxford Polytechnic School of Architecture, 1981/1982.

Callenbach, Ernest, *Ecotopia*, London, Pluto Press, 1978.

Calouste Gulbenkian Foundation, *Community Challenge – A Conference Report*, Calouste Guilbenkian Foundation, UK Branch, 1983.

Capra, Fritjof, *The Turning Point: Science, Society and the Rising Culture*, London, Wildwood House, 1982.

*Christensen, Terry, *Neighbourhood Survival: The Struggle for Covent Garden's Future*, London, Prism Press, 1979.

Cockburn, Cynthia, *The Local State: Management of Cities and People*, London, Pluto Press, 1977.

*Coleman, Alice, *Utopia on Trial: Vision and Reality in Planned Housing*, London, Hilary Shipman, 1985.

Collymore, Peter, *The Architecture of Ralph Erskine*, London, Granada Publishing, 1982.

Community Architecture Working Group (RIBA), *Designing for the Community* (Paper for the 13th World Congress of the UIA, Mexico City), London, RIBA, October 1978.

*Community Land and Workspace Services Ltd (CLAWS), *Planning a Capital Project*, London, Directory of Social Change, 1985.

*Co-operative Development Services, *Building Democracy: Housing Co-operatives on Merseyside*, Liverpool, CDS, 1987.

Co-operative Development Services, *Choosing an Architect*, Liverpool, CDS, c.1982.

Crosby, Theo, *How to Play the Environment Game*, Penguin Books, in association with the Arts Council of Great Britain, 1973.

Curno, Paul, ed., *Political Issues and Community Work*, London, Routledge & Kegan Paul, 1978.

*Davidson, Joan, and McEwen, Anne, *The Liveable City*, London, RIBA Publications Ltd, 1983.

Dennis, Norman, *People and Planning: the Sociology of Housing in Sunderland*, London, Faber, 1970.

Department of the Environment, *Urban Renaissance: a Better Life in Towns* (report on United Kingdom urban policies), London, HMSO, 1980.

Department of the Environment, *Whose Town is it Anyway?* (Proceedings of the Conference held to review the progress of the European Campaign for Urban Renaissance in Britain), London, HMSO, 1982.

Divis Residents Association, *The Divis Report: Set Them Free*, Belfast, DRA, 1986.

Donnison, David, and Ungerson, Clare, *Housing Policy*, Penguin Books, 1982.

Dorfman, Marc, *Making Use of Vacant Land and Buildings*, London TCPA, London Planning Aid Service, 1985.

Dunleavy, Patrick,*The Politics of Mass Housing in Britain, 1945–1975: a Study of Corporate Power and Professional Influence in the Welfare State*, Oxford, OUP (Clarendon Press), 1981.

Dunn, Nell, *Living Like I Do*, Futura, 1977.

Education for Neighbourhood Change, A range of community resource packs including 'Planning for Real', 'The Neighbourhood Fact Bank', 'The Feasibility Pack', 'Turning the Talk into Action', 'Neighbourhood Case Histories and Your Learning Pack', School of Education, University of Nottingham, Nottingham NG7 2RD.

*Eldonian Community Association, *We Know What We Want: a Guide to Help Your Group Get It*, Eldonian Community Association, 1986.

Esher, Lionel, *A Broken Wave: the Rebuilding of England 1940–1980*, London, Allen Lane, 1981.

Falk, Nicholas, and Martinos, Haris, *Inner Cities: Local Government and Economic Renewal*, Fabian Society, 1976.

Fathy, Hassan, *Architecture for the Poor*, University of Chicago Press, 1973.

Fraser, Ross, *Filling the Empties*, London, Shelter, 1986.

Freeman, Hugh, ed., *Mental Health and the Environment*, London, Churchill Livingstone, 1985.

Friedman, Yona, *A Better Life in Towns*, Council of Europe, 1980.

Gibson, Michael S., and Langstaff, Michael J., *An Introduction to Urban Renewal*, London, Hutchinson, 1982.

*Gibson, Tony, *Counterweight: the Neighbourhood Option*, London, Town and Country Planning Association, and Education for Neighbourhood Change, 1984.

Gibson, Tony, *et al.*, *Us Plus Them: How to Use the Experts to Get what People Really Want*, London, Town and Country Planning Association, 1986.

Girardet, Herbert, *Land for the People*, London, Crescent Books, 1976.

Goodman, Paul and Percival, *Communitas: Means of Livelihood and Ways of Life*, New York, Vintage Books, 1960.

Goodman, Robert, *After the Planners*, Penguin Books, 1972.

Grabow, Stephen, *Christopher Alexander: the Search for a New Paradigm in Architecture*, Stocksfield, Northumberland, Oriel Press, 1983.

Greater London Council, *Community Areas Policy: A Record of Achievement*, London, GLC, 1985.

Habeebullah, Mohammed, and Hargreaves, John, with Robert Jeffocate, *Design for Living: The Making of a Multi-cultural Community*, London, Community Projects Foundation, 1986.

*Habraken, N.J., *Supports: an Alternative to Mass Housing*, London, Architectural Press, 1972 (originally published in Dutch in 1961).

Hain, Peter, ed., *Community Politics*, London, John Calder, 1976.

Hardy, Dennis, and Ward, Colin, *Arcadia for All: the Legacy of a Makeshift Landscape*, London, Mansell Publishing, 1984.

Harrison, Paul, *Inside the Inner City: Life under the Cutting Edge*, Penguin Books, 1983.

*Hatch, Richard, ed., *The Scope of Social Architecture*, Wokingham, Berkshire, Van Nostrand Reinhold, 1984.

Hellman, Louis, *A is for Architect*, Trend Publishing (S) Pte Ltd, in cooperation with Lim Chong Keat and Atsco Pte Ltd, 1975.

*Hellman, Louis, *All Hellman Breaks Loose: Architecture Exposed*, Arcus Ltd, 1980.

Hiller, Patricia M., *Analysis of the British Construction Industry*, Macmillan, 1984.

Hillier, Bill and Hanson, Julienne, *The Social Logic of Space*, Cambridge, Cambridge University Press, 1984.

Hillview Residents Association and Hunt Thompson Associates, *Hillview: The Alternative to Demolition*, Hillview Residents Association, 1986.

Holod, Renata, and Rastorfer, Darl, eds., *Architecture and Community: Building in the Islamic World Today*, New York, Aperture, 1983.

Home, Robert K., *Inner City Regeneration*, London, Spon, 1982.

Housing Research Group, *Could Local Authorities be Better Landlords?*, London, The City University, 1981.

Illich, Ivan, *Shadow Work*, London, Marion Boyars, 1981.

Illich, Ivan, *Tools for Conviviality*, London, Calder & Boyars, 1973.

Illich, Ivan, *Energy and Equity: Ideas in Progress*, London, Calder & Boyars, 1974.

Illich, Ivan, *The Right to Useful Employment*, London, Marion Boyars, 1978.

*Illich, Ivan, *Disabling Professions*, London, Marion Boyars, 1977.

*Jacobs, Jane, *The Death and Life of Great American Cities: The Failure of Town Planning*, Penguin Books, in association with Jonathan Cape, 1965 (first published 1961).

Jacobs, Jane, *The Economy of Cities*, Vantage Books, 1970.

Kagan, Paul, *New World Utopias*, Penguin Books, 1975.

King, A., and Clifford, Sue, *Holding your Ground*, Hounslow, Middlesex, Wildwood House, 1985.

Knevitt, Charles, *Space on Earth; Architecture, People and Buildings*, London, Thames-Methuen, in association with Anglia Television and Channel Four TV, 1985.

Knevitt, Charles, ed., *Community Enterprise*, London, *The Times* and the Calouste Gulbenkian Foundation, 1986.

Knevitt, Charles, ed., *Monstrous Carbuncles: a Cartoon Guide to Architecture*, London, Lund Humphries, 1985.

Knight, Barry, and Hayes, Ruth, *Self Help in the Inner City*, London, London Voluntary Service Council, 1981.

Kohr, Leopold, *The Breakdown of Nations*, London, Routledge & Kegan Paul, 1957.

Kroll, Lucien, *The Architecture of Complexity*, London, Batsford, 1986.

*Kropotkin, Peter, *Mutual Aid: a Factor of Evolution*, Porter Sargent Publishers Inc., 1976 (first published 1902).

Kropotkin, Peter, edited by Ward, Colin, *Fields, Factories and Workshops Tomorrow*, London, Allen & Unwin, 1974.

Lambert, Jack, and Pearson, Jenny, *Adventure Playgrounds*, Penguin Books, 1974.

Lees, Ray, and Mayo, Marjorie, *Community Action for Change*, London, Routledge & Kegan Paul, 1984.

McCullough, Jamie, *Meanwhile Gardens*, Calouste Gulbenkian Foundation, 1978.

*McDonald, Alan, for the Weller Streets Housing Cooperative, *The Weller Way*, with a Foreword by HRH The Prince of Wales, London, Faber, 1986.

*MacEwen, Malcolm, *Crisis in Architecture*, London, RIBA Publications, 1974.

McKean, Charles, *Fight Blight*, Kaye & Ward, 1977.

McKean Charles, ed., *Funding the Future: the Report of a Conference Studying New Initiatives in Architecture, Planning and Construction*, London, ERA Publications Board (Eastern Region RIBA), 1977.

Macrae, Norman, *The 2024 Report*, London, Sidgwick & Jackson, 1984.

Manchester City Council, *Deck Access Disaster: Report of the Hulme Conference*, Manchester, 1985.

Markus, Thomas A., ed., *Building Conversion and Rehabilitation: Design for Change in Building Use*, London, Butterworth, 1979.

Marriott, Oliver, *The Property Boom*, London, Hamish Hamilton, 1967.

Marris, Peter, *Community Planning and Conceptions of Change*, London, Routledge & Kegan Paul, 1982.

Matrix, *Making Space: Women and the Man-made Environment*, London, Pluto, 1984.

Mikellides, Byron, ed., *Architecture for People*, London, Studio Vista, 1980.

Ministry of Housing and Local Government, *People and Planning: the Report of the Committee on Public Participation in Planning* (Chairman: A. Skeffington), London, HMSO, 1969.

Moss, Graham, *Britain's Wasting Acres: Land Use in Changing Society*, London, Architectural Press, 1981.

Naisbitt, John, *Megatrends*, London, Futura, 1984.

National Federation of Housing Associations, *Inquiry into British Housing* (Chaired by The Duke of Edinburgh), London, NFHA, July 1985.

New Architecture Movement (Public Design Group), *Community Architecture: A Public Design Service?* (a report to the Minister of Housing and Construction into the provision of architectural services to the community), London, NAM, 1978.

Newman, Oscar, *Community of Interest*, Anchor Press/Doubleday, 1981.

*Newman, Oscar, *Defensible Space: Crime Prevention through Urban Design*, New York, The Macmillan Company, 1972.

Norton, Michael, *The Directory of Social Change*, Hounslow, Middlesex, Wildwood House: Vol. 1, *Education and Play*, 1977; Vol. 2, *Community*, 1977; Vol. 3, *Women*, 1978; Vol. 4, *Housing*, 1980.

Parker, Tony, *The People of Providence: a Housing Estate and Some of its Inhabitants*, London, Hutchinson, 1983.

Pawley, Martin, *Architecture versus Housing*, London, Studio Vista, 1971.

Pawley, Martin, *Home Ownership*, London, Architectural Press, 1978.

Policy for the Inner Cities, London, HMSO, 1977.

*Porritt, Jonathan, *Seeing Green: the Politics of Ecology Explained*, Oxford, Blackwell, 1984.

Portola Institute, *The Last Whole Earth Catalogue*, Penguin Books, 1971.

Postgate, Richard, *Home: a Place for Work?*, London, Calouste Gulbenkian Foundation (UK Branch), 1984.

Power, Anne, *Local Housing Management: a Priority Estates Project Survey*, London, Department of the Environment, 1984.

*Ravetz, Alison, *Remaking Cities: Contradictions of the Recent Urban Development*, London, Croom Helm, 1980.

Ravetz, Alison, *The Government of Space: Town Planning in Modern Society*, London, Faber, 1986.

Reich, Charles A., *The Greening of America*, Penguin Books, 1971.

Report of the Archbishop of Canterbury's Commission on Urban Priority Areas, *Faith in the City: a Call for Action by Church and Nation*, London, Church House Publishing, 1985.

Robertson, James, *The Sane Alternative, a Choice of Futures*, J. Robertson, 9 New Rd, Ironbridge, Telford, Salop.

*Rock, David, *The Grassroot Developers: a Handbook for Town Development Trusts*, London, RIBA Conference Fund, 1980.

Roddewig, Richard, *Green Bans: the Birth of Australian Environmental Politics*, Conservation Foundation (Washington), with Alanheld, Osman & Co., 1978.

Roszak, Theodore, *Person/Planet*, St Albans, Granada Publishing, 1981.

Royal Institute of British Architects, *Highfield Hall: a Community Project*, London, RIBA Publications, 1983.

Royal Institute of British Architects, *A National Urban Renewal Agency: Inner Cities Committee Report*, London, RIBA, 1987.

Royal Institute of British Architects, *The Practice of Community Architecture: the Case for a Community Aid Fund*, London, RIBA, 1978.

Royal Institute of British Architects, *Homes Old and New, a Housing Strategy for the Eighties*, London, RIBA Publications, 1983.

Royal Society of Arts, *Practical Conservation: the Third Force – Environmental Charities as Owners or Managers of Property* (Conference Proceedings), London, RSA, 1985.

Royal Town Planning Institute, *The Public and Planning: Means to Better Participation* (Final Report of the Public Participation Working Party), London, RTPI, 1982.

Saint, Andrew, *The Image of the Architect*, London and New Haven, Yale University Press, 1983.

*Sale, Kirkpatrick, *Human Scale*, London, Secker & Warburg, 1980.

Scarman, Lord, *The Brixton Disorders 10–12 April 1981*, London, HMSO, 1981; Penguin Books, 1982 (under the title *The Scarman Report*).

Schön, Donald, *The Design Studio: an Exploration of its Traditions and Potential*, London, RIBA Publications Ltd, for RIBA Building Industry Trust, 1985.

Schumacher, E. F., *Small is Beautiful: a Study of Economics as if People Mattered*, London, Blond & Briggs, 1973.

Scott, Jim, and Jenks, Mike, *What is the Point of Community Architecture?*, Oxford, Oxford Polytechnic, Department of Town Planning (Working Paper no. 95), 1986.

*Seabrook, Jeremy, *The Idea of Neighbourhood: What Local Politics should be about*, London, Pluto Press, 1984.

Seelig, Michael Y., *The Architecture of Self-help Communities*, New York, Architectural Record Books, 1979.

Sennett, Richard, *The Uses of Disorder: Personal Identity and City Life*, Penguin Books, 1970.

Serrano, José Luis Ospina, *Housing Ourselves – Popular Participation in Housing in Columbia and England*, York, University of York, Institute of Advanced Architectural Studies, 1985.

Sharples, Steve, and Woolley, Tom, *The Nature of Community Technical Aid and the Contribution Made to it by the DOE's Special Grants Programme* (A research report prepared for the Department of the Environment by the Housing and Rehabilitation Research Unit) Glasgow, University of Strathclyde, Department of Architecture and Building Science, 1987.

Skeffington, A., see Ministry of Housing and Local Government.

Smiles, Samuel, *Self-Help*, Penguin Books, 1986 (first published 1869).

Smith, Adam, *The Wealth of Nations: Books I–III*, Penguin Books, 1983 (first published 1776).

Smith, Jerry, *Urban Renewal: Securing Community Involvement*, London, Community Projects Foundation, 1983.

Smith, Neil, and Williams, Peter, eds., *Gentrification of the City*, London, Allen & Unwin, 1986.

*Sneddon, Jim, and Theobald, Caroline, eds., *Building Communities: the First International Conference on Community Architecture, Planning and Design* (conference proceedings), London, Community Architecture Information Services, in association with RIBA Publications, 1987.

Spretnak, Charlene and Capra, Fritjof, *Green Politics: the Global Promise*, London, Hutchinson, 1984.

Stead, Peter, *Self-build Housing Groups and Co-operatives: Ideas in Practice*, London, Anglo-German Foundation for the Study of Industrial Society, 1979.

Stead, Peter, ed., *Local Initiatives in Great Britain: Vol. III, Housing*, Banbury, Oxon, New Foundations for Local Initiative Support, 1982.

Stephenson, Jane, and Rawson, Jill, *Community Buildings Project Pack*, National Council for Voluntary Organizations, London, 1983.

Stokes, Bruce, *Helping Ourselves: Local Solutions to Global Problems*, Norton/Worldwatch Books, 1981.

Sullivan, Andrew, *Greening the Tories: New Policies on the Environment* (Policy Study no. 72), London, Centre for Policy Studies, 1985.

Talbot, Michael, *Reviving Buildings and Communities: a Manual of Renewal*, Newton Abbott, David & Charles, 1986.

Taylor, Marilyn, *Resource Centres for Community Groups*, London,

Community Projects Foundation and Calouste Gulbenkian Foundation, 1983.

*Thompson, John, *Community Architecture: the Story of Lea View House, Hackney*, London, RIBA Publications, 1985.

Toffler, Alvin, *The Third Wave*, London, Collins, 1980.

Toffler, Alvin, *Future Shock*, London, Bodley Head, 1970; Pan Books, 1971.

Town and Country Planning Association, *Whose Responsibility? Reclaiming the Inner Cities* (Inner City Report), London, TCPA, 1986.

Town and Country Planning Association, *Community Technical Aid Centre, Places for People: How to Start a Community Project*, London, TCPA, 1986.

Townsend, Peter, ed., *Art within Reach: Artists and Craftworkers, Architects and Patrons in the Making of Public Art*, London, Thames & Hudson, 1984.

Trombley, Stephen, ed., *Architecture for Developing Countries* (Architectural Education 2), London, RIBA Magazines, 1983.

*Turner, Bertha, ed., *Building Community: a Third World Casebook*, Habitat International Council, The Hague, and Habitat Forum, Berlin, in association with Intermediate Technology (IT) Publications, London, 1987.

*Turner, John F. C., *Housing by People – Towards Autonomy in Building Environments*, London, Marion Boyars, 1976.

* Turner, John F. C., and Fichter, Robert, eds., *Freedom to Build: Dweller Control of the Housing Process*, London, Collier-Macmillan, 1972.

Warburton, Diane, ed., *Community Landscapes: Making Your Mark on Manchester*, Manchester, Manchester City Council/Think Green/ Partnership Ltd, 1986.

Warburton, Diane, ed., *Raising Money for Environmental Improvements*, Peterborough, Shell Better Britain Campaign, 1986.

*Ward, Colin, *Housing: an Anarchist Approach*, London, Freedom Press, 1976.

Ward, Colin, *The Child in the City*, London, Architectural Press, 1978; Penguin Books, 1979.

Ward, Colin, *Utopia: Human Space*, Penguin Books, 1974.

*Ward, Colin, *When We Build Again: Let's Have Housing That Works!*, London, Pluto Press, 1985.

Ward, Colin, *Tenants Take Over*, London, Architectural Press, 1974.

Ward, Colin, and Fyson, Anthony, *Streetwork the Exploding School*, London, Routledge & Kegan Paul, 1973.

Ward, Peter M., ed., *Self-help Housing: a Critique*, London, Mansell Publishing, 1982.

Wates, Nick, *The Battle for Tolmers Square*, London, Routledge & Kegan Paul, 1976.

Wates, Nick, ed., *The Limehouse Petition*, London, Limehouse Development Group, in association with the Town and Country Planning Association, 1986.

Wates, Nick, and Wolmar, Christian, eds., *Squatting: the Real Story*, London, Bay Leaf Books, 1980.

Watkin, David, *The Rise of Architectural History*, London, The Architectural Press, 1980.

Wilcox, David, and Richards, David, *The Heartless City – London*, London, Thames Television/Argus Books, 1977.

Willmott, Peter, and Young, Michael, *Family and Kinship in East London*, London, Routledge & Kegan Paul, 1957; Penguin Books, 1962.

Wilson, Des, ed., *The Environmental Crisis: a Handbook for all Friends of the Earth* (with an introduction by David Bellamy), London, Heinemann, 1984.

Wilson, Des, with Andrews, Leighton, and Franlez, Maurice, *Citizen Action: Taking Action in Your Community*, London, Longman, 1986.

Wirksworth Project, in association with the Civic Trust, *The Wirksworth Story: New Life for an Old Town – The Report on the First Stages of a Town Regeneration Project*, London, Civic Trust, 1984.

Wolfe, Tom, *From Bauhaus to Our House*, London, Jonathan Cape, 1982.

Woolley, Tom, Community Architecture: an Evaluation of the Case for User Participation in Architectural Design, Department of Architecture, Oxford Polytechnic, 1985.

Woolley, Tom, ed., *The Characteristics of Community Architecture and Community Technical Aid*, Glasgow, University of Strathclyde (Department of Architecture and Building Science occasional paper), 1985.

Young, Tim, ed., *Community Technical Aid: a Directory of Technical Aid Centres Serving Community Groups in London*, London, London Voluntary Service Council, 1984.

ARTICLES

(*AJ* = *Architects' Journal*; *BD* = *Building Design*)

Anson, Brian, 'City under siege: report on the plight of residents of the Divis flats in Belfast', *AJ*, 9 July 1986.

Architectural Design, special issues: 'Dwelling Resources in Latin America', August 1963.

'Alternative Approaches to Human Settlements', April 1976.

'Habitat Reconsidered', October 1976.

Architectural Review, special issues: 'Architecture and Community', April 1985; 'Architecture of Commitment', March 1987.

Architektur Wittbewerbe, special issue: 'The Architect as Enabler of User House Planning and Design: International Competition for Students of Architecture Unesco Prize 1974', Stuttgart, Karl Kramer Verlag, 1985.

Arnstein, Sherry, 'A ladder of public participation', *Journal of the American Institute of Planners*, July 1969.

Barnard, Roger, 'Community action in a twilight zone', *RIBA Journal*, October 1970.

Bennet, Graham, and Rutherford, Stuart, 'A site better off: special report on small vacant sites', *AJ*, 31 January 1979.

Broome, Jon, 'The Segal method', *AJ* (special issue), 5 November 1986.

Brown, Anthony, 'Rod Hackney's people buildings', *Reader's Digest*, July 1987.

Building Design, special issues for Building Communities Conference, 21 and 28 November 1986.

Charles, HRH The Prince of Wales, 'Give us design with feeling', *The Times*, 31 May 1984.

'Paradise regained', *The Times*, 13 June 1986.

'A four-point plan for the cities', *The Times*, 14 June 1986.

Clare, John, 'Grass roots advice', *BD*, 11 March 1977.

Community Action Magazine, many relevant articles.

Community Network, a regular newsletter on community planning, architecture, design and technical aid from the Town and Country Planning Association (launched 1987).

Cowan, Rob, 'Developing Planning Aid' (special report), *Town and Country Planning*, October 1980.

'Meat and gravy: Martlett Court, Westminster, and the Doddington Estate, Wandsworth', *AJ*, 29 April 1987.

Darke, Jane, 'Architects and user requirements in public sector housing: towards an adequate understanding of user requirements in housing', *Planning and Design*, vol. 11, 1984.

Ellis, Charlotte, 'Do-it-yourself vernacular', *AJ*, 17 December 1980.

Falk, Nicholas, 'Community as developer', *Built Environment*, April 1974.

'Enabling change', *Built Environment*, vol. 5, no. 3, 1979.

'Our industrial heritage: a resource for the future', *The Planner*, October 1985.

'Baltimore and Lowell: two American approaches', *Built Environment*, vol. 12, no. 3.

Fogg, Eva, 'Self-build and self-extension', *AJ*, 23 January 1985.

Francis, Mark, 'Community design', *Journal of Architectural Education*, no. 37, 1983.

Gibson, Tony, 'Decision-making in neighbourhood design and development', *Design Studies*, vol. 7, no. 3, July 1986.

Gorman, Fiona, 'Putting the heart into Hoxton', *Building Design*, 14 February 1986.

Gregory, Jules, and Lewis, David, eds., 'Community Design by the People', *Process: Architecture no. 3* (special issue), Tokyo, Process Architecture Publishing, 1977.

Gundry, Walter, 'Architects in the community', *RIBA Journal*, January 1971.

Hackney, Rod, 'The Black Road improvement area', *Royal Society of Health Journal*, no. 1, 1975.

'Using the media', *AJ*, 3, 10 and 17 November 1982.

'A design for Britain with people in mind', *Guardian*, 26 August 1985.

'How to give cities new life', *The Times*, 25 October 1985.

'A manifesto for architecture', *BD*, 3 July 1987.

Hannay, Patrick, and Ravetz, Alison, 'Double take: participation in design in Glasgow and Austria', *AJ*, 3 December 1986.

Hannay, Patrick, and Wates, Nick, eds., 'Co-op dividends: architects, managers and independent critics: Hesketh Street co-op in Liverpool', *AJ*, 18 July 1984.

Hellman, Louis, 'Housing and community', *Built Environment*, June 1973.

'Democracy for architects', *RIBA Journal*, August 1973.

'Focus for a better future: the Beomund Centre, Bermondsey', *AJ*, 2 April 1986.

Higgins, Sandra, ed., 'The city Green Movement', *AJ*, 5 February 1986.

Hook, Michael, 'Housing co-operatives', *AJ*, 29 June 1977.

Hunter, James, 'Self help planning', *Architecture and Building News*, 20 November 1969.

Johaentyes, Karl, 'Self-build housing in Hanover, West Germany', *AJ*, 10 September 1986.

Jones, Peter Blundell, 'Student self-build in Hanover, West Germany', *AJ*, 27 July 1983.

'Voyage of discovery', *AJ*, 23 January 1985.

Journal of Architectural and Planning Research, special issue: 'Design and Democracy', 1987.

Knevitt, Charles, 'Community architect, mark 1 – profile of Rod Hackney', *BD*, 11 July 1975.

'Down your way: current projects by Rod Hackney', *AJ*, 5 October 1977.

'"It is only working-class conservation" – profile of Rod Hackney', *The Times*, 18 May 1984.

'Royal work in the inner cities', *The Times*, 6 June 1986.

'The architect as anti-hero', *The Times*, 7 February 1986.

Knevitt, Charles and Wates, Nick, 'Power to the people of the twilight world', *The Times*, 18 April 1985.

Lubbock, Jules, 'A design for Britain with people in mind', *Guardian*, 26 August 1985.

'Lambeth Community Care Centre, a patient revolution', *AJ* (special issue), 16 October 1985.

'The GLC's community area policy', *AJ*, 2 April 1986.

Mangin, William, 'Squatter settlements: problem or solution?', *Scientific American*, no. 217, 1967.

Mijares, Carlos, 'Speaking in foreign tongues', *AJ*, 23 January 1985.

Open House International, many relevant articles.

Owens, Ruth, 'Participation panacea', *AJ*, 11 June 1986; 'Dreams and realities: Bramley Housing Co-op', *AJ*, 29 April 1987.

Pawley, Martin, 'Fallen arches of the barefoot architect', *Guardian*, 12 August 1985.

Pooley, Fred, 'A mirror to architecture today: toward a community architecture' (inaugural address as RIBA president), *RIBA Journal*, December 1973.

Reeder, Joan, 'The Pied Piper of Black Road', *Woman*, 20 October 1982.

Smith, Douglas, and Poynton, Robert, 'Practising community architecture', *RIBA Journal*, September 1985.

Swain, Henry, 'The Ollerton shop', *AJ*, 21 July 1982.

Tegin, Harry, 'New life for Wirksworth', *AJ*, 8 June 1983.

Thornton, Michael, 'ASSIST: three-part series on community-based approach to rehabilitation in Glasgow', *AJ*, 10 November and 8 December 1976, and 9 February 1977.

Tighe, Chris, 'Working wonders in Newcastle' *BD*, 11 June 1982.

Turner, John, 'Barriers and channels for housing development in modernizing countries', *Journal of the American Institute of Planners*, May 1967.

'Uncontrolled urban settlement: problems and policies', *International Social Development Review*, New York, no. 1, 1968.

'A design for Britain with people in mind', *Guardian*, 26 August 1985.

Wates, Nick, 'Netherlands' neighbourhood architects', *AJ*, 30 August 1987.

'Kirkland comes alive', *AJ*, 28 October 1981.

'CA is here to stay', *AJ*, 9 June 1982.

'Shaping a service in Manchester', *AJ*, 4 August 1982.

'The Liverpool breakthrough', *AJ*, 8 September 1982.

'ACTAC in action', *AJ*, 12 October 1983.

'Community catalysts: report on the RIBA's Community Projects Fund', *RIBA Journal*, October 1984.

'The Hackney phenomenon', *AJ*, 20 February 1985.

Community Architecture Column, *BD*, 29 March 1985, 26 April 1985, 12 July 1985, 16 August 1985, 4 October 1985, 15 November 1985, 31 January 1986, 28 February 1986.

— , ed., 'Radical alternatives', *AJ* (special issue), 19 October 1977.

Woolley, Tom, 'Community architecture', *Slate*, 5 June 1977.

'Where will the money come from?', *AJ*, 9 June 1982.

'Prefab pioneers', *AJ*, 20 October 1982.

'Community architects: in it for the fees?', *Community Action Magazine*, July 1985.

'1:1 and face to face', *AJ*, 29 April 1987.

SPEECHES

Charles, HRH The Prince of Wales

Speech to Royal Institute of British Architects, Hampton Court Palace, 30 May 1984.

Speech to the Institute of Directors, Royal Albert Hall, London, 26 February 1985.

Speech to the Stone Federation, London, 13 December 1985.

Speech to the National House Building Council, London, 28 October 1986.

Speech to Building Communities: The First International Conference on Community Architecture, Planning and Design, London, 27 November 1986.

Speech at *The Times*/RIBA Community Enterprise Awards ceremony, 13 June 1986.

Speech at *The Times*/RIBA Community Enterprise Awards ceremony, 3 July 1987.

Lubetkin, Berthold, in collaboration with John Allan, RIBA President's Invitation Lecture, 11 June 1985.

FILMS

The House that Mum and Dad Built, BBC Open Door, 1985.

The Pride Factor – Community Architecture in Action, Mirageland Productions, 1985.

Community Architecture: The Story of Lea View House, Hackney, Hunt Thompson Associates, 1985.

Designed for Living, World in Action, Granada Television, 1985.

Housing Cooperatives; The Liverpool Pioneers, Cooperative Development Services, Liverpool, 1985.

Towards Urban Cooperatives, Building and Social Housing Foundation, 1985.

United We Are Strong, Building and Social Housing Foundation, 1985.

Groundwork in Action, BBC, 1986.

Design Matters: Why Can't We Live and Let Live, Channel 4, 1986.

Back to the Future, Calvay Cooperative, Glasgow, 1986.

A Change for the Better, Department of the Environment, 1986.

Building a Better Barrowfield, James Cunning, Young & Partners, Glasgow, 1986.

The Hackney Way, BBC Omnibus, 1986.

Index

205